FINGER PAINTING 101

"Are those paints?" I got down on the floor next to Luc and picked up a small container. "Finger paints? I haven't finger painted since—" I frowned. Actually, I couldn't ever remember doing it before.

"That's why I got them. You need some fun in your life. You're too serious."

"I am not. I have fun all the time."

Luc gave me the shortest sidelong glance ever. "Like when?"

"Like at work."

"Work is work. It's not entertainment. Here." He handed me a piece of paper. "Let loose. Humor me."

Intent on drawing a snake with Luc's face, I didn't register the feeling of cold wetness tickling my leg until it was too late. I glanced down and gasped at the blue streak on my bare leg.

Luc grinned, looking like a mischievous little boy. "It looked like it needed color . . ."

I shrieked when he grabbed me and set me on his lap. Holding my leg in place with his, he began to write on it. I bent over to read what he was writing. *KM has cooties* . . . "Oh, really mature, Luc."

I don't know the exact moment it happened, but suddenly things changed. His fingers stroked rather than painted. I knew then I was going to do something stupid. Like push my paint-coated fingers into his hair and pull him down so I could find out exactly what the girls were talking about in high school when they whispered how he had such an excellent mouth. . . .

Project
Daddy

Kate Perry

ZEBRA BOOKS
KENSINGTON PUBLISHING CORP.
www.kensingtonbooks.com

ZEBRA BOOKS are published by

Kensington Publishing Corp.
850 Third Avenue
New York, NY 10022

All Kensington titles, imprints, and distributed lines are available at special quantity discounts for bulk purchases for sales promotion, premiums, fund-raising, educational, or institutional use.

Special book excerpts or customized printings can also be created to fit specific needs. For details, write or phone the office of the Kensington Special Sales Manager: Attn. Special Sales Department. Kensington Publishing Corp., 850 Third Avenue, New York, NY 10022. Phone: 1-800-221-2647.

Zebra and the Z logo Reg. U.S. Pat. & TM Off.

ISBN 0-8217-8028-X

First Printing: May 2006
10 9 8 7 6 5 4 3 2 1

Printed in the United States of America

To
Nate and Parisa
both.

Equally.

I love you.

Acknowledgments

If I listed everyone who deserved thanks, this would read like a novel. But there are a few people who need to be mentioned . . .

Melissa Ramirez, Susan Hatler, Allison Brennan, and Michele Acker, without whom I'd be twitching in a dark corner. (Special thanks to Melissa for critiquing above and beyond beyond the call of duty.)

Parisa Zolfaghari and Chuck Jaffee, who both insisted this was the story I should write.

Steve Grant, who champions my work and doesn't complain that I'm a pest (at least not to my face).

Ron Cherry, Joyce Starling, Laurie Zmrzel, and Bob Heinrich, who listen to my very rough drafts and manage not to gag—for the most part. (Babette, Gina, and Larry, too.)

Everyone in Sierra Writers and Sacramento Valley Rose, with a special shout out to Lisa Sorenson and Phylis Warady.

But especially Nate Perry-Thistle, who believed with unwavering faith that this day would come.

Chapter One

My boss is a crazy bitch.

No, that's not true. She isn't really crazy. She's driven. Focused. Often obsessive. But there usually is method to her madness.

So let me rephrase that statement: my boss is a heinous bitch.

Tonight, that's my mantra. Lydia Ashworth, CEO of Ashworth Communications, Inc., my esteemed boss and role model (God help me) is a heinous bitch.

But it didn't matter how much I resented Lydia and the assignment she gave me—I just had to get it done.

I sighed and turned to the guy standing next to me at the bar. I stared at his cheeks, wondering if he had dimples. "Excuse me."

He glanced down at me.

Blue eyes—at least he had that going for him. "Does your family have a history of mental illness?"

His lovely eyes widened with something reminiscent of horror. He snatched his drink and hurried away.

Maybe that wasn't such a great opening question.

I rummaged through my Coach bag—I got it from a thrift store on Fillmore for a steal—and pulled out my handheld. I turned it on and accessed the spreadsheet I'd put together earlier that afternoon. With a few clicks, I rearranged the questions on my list.

Better.

I smoothed down my straight black skirt, straightened the strand of faux pearls I'd added to dress up the outfit, pushed my wire-rim glasses up my nose, and looked for my next victim—uh, candidate. I needed to find a man and I didn't have much time.

At the end of the bar, there were two men standing together watching the dancers on the floor. They looked friendly and open-minded.

Gripping my handheld, I pushed through the masses to them.

"Hi," I squeaked when I reached them.

The blond guy glanced at me and looked away without saying a word. The other guy smiled and nodded.

This was going to be easier than I thought. Heartened, I forged on. "Uh, I was wondering, um . . ." I looked down at my spreadsheet. Shoot, I was going to ruin what was left of my eyesight trying to read in here.

He looked at me kindly. "Can I help you?"

"Well, yes, actually. Do you smoke?"

"No, sorry. But there's a store around the corner. I'm sure they have cigarettes."

I turned to look where he was pointing. "Oh. Oh, well. Thanks." I checked "No" next to that question on my survey and jotted down that he was helpful and solicitous in the Notes area.

Next question. "Where did you go to college?"

He squinted at me in confusion. "SF State. How about you?"

"Stanford." Educated. I marked that down. "Did you know at Stanford it's tradition for seniors to kiss freshmen at midnight under the first full moon of autumn quarter?"

He squinted at me, so I noted that he had poor eyesight.

"Have you ever sired any children?"

His face scrunched but before I could say anything, his friend poked him in the ribs and they disappeared into the crowd.

"Well." I hit Close, opened a fresh spreadsheet, and surveyed the club.

If I had to picture hell, it would be like this, only less scary. There was a diffused red glow and loud thumping bass accompanying the music. At least I thought it did—the thumping was all I registered. I could make out the outlines of figures, but they looked otherworldly.

"What am I doing here?" I murmured, shaking my head.

I had no one to blame but myself. It was my brilliant idea to come to GY-R8. This afternoon when I cooked up my plan, it seemed so simple. I'd go to the hottest club in town, find a man, and go home happy.

I should have known it wouldn't work out that way.

"Suck it up, kiddo," I told myself. "This is your ticket to the big times."

All these years, that was what I wanted—a chance to strut my stuff. The opportunity to prove that I, Katherine Murphy, was capable and worthy. Lydia had handed it to me on a silver platter and all I could think of doing was shoving it back with a polite "no, thank you."

I sighed again and considered ordering a stiff drink. Only I have zero tolerance for alcohol. The fumes from all the drinks around me were making me tipsy.

I waved at one of the bartenders. He finished flirting with a tall blonde and came over.

He gave me one of those thorough look-overs that guys give women—minus the sexual appreciation—and said, "The librarian's convention is down the street at the Hilton."

So I wasn't exactly dressed for a night of boogying to what the masses called music these days, but neither was I a hag. I was wearing my best Ferragamo pumps (from Nordstrom Rack—so deeply discounted I bought two pairs to alternate during the week).

I gave him my fiercest "you better do as I say or I'll eat your lunch" look that I learned from Lydia and waved my hand in front of his face. "You *will* get me a Shirley Temple."

Hey—it worked for Obi-Wan.

With a few quick movements, he whipped up my drink and slid it across the bar.

That's more like it.

I took out a few dollars and handed them over reluctantly. At least I'd be able to expense this, and the twenty I'd spent on the cover charge. "Did you know Shirley Temple always had exactly fifty-six curls in her hair?"

He looked me over again and shook his head before moving along to a more trendily dressed, better-endowed woman.

"Hmm." I took a sip and looked down the bar.

Most of the men were in groups of four or more. I cringed. There was no way I could approach a large group. My stomach flopped at the thought.

Then I saw a guy seated all by himself at the other end of the bar. Even better, he had a goatee. I enthusiastically checked that box on my survey.

"I knew I was going to get lucky." I pushed my way through the crowd, stopping every now and then to make notes. Like that he was drinking a beer, sipping not guzzling. He was dressed in a custom-made suit (working for Lydia I'd learned a thing or two about expensive clothes).

Fortunately, the tall stool next to him was unoccupied. Unfortunately, I overcompensated for my purse, which really doesn't weigh as much as most people say, and almost fell off the other side.

"Careful." He reached out to steady me, helping me settle on the stool.

My hands got sweaty with excitement. Deep voice, big hands. Big hands had to count for a lot, right? I tapped it into the Notes area.

I could feel his gaze on me, so I looked up and genuinely smiled—that's how excited I was. "Hi."

He grinned. "Hi."

My, he was lovely. "Do you come here often?" A

clichéd question, yes, but I needed to know how much of a partier he was. I wasn't looking for someone who habitually frequented bars.

"No, actually. I usually work late and go to the gym afterward."

My heart beat faster and I could barely keep from squirming. A workaholic who kept in shape? Could he be more perfect?

"What type of work do you do?"

"I'm an attorney."

Yes, he was more perfect.

"What type of law do you practice?"

"International finance."

I was so excited I almost forgot to note that. "You must have to travel often." I was very proud of myself. And Luc said I was an abysmal conversationalist.

"Yes, though not much in August. This time of year is slow."

I leaned closer to him. Just as I opened my mouth to ask him about his family, a tall blonde swooped down from behind.

"Hi, baby," she drawled and kissed him.

Goodness, it was voracious.

My ears went red, but I watched avidly. Maybe I could learn a thing or two.

When they finally broke apart, she glanced down at me. Apparently I wasn't considered a threat because she dismissed me with a casual flip of her hair. She tugged on the guy's sleeve. "Come on."

He smiled at me and said, "It was nice talking to you," and disappeared into the crowd with the bim— er, woman.

"That was *my* man," I protested, deleting his

questionnaire. Sighing, I turned to search for another candidate.

For a brief moment, I was tempted to order myself a stronger drink for fortification. It was a fleeting thought, though. The last time I'd imbibed, it was only half a beer, and I still don't remember how I ended up at the beach.

"Okay," I mumbled under my breath. "The One is in here. Somewhere. I just need to find him."

I studied the scene. Easier said than done.

"I can do this." I took a swig of my Shirley Temple for courage.

A man leaned onto the bar next to me, trying to get the bartender's attention. I pursed my lips in consideration. Not bad. He didn't have a goatee, but he was dressed nicely and was handsome enough.

He must have felt my stare because he glanced at me. I attacked before I lost my nerve.

"Have you ever had any social diseases?"

His skin paled and he rushed away from me, heading toward the back where the bathrooms were.

"Poor guy." I shook my head. "Probably had too much to drink."

Chapter Two

"I'm going to be sick." I stared at Lydia's office door and pressed a hand to my stomach, willing it to stop flopping.

Jessica, Lydia's personal assistant, frowned at me. "Lydia said she'll see you now," she repeated.

No kidding. I heard her the first time. I knew it was part of her job description to keep Lydia's schedule on track, but she didn't have to rush me. I wanted to tell her to back off but I just smiled and said, "Thank you, Jessica."

Clutching a manila folder, I took a deep breath and walked in.

Lydia glanced up from her laptop. "Sit down, Katherine. I'll be right with you." She continued typing the whole time.

"Thank you." How did she keep her manicure from chipping? I looked down at my own short nails and wondered what they'd look like with a manicure.

I took a seat across from her. I ran my hands first on the leather of the chair and then the cool chrome of the armrest. Lovely. Rich. One day . . .

I have an office too, but I suspect it was a janitorial closet until they needed the additional space. It barely fits my desk, has no windows, and has the lingering scent of Lysol no amount of air freshener will ever erase. Still, it was better than a cubicle.

Until I saw Lydia's office. It's bigger than my apartment, furnished in modern retro with leather, metal, and glass. It represented what I wanted: money—lots of it.

"Okay." Lydia closed her laptop and sat back. "What do you have for me?"

My nerves flared as the impossibility of my assignment hit me again. I stifled the urge to tell her that there were 384 fertility clinics in operation in 2001—probably more now—that'd be able to help her better than I could.

"I made a questionnaire—here, I have a copy for you." Somehow I managed to sound professional and cool despite the panic. I opened the manila folder and pushed the spreadsheet across the glass tabletop.

Lydia barely glanced at it, keeping her unnerving, cool gray gaze focused on me. "A questionnaire?"

I nodded. "I thought the most efficient way to interview the—uh—candidates would be to make a survey with all the criteria you requested." I scooted to the edge of my seat and pointed out the list. "I've organized it in order of importance, according to the list you gave me yesterday."

"Good." She leaned back in her throne—uh, chair—and crossed her long, Wolford-clad legs. "And what progress have you made?"

Progress? I was good, but not that good. She gave me the assignment yesterday. What did she expect—that I had a sperm donor lined up in one evening? I cleared my throat. "Well, I did interview a few—uh—men last night—"

"Great." Flicking her smooth blond hair over her shoulder, she tapped her foot on the hardwood floor. Her shoes made my Ferragamos look like Kmart blue light specials.

"—but, uh, none of them were promising."

"I see." Lydia said it blandly, but I could hear a world of meaning in those two tiny words.

"I think, though, since it's been less than twenty-four hours since you gave me the assignment, that I've made adequate progress—"

"Katherine, do you know why I gave you this assignment?"

Because you wanted to make my life a living hell?
"No, actually."

It did seem bizarre to trust an employee you barely knew with the task of finding a father for your baby. Why did someone as gorgeous and successful as Lydia need someone to find her a mate anyway? All she had to do was crook her finger and any man would prostrate himself on the altar of her love.

Fortunately, mind reading wasn't one of her innumerable skills. "I've watched you for the seven years you've worked for me—"

Eight years in a month, but who's counting?

"—and I've been impressed with your tenacity.

You've steadily climbed up the ladder to director of research. Not a small feat."

"Thank you." I had to keep myself from puffing up with pride. It wouldn't do to preen in front of the boss, even if she had just given an uncharacteristic compliment.

"Besides being the best researcher this company has seen since its inception, you get the job done, quietly and with a minimum of fuss. That alone made you the most logical candidate to take care of this job for me."

I opened my mouth but had no idea what to say. I closed it again, hoping I resembled a competent employee rather than a fish.

Lydia leaned forward. I felt a wave of energy from her—intense and impatient. "I can't stress the importance of this matter enough, Katherine. I've entrusted you with my dream."

Uh-oh. Here it comes. This was why AshComm was so successful—the power of Lydia's speeches. She made Joan of Arc look like a candidate for Toastmasters.

She came around her desk to pace in front of me. Her designer suit gently fell into place, not a wrinkle marring the expensive fabric. I bet the suit cost more than what I made in a month, and she had a closet full of them.

"I've built this company from scratch, paying for it with my own blood and sweat rather than using a penny of my father's capital."

Her dad was loaded. I would've used his money.

"To get to this point, I had to make a lot of sacrifices. Unfortunately, one of those sacrifices was having a family." She leaned her beautifully encased derriére on the top of her desk. Even if I worked out three hours a day I'd still have a scrawny butt.

I couldn't help interjecting at this point. "You're hardly too old."

"I'm thirty-eight," she said flatly. "And, to tell you the truth, I don't have the patience to go through the trouble of finding a husband. Men are needy and demanding, and my work doesn't permit that kind of drain on my time. But then I realized I didn't need a man to achieve my goal."

It was hard to come by a penis that wasn't attached to a man. But obviously she'd realized this because here I was, sitting in front of her.

I could understand the ticking biological clock, and that hers was set to self-destruct any second now, but I didn't get one thing. "Forgive me for asking, but have you considered going to a sperm bank? Between January 2000 and August 2003, five hundred fifty-nine women conceived with donor sperm from the Sperm Bank of California."

She cocked a perfect, blond eyebrow. "Of course I considered it; however, I wouldn't have control over the choice. While they assure their records of donors are accurate, I feel more comfortable making my own selection."

Right. She was ignoring the fact that *she* wasn't going to be the one doing the selecting.

"That's where you come in." She picked a nonexistent fleck of lint off her skirt. "Your research is impeccable. I have utmost faith that you'll be able to find me a handful of suitable donors."

"Yes, but—"

"I know I don't have to reiterate my urgency in

getting this matter settled. I'd like to begin my family by my thirty-ninth birthday."

I almost sighed in relief. She was giving me some time. I'd have to reconsider the heinous bitch comment. "And that is?"

"In three weeks."

Three weeks? She wanted me to find a father for her baby in three weeks?

Delusional.

Okay. I took a deep breath. There were more impossible things to accomplish in this world. At the moment, I was hard pressed to come up with one, but I knew they existed. Pointing out that she might have given me the time constraints yesterday, or perhaps assigned me this task five months ago, barely entered my mind.

Lydia continued like she was asking me to research the history of the Pez dispenser. "Like I said, I have faith in you, Katherine. And there will be adequate compensation—"

God, I hoped so. I'd deserve sainthood for getting this job done.

"—starting with a promotion. I know you've had your eye on the VP spot that's recently opened."

Forget sainthood. I wanted VP.

I gripped the armrests to keep from jumping up and screaming *Yes!* I tilted my head to one side—I'd seen Lydia do it and practiced in the mirror until I got just the right amount of coy—and said, "The thought had crossed my mind."

Wow—what an understatement. For the last eight years, that was all I had existed for.

It wasn't the actual job that jump-started my boat. It wasn't the corner office or the fact that I'd have a lackey—excuse me, an executive assistant. Being VP of research meant I'd have a six-figure salary, which meant I'd be able to save more money, which meant I'd be able to realize my dream of owning a home that much sooner.

Lydia gave me a look that said she recognized I was about to burst with excitement despite my cool exterior. "The way I see it, Katherine, this assignment is the ultimate research project. Find me a viable candidate to father my child and the position is yours."

My heart raced and sweat made my palms sticky. I forgot all my misgivings and fears. All I could taste was the sweetness of having my own home.

Surreptitiously, I wiped my hands on my skirt. "That certainly provides incentive."

Lydia's perfectly bowed lips turned up in a little smile. "Good." She gracefully slinked back to her chair and lifted the top of her computer. "I expect daily progress reports as well as a list of potentials at the end of each week, this week excluded."

The haziness of my dream faded abruptly into the reality of what I had to do. How was I going to find viable sperm donors for her when I practically hyperventilated each time I had to ask a stranger for directions? At least she gave me a reprieve this week. I could come up with something by next week. I hoped. Maybe.

I gulped and resisted stating that over fifteen hundred children had been born to the Sperm Bank of California.

Because Lydia started tapping away at her keys, I figured I was dismissed. I stood, collected my folder, and turned to leave.

"Katherine."

I looked back.

Without lifting her gaze from the screen, Lydia said, "Failing isn't an option. I'm sure I don't have to tell you there are other qualified applicants for both the VP position as well as director of research." She glanced up and the brief contact of her eyes reinforced the threat like nothing else could have.

I straightened my spine. "Failing never entered my mind." Ha! Complete lie. Sometimes I thought the idea of failing had lived inside me forever. And now it was planning on expanding its territory.

"Good." She went back to work.

I closed the door with a soft snick on my way out. Calmly, I walked to the elevator, took it down to my floor, and strode into my closet of an office. I shut the door and collapsed against it.

Oh God. I was in deep trouble.

By midafternoon I was in a state of sheer panic, so I did what I've always done when I've had a dilemma—at least for the last fifteen years. I went to Luc's.

Lucas Fiorelli has been my best friend since the first day of ninth grade. We met in theology class at St. Margaret's Catholic School. I was sitting in the back, trying not to throw up from nerves. Luc walked in after the bell rang, sat down next to me, and proceeded to whisper every knock-knock joke he'd ever heard. Annoying, but even in my freaked-out state I recognized it was deliberate—to set me at ease. When he asked me to have lunch with him I happily said okay.

If we hadn't met at the very beginning of high school, I doubt we'd have become friends. We were as far apart on the high school spectrum as we could be. I was the geek no one knew existed; Luc was the golden boy everyone looked up to. I was there on an academic scholarship; Luc was there because his family had paid for the science wing.

That wasn't to say he's a dunce. Luc's way smarter than me. You could bring up the most obscure topic and Luc would know everything there is to know about it. He just didn't apply himself in school. I've always thought he could be a Nobel laureate if he got up the gumption.

I blame Luc's father for his lack of motivation. Mr. Fiorelli makes Genghis Khan look like Mr. Rogers. If I had a father like that, I'd be a major slacker too.

Maybe I'm painting the wrong picture of Luc. I don't mean to make it sound like he sits around all day eating bonbons. He doesn't. He's a massage therapist with a thriving practice. He's in demand, but he's not driven. He gets by well enough to afford a great loft south of Market (or SoMa as those of us who live in San Francisco like to call it) with an attached studio he uses to see his clients.

Anyway, I maintain he could easily become a mogul if he put his mind to it. It's not often Luc really wants something, but when he gets it in his head, there's no stopping him.

I let myself into his building with my key. I have a key to his loft too, but I always knock. It's the polite thing to do. Luc rolls his eyes and says I should just come in, but I know the one time I do I'll catch him browsing Internet porn or something.

I banged my fist on the door, hoping he wasn't next door with a client. Muttering curses under my breath, I shook out my hand. His door is an original one from the warehouse—ergo, thick metal. It's like knocking on the door of an industrial refrigerator.

He must not have had any clients because he opened up immediately. "Kat. This is a surprise."

The familiar way his smile lit his face and his blue eyes sparkled eased the tightness in my chest a little.

"Are you busy?" I asked, knowing the answer.

" 'Course not." He pulled me in and hugged me. Luc gave the best hugs. "Let me save the changes I'm making to my schedule and then I'm yours."

Right. He'd never be mine. Yes, I was attractive (and quite witty), but I'd never deluded myself to think I was his type—leggy and blond.

Still, Luc is one of those really nice guys who also happens to be drop-dead gorgeous. He has thick, wavy Matthew McConaughey hair and a lean, muscled body from swimming and windsurfing. Combined with his intellect, humor, and talent for massages, he was a woman's dream date. One day I wanted a man just like him.

I followed him to the area he had sectioned off for an office. He slouched back down in his space-age ergo chair. I paced back and forth behind him while he poked at the keyboard. I was just about to shove him aside and do it myself when he finally turned around. "Okay. Tell me what's wrong."

That's the great thing about Luc. He knows me. And he didn't hold it against me that I hadn't had free time to hang out with him the past few months.

All right—fine. I admit it'd been more than a few months. If I wanted the VP salary, I had to prove that I could work like one. Which meant long hours and no time for socializing.

I swallowed my guilt at being such a poor, undeserving friend and forged ahead. "I'm desperate. I need your help. I want to employ your services."

"What? You need a massage?"

"No, I need a man to stud."

"What?" He jumped out of his chair so quickly it toppled over. I found the spinning wheels oddly mesmerizing. He paid no attention to it, his eyes riveted on me.

Did I mention that he could really focus when he wanted to?

"I need someone to father a baby." I realized how this sounded when his eyes bugged out. "Not for me, you idiot. For Lydia—my boss."

He relaxed, his shoulders slumped in his typical slacker pose. "That's a relief."

I frowned. "What does that mean?"

He wrapped an arm around my neck and gave me a noogie. "Just that I don't think I'm ready for you to get settled, squirt."

I hate it when he calls me that. Usually, I remind him that, at five foot four, by medieval standards I was of Amazonian proportions, but today I shut up. I needed his help—bad. There was no way I could accomplish this without him, and I wasn't about to antagonize my only hope. "So are you going to help me or not?"

He righted his chair and plopped onto it, leaning back until the front wheels were six inches off the ground. I bit my lip to keep from telling him he was going to fall backward and crack his head open. (Accidental falls in the home kill one person every five hours.)

He studied me, his chin tipped to one side. He took my right hand and gently rubbed it, starting at the base of my palm and working his way out to my fingertips.

I tried not to melt but it was awfully hard. Tingles shot up my arm and down my spine, pooling in a pit right at the center of me.

But I was here on business, so I pushed the warm Luc feeling aside and pulled my hand from his. "Well?"

"This is important to you?"

"If I do this, I get my promotion."

He nodded. "And this promotion is what you really want?"

"It means more money, which means I'd be that much closer to being able to buy a home." He knew buying a home is all I've ever wanted.

"With the way you pinch and save, I'd think you'd have enough to put down on a place. Maybe not in the City, given the cost of housing, but definitely in the East Bay."

"Well . . ." I gave a little laugh and cleared my throat.

Luc's eyes narrowed. "Kat, your father's not still hitting you up for money, is he?"

Oh no. I hated when this came up. I knew he was just being protective of me, but I wished he understood that I couldn't *not* help my dad. But given Luc's relationship with his father, his reaction was to be expected. "The issue here is my promotion."

Read: this subject is not up for debate.

He stared at me for what seemed like forever.

"Isn't finding your boss a sperm donor beyond the call of duty? You already deserve the promotion, if you ask me."

"It's what she wants me to do." I forced a smile. "It's the ultimate research project. If I do this, I'm worthy."

He scowled. "You're worthy anyway."

Luc was so sweet.

"And why can't she do what normal people do and go to a sperm bank?"

"She doesn't want to. She's worried about quality control, and I don't blame her."

Actually, I didn't really understand what the big deal was about a sperm bank either. Except that there was a possibility that her child could have dozens of other brothers and sisters. Or that her child's father could be a psycho.

I shook my head. None of that mattered. "I have three weeks to find her a viable candidate or I'm fired."

"What?" Luc's scowl deepened. "She can't do that. Want me to talk to her?"

I sighed. "No, I want you to help me find a sperm donor. You know how I am around people I don't know."

He grinned. "You mean inept?"

"I just get a little tongue-tied."

"You don't get tongue-tied. You spew. Remember the time I took you to my friend's Christmas party and you pointed out to his wife that her shoes were made from an animal on the endangered species list?"

"Well, they were."

"And the time we went to that concert in Golden Gate Park—"

I groaned.

"—and that guy next to us tried picking you up, but you kept quoting facts on how our generation was going to experience hearing loss at an alarming rate due to the loud music we listen to."

"It's true." Of the 28 million Americans who have hearing loss, one-third can attribute it to noise.

"And then—"

"Stop." I held up my hand. "I think we've established that I have no social skills."

He tugged on one of my runaway curls. "I wouldn't go that far."

I batted his hand away and tucked my hair back into its bun.

"You should wear your hair down more. It's beautiful."

I snorted. "It's frizzy and out of control."

Luc crossed his arms and studied me. "It's not frizzy. And is being in control that important?"

I shrugged. "It is if it'll get me my house."

He didn't say anything but I could read his thoughts. I didn't doubt that he understood how important my dream was to me. But sometimes I wondered if he could *really* appreciate what it meant. I mean, he grew up in a mansion—the same home with the same staff all his life. My father and I moved every few months, always to a tiny apartment that was worse than the one before it. I just wanted a place that was *mine*. A home instead of a hovel, one that I'd never have to leave.

"Okay." He nodded.

"Okay what?"

"Okay, I'll help you."

"Thank God." I heaved a sigh of relief. Luc was full of charisma. Strangers flocked to talk to him all the time—men as well as women. With him helping, I was sure to compile my list in no time.

He leaned back in his chair again. "So what's the plan, squirt?"

I ignored the "squirt" only because he'd just agreed to help me. "We need to meet some men. I have a list of criteria here. It's organized by order of importance." I pulled out my handheld, brought up the characteristics Lydia wanted in her donor, and handed it to him.

He read it out loud. " 'Blue eyes (any shade), dimples, successful in business, busy work schedule, good parentage, intelligent, and attractive, with a goatee.' " He stared at me incredulously. "A goatee? Why does she want a goatee?"

I shrugged. "Beats me."

"You don't find that odd?"

I found this whole endeavor odd, but if it meant me getting my promotion I wasn't going to question it. "I'm sure Lydia has her reasons."

Luc shook his head in disbelief. "No wonder she can't find her own husband."

"She doesn't want a husband. She just wants a sperm donor."

"Whatever. So what's the plan?"

"I was hoping you'd be able to help me with that." I smiled. I hoped I looked innocently appealing and not like I was baring my teeth at him. "I need a list of potential candidates by next Friday morning."

"Eight days, huh?" He shook his head and

grabbed my hand—the left one this time—and massaged it as thoroughly as my right one. I tried to pull away but he held fast.

Luc touches. All the time. He always has. It's how he communicates.

I'm uncomfortable with the touchy-feely stuff. You'd think I'd be used to it by now—we *had* been friends for fifteen years, after all. I guess it's because I didn't grow up with it (at least not since I was six, before my mom died). When Luc touches me so casually I'm torn between needing to put space between us and wanting to curl into him and let him pet me all over.

I flushed beet red. That was *not* something I needed to think about.

I tugged my hand. "Well?"

"I'm thinking." His fingers pressed a particularly sensitive spot.

I clamped my lips on the moan that rose in my throat.

Space—need to get free. I jerked my hand hard. Luc chose that moment to release it and I flew back into his desk.

He frowned at me. "What's the problem?"

"Nothing." No way was I telling my best friend he was making my nerves tingle in places I didn't realize I had nerves.

He rolled his eyes. "You're weird sometimes, Kat. Okay, here's what we're going to do. You meet me at a club of my choosing tomorrow night and I'll show you how to meet people."

"Are you going to introduce me to your friends?"

"Hell no." He shook his head vigorously. "Leave my friends out of this. I like that they talk to me."

"Okay." I shrugged. I'd take whatever he'd give me.

Luc leaned back in his chair. "What do I get for helping you?"

I frowned. "What do you want?"

A wicked gleam lit his eyes. "A boon."

"A boon?" I scowled. "What the hell does that mean?"

"It means I'll help you make your list and you'll give me whatever I ask for."

His satisfied smile made me nervous. "You aren't going to want my firstborn or anything, are you?"

"And if I did?"

The way he looked at me made me understand how Little Red Riding Hood felt in the wolf's presence. "That's not exactly reassuring."

"Would I ever hurt you?"

"No." I didn't have to think about that.

"Then what's to worry?"

He had me there. I hated when Luc outmaneuvered me. "Fine."

He grinned. "Shake on it."

I reluctantly took his hand. Somehow, I knew this was going to come back and bite me in the ass.

Chapter Three

By Friday night, I was eager to get cracking. I felt on the verge. I could almost smell the fresh paint of my new home. It was time.

Instead of dawdling at work (like I did most nights), I rushed to my apartment to change. I unlocked the security gate at the steps of my building, making sure it closed behind me before unlocking the next series of locks that let me into the lobby.

My apartment was in the heart of the Mission District. Personally, I don't think the neighborhood is *that* bad. Luc says it isn't—not if you want to score some crystal meth.

Okay, I've got to agree that it's not the optimal place to live, but my rent is cheap, which allows me to save more. And the high-security prison–like atmosphere of the building I live in deters any kind of crime.

I flew up three flights of stairs and changed into casual clothes, just like Luc suggested, before running right back out. I'd just finished locking both deadbolts when the door to my left opened up and my neighbor peeked her head out.

"Hey, Kath!"

I gritted my teeth. "Hello, Rainbow."

She beamed at me, like I'd given her the greatest gift. "How're things going?"

"Fine. Thank you."

"Cool." Rainbow smiled wide. I watched in morbid fascination as the piercings (yes, plural) in her bottom lip caught the light and flashed.

I waited for Rainbow to say something else, but she just stood there, grinning. Since I was afraid my face would freeze in the grim smile I'd pasted on, I dropped my keys into my purse and edged away. "Well, I guess I'll just—"

"Want to come over?" Rainbow asked hurriedly.

"Um—"

"I got a great bottle of wine at Trader Joe's—"

"I don't—"

"—and I thought we could chat and get to know each other a little. 'Cause we're neighbors and all."

She looked like an eager puppy, with her wide, imploring eyes. For a second—maybe a split second—I was tempted to give in and accept her invitation. After all, she'd been asking me since she moved in almost a year ago.

But then I snapped out of it. "Sorry, Rainbow. I already have plans for this evening."

Her grin collapsed. "Oh. Okay. I understand."

"Maybe another time." I resisted feeling guilty.

"Right." Her smile conveyed her disbelief. Her shoulders slumped and she scuffled into her apartment.

"Wait." I don't know what came over me. I couldn't stop the words from escaping my mouth. "How about Sunday?"

The joy that leaped into her eyes was painful to behold. "That's so cool! I can't wait. Come over about seven, okay? I'll make some hors d'oeuvres to go with the wine."

Ugh. Well, how bad could her hors d'oeuvres be? It couldn't be any worse than my usual dinner of Top Ramen and tuna fish, right? "Sure. See you at seven."

Rainbow beamed at me and disappeared into her apartment. As I closed my door, I swear I heard a jubilant "Yes!"

Oh boy. What had I gotten myself into?

The Muni bus arrived as I got to the stop—a fluke, trust me. (The City's public transportation left much to be desired.) Because I wasn't in a hurry, having allowed plenty of time to get to the bar, the trip took a fraction of what it normally would. Which meant I arrived too early.

I bit my lip. Did I wait outside or go in? If I stayed outside, people walking by might confuse me for one of the strippers from the clubs that lined the street. And it wasn't safe. Thirty-seven percent of all attacks against women occurred between 6:00 P.M. and midnight.

I looked at my watch. Right. Inside.

The bar was located up an alley off Broadway near Columbus. The doorman checked my ID and waved me in. I stepped through a velvet curtain and into the dimly lit bar.

At least it wasn't as hell-like as the one I went to Wednesday night. It was pretty crowded, but it didn't have the frenetic, meat-market quality the other one did.

I relaxed. I could wait here, no problem. I walked up to the bar, set my bag on the floor, and took a seat.

The bartender came up to me right away. She smiled. "Hey there. What can I get you?"

"A Shirley Temple, please."

Her brow wrinkled but she got my drink without a comment. She set it on the bar top and leaned over. "I've never seen you here before."

"There are over five hundred bars in a thirty-mile radius of the City. It'd take a person almost two years to go to all of them if you went to a new one each day."

"Uh—" She looked confused.

I shrugged. Math wasn't everyone's forte.

I felt a hand on my back and was about to elbow the hell out of my assailant when I heard his voice.

"Been waiting long?" Luc slid onto the stool next to me and leaned over to peck me on the cheek. He stopped in midmotion and frowned at me. "I thought I told you to dress casual."

"I did." I looked down at myself. I'd changed out of my suit and into a pair of wool slacks and a long-sleeved green silk shirt. And a wool jacket, of course—it was cold out.

Luc shook his head. "That's casual." He pointed at the bartender. "You look like you stepped out of *Forbes* magazine."

I glanced at the bartender. She wore a white tank top, showing off her toned arms and prominent nipples. I shook my head. No way was I letting people stare at my nipples. "I'm casual enough, thanks."

"No, you aren't." He unbuttoned the two top buttons of my shirt and reached around to pull the pins out of my hair.

"Hey!" I slapped his hands away. "Stop undressing me."

"You need to loosen up, Kat."

"I do not."

"At least the color is great on you." He ran a finger under the wire rim of my glasses. "It makes your eyes look like big emeralds."

"Does not." My eyes are murky green at best. I pushed his hand away.

The bartender watched us with pouty interest. She tipped her head toward me but looked at Luc. "Your girlfriend, huh?"

Luc grinned. "Sorry."

"Damn."

I looked back and forth between them. What were they talking about?

"Do you have Sierra Nevada on tap?"

The bartender nodded. "Sure thing."

She got busy filling Luc's order, so I leaned closer to him and whispered, "What was that about?"

He chuckled. "You made a conquest."

"Huh?"

"She wanted to ask you out."

I wrinkled my nose and stared at the woman. "Really? Why?"

He shook his head. "You're really dense for being so smart."

Luc paid her after she set his beer in front of him. I looked down, conscious of her eyes on me.

It made me uncomfortable. It wasn't a lesbian thing—anyone paying attention to me made me feel anxious.

I gripped Luc's hand. "Did you know the Aztecs had a god who was the patron of homosexuals?"

He rubbed my knuckles. "There's nothing to feel uncomfortable about. People notice you're an attractive woman even though you camouflage yourself." He sipped his beer and looked out into the crowd. "Okay, where do we start?"

I surveyed the club. Small groups of people gathered around tables, some laughing and having fun, some in heated conversations.

I felt a pang, wishing I had a group of friends to hang out and have fun with. I had Luc, though, and that was great. Only we hardly ever hung out anymore because I was always working.

I shook my head. Focus. I had a mission to get underway. "How are we going to do this?"

Luc glanced at me. "I'll put you in front of people. You say hi, smile, and find out if they suit your qualifications."

"But what do I say?" My palms were already starting to get clammy. "Ask them if they'd be willing to be sperm donors?"

Luc rubbed his chin. "Going up to guys and asking them how they'd feel about giving up some spunk? Direct. Could work." He nodded. "How about the guys shooting pool?"

I pushed my glasses up and looked over. There were four guys around the pool table. Three women too, but they didn't count. "I can't tell. They have to have blue eyes."

"Well, let's go over and check them out." He

stood and helped me off my stool. I hefted my purse, picked up my drink, and headed toward the pool table.

He slipped his arm around my waist. "I love it when your heels clack with purpose."

I ignored him and kept walking. Sometimes I wished he'd take things more seriously. This was important—all the dreams I've ever had rode on successfully completing this mission.

Next thing I knew, I stood next to the pool table. The women stared at me. One snickered. I froze, unsure of what to do next.

I turned to Luc, who was still behind me. "Did you know billiards is one of the safest sports in the world?"

He rolled his eyes. Pulling me closer, he walked up to one of the men holding a cue stick. "Hey. How's it going?"

The man nodded and they did some guy hand-shake thing.

I frowned. Did Luc know him?

"Can we join you guys?" I heard Luc ask.

I started to protest that I didn't know how to shoot pool but the man's blue eyes distracted me. I set my drink down and reached into my purse for my handheld.

"Sure. We can work you into the rotation." He smiled.

Oh! Blue eyes *and* dimples. A candidate. I quickly turned on my handheld and keyed in my password. I had to jot this down. He didn't have a goatee, but maybe he could grow one really quickly.

My handheld was jerked out of my palm in mid-stroke. "Hey! What—"

"No." Luc shut it off and dropped it back in my purse. "Tonight you're going to interact with humans instead of machines."

"Fine." I knew he thought I couldn't do it but I'd show him.

My candidate gaped at us like we were insane.

Luc elbowed me.

That was my cue, I guess. I smiled stiffly and said, "Did you know pool evolved from croquet? It was played on lawn. The green felt on the table represents the grass."

The guy nodded, his eyebrows raised. "Right."

Luc sighed like he was deeply put upon. I glared at him. What? What did he want me to do? That was friendly. I'd smiled. Kind of.

A shout of exaltation drew our attention. A trendy woman did a victory lap around the table while another dimpled man grinned.

So many dimples, so little time. My fingers itched to get a hold of my handheld.

The two losers groaned comically, loudly protesting having to buy the next round of drinks. Luc wandered over to them and struck up a conversation. Just like that.

I shook my head. I just didn't get it. He could be thrown in a pit of vipers and he'd end up charming them all with a minimum of effort.

I became aware of the candidate standing next to me. He stared at me like he wasn't sure I'd understand him if he spoke, as if I were from a different planet.

I sighed. "I do speak English, you know."

"Huh?" His forehead crinkled up.

Well, gee—if that statement was too complex

for him I doubted he'd be a good choice for Lydia. I scratched him off my mental list.

"I speak English," I repeated slowly, enunciating each word so he'd be sure to understand.

He looked even more confused. I sighed and thought about trying sign language when Luc grabbed my elbow. "Kat, there's someone over here you should meet."

I wiggled my fingers at the ex-candidate and let Luc drag me away.

"What are you doing?" Luc's voice was a low hiss in my ear.

"I'm being conversational."

He muttered something under his breath. It sounded suspiciously like "if you're a hermit" but I wasn't sure I heard correctly.

"Everyone, this is my friend Katherine." Luc ran through a half dozen names before I could blink.

They seemed to be waiting for something from me. The three women stared at me in a way that made me feel inadequate. The guys seemed more casual, though.

"Hi." I glanced at Luc. See—I could be friendly.

"Luc, do you want to play on my team?"

I frowned at the blonde who spoke. Her voice was falsely honeyed, and when she spoke she jiggled her wares. I had the distinct impression she was inviting Luc to a whole lot more than a game of pool. And I didn't like it one bit.

"I'd love to." Luc smiled at her.

Poor Luc. He was probably just being really nice. That was Luc for you—always the good guy.

He gave me a look and went over to pick a stick

from the rack on the wall. The blonde followed him, jiggling all the way.

I curled my fingers to keep from jumping on her and clawing her back. To save Luc, of course. Gritting my teeth in a smile, I turned to the three guys. "Hi."

Two of them exchanged a look and walked away. The third grinned. "Hi."

He had a dimple in his right cheek! I relaxed and smiled, genuinely this time. "Hi."

He laughed. "You're cute."

I was obviously dealing with a very intelligent man here. It was too bad his eyes were brown, but nobody was perfect. "Would you say you're successful at your work?"

"I do well."

"How do you feel about children?"

The laughter faded abruptly from his face. "What?"

"Children," I shouted.

He shrugged. "I can't see myself as a father right now."

Great. I bit my lip, wondering how to proceed. Luc said directness was good. So I grabbed his shirt, pulled him down, and whispered in his ear, "I have a proposition for you."

"Really."

He looked intrigued. Emboldened, I continued. "I have to find a sperm donor and I think you might fit the bill."

He blinked a few times. Probably the smoke in here. Behind my glasses, my eyes were watering too. Mental note: inform the proper authorities that the no-smoking ordinance was being broken.

He leaned in, snaking an arm around my waist. "Would it involve sex?"

Hmm. I took a sip of my Shirley Temple to give me a moment to think. That was a good question. "I'm not sure."

"Well, I'd be interested," he said against my ear.

I resisted the urge to shout in triumph. But I couldn't help wiping away the residue of his moist breath on my skin. "Great. I just need to get your name and contact information."

"My name is James."

James. A very regal-sounding name. I pushed him back, set my drink on the counter behind me, and dug in my purse for a pen and pad.

Playing it cool, I watched him jot down his full name and phone numbers. At this rate, I'd be able to put together an adequate list before my three weeks were up.

I owed Luc big-time. I should take him out to dinner or something when this was over.

I had a niggling sense of being watched. I looked up to find Luc glaring from the other side of the pool table. I gave him a thumbs-up.

This was going to be easier than I thought.

Chapter Four

6:54 Sunday evening. All I wanted to do was crawl into bed, pull the covers over my head, and sleep for the next two months. I'd gone out again with Luc last night. Different bar, same objective, and the only thing I had to show for it was a huge blister on the heel of my left foot.

I entertained the idea of calling Rainbow to cancel our get-together, but there were two problems with that. One: I'd promised her I'd go and I didn't think I could bear her kicked-puppy pout if I didn't. Two: I didn't have her phone number.

I just had to buck up and go over, I decided as I slipped my feet into the Ferragamos.

I stood up with a sigh. It wasn't going to be that bad. Certainly not worse than a company party. (Shudder.)

I picked up my keys, which I always leave hanging on a hook by the door, and debated taking my purse. In the end I grabbed it. You never know when you might need an emergency sewing kit or clear nail polish (amazing how useful it is for any number of things).

Locking the door, I sighed again, strode to Rainbow's, and knocked. As I waited, I shifted my weight from one foot to the other to alleviate the radiating pain of the blister.

One thousand one.

One thousand two.

One thousand three.

One thousand four.

One thousand five.

No answer.

"Hmm." I pressed my ear to the door. Nothing. What if she wasn't home? Did she forget?

I banged my fist on the door and held my breath. I was just starting to get my hopes up when the door swung open and there she was, dressed just like her name.

"Hey, Kath!" She beamed. Before I could say or do anything, she yanked me into her apartment and slammed the door. "Come on in."

Setting my purse on the floor, I stepped over a pile of shoes to avoid tripping. "Um, thank you."

"Have a seat. I'll pop open the wine and join you in a sec."

I stopped her before she flitted off to the kitchenette. "Rainbow, I don't drink alcohol."

Her face fell. But only a touch before she perked right up. "No problem. How about some tea? I got this great blend from my acupuncturist. Straight from China."

"Sure. That'd be fine."

"Groovy." She gestured to the living room as she walked away. "Make yourself at home."

She didn't have to point the way—her apartment was the mirror image of mine. And calling it a living room was generous. It was more of a long hallway between the front door and the bedroom (a.k.a. glorified closet).

If I had any doubts about finding it, all I had to do was follow the stench.

God, what was that? Pinching my nose with two fingers, I inched forward. And stopped.

Oh my God, it was a mess. Mounds of magazines piled on the table—at least I think there was a table underneath. Scarves draped over lamps, and the bookshelf overflowed onto the floor with paperbacks. It was so different from my orderly apartment that I felt like I'd entered a foreign country.

Then I found it.

There—on the crate-slash-table by the futon-slash-couch. A thick plume of smoke languidly drifted up.

Incense.

In college, one of the girls in my dorm burned incense night and day. It hid the smell of all the pot she smoked.

But where that was light and fruity, Rainbow's was heavy and perfumed, kind of like I'd imagine a South American prostitute would smell. It made me wonder what she was trying to cover up.

Still holding my nose, I picked up the long brass holder and burning stick and looked around for a place to relocate it. It needed to go away. Far away.

"I'm so glad you could make it," Rainbow yelled from the kitchenette.

I jumped. Guilty? Not me. "Um, yes, me too."

"I pulled out all the stops tonight. I hope you like it."

"I'm sure I will." I needed to find a hiding place—fast. I wondered if she'd notice if I put it outside on the decrepit fire escape.

"Here we are. Oh, do you like the incense?"

I whirled around as Rainbow skipped in, carrying a small tray laden with food and mismatched china. Dark gray ash floated to the floor, but I doubted she'd notice given the state of her apartment. "Uh—"

"I *knew* you'd like it. I picked it especially for you. It goes with your aura. Here." She snatched it out of my hand. "Let's put it here so it's close to you."

I was proud that I didn't wince when she set it back down on the crate.

She waved in my general direction. "Sit. I'll get the tea."

My nose twitching, I pushed aside the clothes covering the futon (*please let them be clean*) and perched on the edge, smoothing my skirt over my L'eggs nylons.

Rainbow came back promptly with two steaming mugs. She set one in front of me on top of a precarious stack of magazines before sitting Indian-style on the floor across from me.

Cupping her mug in her hand, she grinned again. "I just can't believe you're here. After all this time."

Guilt pierced me. It was true—I'd been avoiding her invitations for over a year now, ever since she moved in. "It's been a busy year."

She nodded. "I've noticed you work all the time.

That isn't good for you, you know. Your chakras are probably all imbalanced."

Because I didn't know what to say to that, I took a sip of my tea. And choked.

Yuck! I frowned at it. What was this? It tasted like stewed grass.

"Do you like it?"

I looked at Rainbow's eager, cherubic face and bit my lip. "It's quite interesting."

"My acupuncturist swears by it."

I didn't know whether to be impressed that she let someone poke needles into her or to think she was a freak. I decided to reserve judgment for the time being.

"You look so nice, but you didn't have to get dressed up to come over." She sipped her tea.

"Oh." I looked down at my outfit. I didn't get dressed up. "I, uh, came from work."

"On a Sunday? You work for a big conglomerate, don't you?" she asked accusingly.

"I don't. Ashworth Communications is a privately held corporation." For some reason I felt compelled to defend myself and AshComm. "We put back a lot into the community. Last Christmas season we collected enough presents for over eight hundred boys and girls."

Rainbow shrugged. "Christmas is a capitalistic holiday."

"What do you do?" I asked to divert her. "For work."

She shrugged again. "I dabble in aromatherapy."

Read: slacker.

Not that I was surprised. I doubted I could find anyone less ambitious than Rainbow. Even Luc had his own business—small, albeit enough to afford him a huge loft and a comfortable living. Rainbow lived in a dump in the Mission.

But I pasted a smile on my face. "Sounds interesting."

"I love it." She licked an errant drop of tea dripping down her mug. "So did you have a good time Friday night?"

I tried not to be distracted by the tiny clank the stud in her tongue made. (Did it heat up with the hot tea?) "Um, yes, Friday night was successful."

"Successful?" She wrinkled her nose, which made the stud in her nostril wink at me. "Did you get laid?"

"Excuse me?" I knew I must have been gaping, but her question was totally invasive. I mean, I hardly knew the woman and she was asking me if I had sex.

"Did you meet someone?" She scooted closer, her eyes wide and sparkling. "Have a fling?"

"No! No way." I shook my head. I'd never had a fling in my life.

Don't get me wrong—I've had sex. Kind of. Twice. A decade ago. But never a fling. I tried not to pout.

"Oh." She visibly drooped. "But you had fun anyway?"

"It was informative."

Her nose wrinkled again. "Informative? What does that mean?"

"It means 'serving to enlighten or inform.'"

Rainbow laughed. "You crack me up, Kath."

What did that mean? I hid my frown in the so-called tea.

"So did you go out with friends?"

"Just my friend Luc."

"Your boyfriend?"

Why was she so interested in my private life? It made me suspicious. "He's just my best friend."

"Is he hot?"

"No, he's Luc." Luc hot? In my mind, I saw the way his eyes lit with humor and felt the way his hands touched mine, and I flushed. I set my tea down. It was overheating me. "No, Luc's definitely not hot."

"That's too bad. Do you have a boyfriend?"

"No."

"Have an hors d'oeuvres. I made hummus, mostly from scratch, and tofu spinach dip." She pushed the tray closer. The magazines shifted, and for a moment I thought my Ferragamos were going to be doused in yellowish chickpea paste.

I picked up a carrot chunk and nibbled on it.

"I used to have a boyfriend. For a long time, but I dumped him a couple months ago." Rainbow sighed dramatically, drowned a cracker in the hummus, and stuck it in her mouth.

I wondered what the statistics were on breaking a tooth by biting down on a tongue piercing.

"It's just as well that he's gone. He was an asshole," she said as she chewed.

She seemed to be waiting for me to say something, so I did. "Oh?"

I guess it was the right thing because she continued. (And Luc said I was an abysmal conversationalist.) "Yeah, total bastard. I keep my money in a hollowed-out book by my bed"—she waved toward her bedroom—"and he used to help himself to it. When I confronted him about it, he had the nerve to deny it. Then he charmed it out of me by promising he wouldn't do it again."

I froze mid nibble. I knew this story. I lived it still.

"Every time he'd say it was the last time." She snorted so loudly it startled me. "I let him take money from me. You must think I'm such an idiot for believing him."

I bit my lip and shifted, smoothing my skirt down over my knees. If she was an idiot, what did that make me? "Um, no. You're not."

"Oh, I am." Her natty hair bounced dully with each nod.

"Rainbow, I have to go." I stood up. I needed to get out of there. I held out my hand. "Thanks for inviting me over."

She frowned but took my hand. Instead of shaking it like I meant, she levered herself up from the floor. "Oh, well, okay."

I blocked out the confused-bunny look in her big eyes. I just needed some space to think. "Uh, thank you. See you later." I edged around the magazines, grabbed my purse, and hurdled over the shoes right out the door.

I fumbled with my locks. When I finally managed to open them, I slipped inside and slammed the door shut, like there was something chasing me.

Leaning against the door, I took my glasses off and pressed the bridge of my nose. I went over to Rainbow's thinking we had nothing in common. That I was superior. I mean, here she was—dreads and piercings, living in a pig sty, doing nothing with her life. She didn't even have a real job—she *dabbled.* I had the job, the big ambitions, the goal. But in the end, Rainbow and I were the same.

No, Rainbow was better, because at least she told her bastard boyfriend he couldn't have any more money from her. I couldn't even do that. Sure, I was supplying my father, not a random guy I'd met, but still.

I went to my bedroom. Without turning on the lights, I got out of my clothes and automatically hung them up. I got into one of Luc's old massage school T-shirts, crawled under my covers, and huddled there. They were so threadbare, I could see the neon lights that slipped through the wide gaps of my blinds.

I screwed my eyes shut and tried to block it all out, but scene after scene flashed in my mind. When I was seven and my dad snuck into my room, thinking I was asleep, to raid my piggy bank. When I was ten and I opened the household purse to pay our landlord, who waited at the door, and found only three pennies and a dime inside. When I was thirteen and had to pawn my mom's pearl necklace—the necklace she gave me eight years before when she realized her cancer wasn't treatable—to pay the rent so we could stay in the current dump one more month.

And then there was junior year in high school when I had to hock the sleek, top-of-the-line calculator Luc gave me for Christmas. I'd loved that calculator—it practically did my precalculus homework on its own. It was a huge step up from the ancient Texas Instruments I'd been using. When Luc found out—well, let's just say I'd never known he could get so angry. Not at me but at my dad. He bought me a replacement and made me promise that if I needed money I'd ask him for it instead. I'd promised, kept the beloved calculator, and started tutoring to earn the extra money I needed.

Sighing, I punched my pillow. Rainbow had wised up. I should have wised up by now too (according to Luc anyway), but whenever my dad came around I gave him what he wanted without a struggle. What could I do? He was my dad.

I rolled over and tried not to think about how different it all would have been if my mom had lived.

Thinking about my father was a mistake because it made him materialize on my doorstep late the next evening.

I was going through all the junk mail on my way up to my apartment. It was after eight and I still had a ton of work to do—mostly on my secret mission. (I found that if I thought of it like I was a super spy it made the whole thing more bearable.) But as I rounded the corner after the last flight of stairs there he was, sitting in front of my door, his legs spread out in front of him.

"Katie bug." He beamed at me and hopped up. "Give your old man a hug."

He wrapped me in his arms and for a moment I was five again and my daddy was king of the world.

Mom and I used to wait for him to come home, peeking out the window. When he drove up to our home, we'd run to greet him. He'd lift me into his arms as he kissed my mom and we'd move into the family room, me curled on his lap and my mom curled next to him. He'd tell us stories from his day at the brokerage—funny stories about his odd clients—that made us giggle uncontrollably.

I burrowed into his chest, imagining him as the conquering hero returning home. Like he used to be before my mom died and he started drinking.

And then I smelled the alcohol on his breath. I pulled away and really looked at him. His hair was unkempt with a dull, dirty cast, his clothes had that wrinkled look like he'd been wearing them for days, and his eyes—the same color as mine—were bloodshot.

Why did I always think things would change? This Pollyanna optimism had to be my most unattractive feature. Next to my frizzy auburn hair, that is.

"I'm surprised to see you here, Dad." I unlocked the door and let him enter before I did.

"Can't a man visit his only offspring?" He walked straight for the old couch Luc gave me (if it weren't for Luc's castoffs I'd have no furniture). He tossed his coat onto the floor and plopped down.

"So you just came here to visit?" I picked up his coat and draped it across the arm of the couch.

"Well . . . you know. That and a bit of business."

I felt my shoulders knot up more than they already were. "Business?" I asked, knowing exactly what kind of business brought him here out of the blue. I set my Coach bag on the rickety coffee table and huddled in the chair across from him. The thought that my suit coat was becoming horribly wrinkled flitted across my mind, but I didn't care. I needed the warmth, even if its lining was wearing away as we spoke.

"We can get to that later. First tell your old dad what you've been up to." He craned his neck and looked around. "I see you haven't settled in yet. You've lived here, what, five years?"

"Seven."

"I'll have to bring some pictures over sometime." He grinned. "Can't have you forget what your parents look like, can I?"

"I'd never forget what you look like, Dad." My stomach rumbled. I ignored it. It wasn't like it'd eat itself. It'd only digest itself if it stopped producing its protective layer of mucus.

"You're hungry. How about if I whip together a little dinner for us?" He jumped up. "Just like the old days."

I instantly started to salivate thinking about his mac and cheese. He used to make it every Sunday night, and it was creamy and delicious. My mom used to say his mac and cheese was so spectacular it warranted getting dressed up, so while he cooked we fixed our hair in fancy upsweeps and put on our best dresses. I even got to wear a little lipstick.

But those days were gone, and all I had in my cupboards was tuna fish and Top Ramen. "That's okay. I just wanted to go to bed tonight. I'm tired."

"You gotta eat, Katie bug." He wagged his finger at me. "You're wasting away."

Actually, I chose to think of it as my fitness regimen. Why pay someone good money to put you on a strict diet? "So, what's going on with you, Dad?"

"You know. A little bit of this, a little bit of that." Right.

"Actually, that's what I wanted to talk to you about."

Shit. I braced myself.

"I'm in this bit of a spot and need to borrow some money." He quickly hurried on, as if he wanted to get all his thoughts out before I interrupted. "It's the last time—I swear. I've learned my lesson. I'd take care of this myself but Ivan is really leaning on me—"

I groaned. "Ivan again, Dad?"

"I know. I know. But I was on a winning streak, and I had this incredible hand." He held up his hands like he still had the cards in them. "Who would have guessed Ivan would have a royal flush?"

"How much is it this time?"

He ducked his head and mumbled into his chest.

"What?" I frowned. "How much did you say?"

He said it more clearly this time.

I almost fell out of my chair. "Dad!"

He sighed and looked at me mournfully. "I had such a great hand."

I briefly entertained the thought of letting Ivan tie my dad to the train tracks again. But only for a second.

Okay, maybe for a touch more. But that's all. I swear.

Sighing, I reached for my purse.

"God bless you, Katie bug." He smiled in relief. "I knew you'd come through for me."

I wanted to growl but I just smiled and got my checkbook out.

"How's Luc?"

I looked up with narrowed eyes. "Why do you ask?"

"Just wondering. He's still your friend, isn't he?"

I stared at him a moment longer before going

back to writing out the check. "Yes, he's still my friend."

"Always liked that boy." He tapped his foot against the table. "I'm surprised he hasn't snapped you up yet."

"He wouldn't go for me, Dad," I said absently as I filled in the date.

"You're a girl. Of course he'd go for you. He's not queer, is he?"

"Dad!"

"Unless he's a flaming fruit, you're his type. Trust me."

Like I was going to listen to advice from a man who hadn't had a relationship in over twenty years. I shook my head, took a deep breath, and forced myself to write in the amount. With each zero I added, my home moved further out of my reach.

I'd just have to work harder to find Lydia a sperm donor. With the increase in pay the promotion would bring, I could make up this setback in no time.

"You know, Luc has my blessing should he pop the question."

"*Dad!*"

"What?" he asked innocently.

I sighed. There was no point in trying to explain to him that Luc was my best friend. You don't date friends. Especially your best friend. When things don't work out, you'd not only be out a date but also the person who means the most to you.

"Here." I handed him the check. "But next time—"

"I promise, Katie bug. No more." He made a cross over his heart. He looked at the check and grinned. "You're an angel, honey. I owe you big for this."

God, did he ever.

"Well, I should be off." He bounced up and grabbed his coat. Carefully, he folded the check and put it in his pocket. He smiled at me and dropped a kiss on my forehead. "I swear this is the last time, Katie bug."

If only I had a dime for every time I heard that one.

Chapter Five

"Why do I have to be here?"

Luc held fast to my arm as I tried to back away from the art gallery's front door. "Don't you have to turn in a list to your boss by tomorrow morning?"

I pouted.

"Well, this is a great place to meet men."

"It is?" I couldn't help the suspicious note in my voice. I had the feeling Luc had ulterior motives for getting me there.

"Hell yeah. Guys go trolling for women in galleries all the time."

"They do?"

"Sure."

Call me skeptical, but I had doubts. Still, I let him drag me through the door.

The second we entered Zar Gallery, champagne-drinking intellectuals with perfect hair and expensive clothes closed in around us.

"I can't do this." I turned on my heels and tried to leave.

"Kat." Luc grabbed me around the waist.

"I can't do this." I tried to pry off his arm but it was like a steel vise. Massage work sure does make a person buff.

"What do you mean?" He pulled me closer and soothed my back. "Jesus, Kat, you're tense."

No kidding. "Did you know when opossums play possum they aren't playing? They actually pass out from sheer terror."

He looked around. "There're a lot of people here, but it's not that bad."

"Not if you're a sardine," I murmured. "Then it's almost roomy."

Luc laughed, uninhibited and bright. Several people around us turned to look. The women's gazes lingered so long I had to glare to get them to stop visually mauling Luc.

"Come on. You fit in just right." He didn't say *for a change*, but I could hear it in his voice.

I straightened my suit coat and smoothed back a curl that had gotten loose from my chignon. "I don't know—"

"Don't chicken out." He smiled and took my hand. How was it his hands were always so warm? "I want you to meet my friend Gary."

I sighed. "After I meet Gary, if I'm really uncomfortable, I can leave?"

He put his arm around my shoulder and pulled me into his side. "If you're really uncomfortable, we'll both go. I'll take you to dinner."

I perked up. "You will?"

"Would I lie?"

No, he wouldn't. And Luc liked to eat, so when he said he'd take me to dinner he didn't mean McDonald's.

Going out to eat was a treat. That it was with Luc made it doubly so, and that it'd probably be his favorite Italian restaurant was icing on a rich double-chocolate cake.

I never went out to eat. With my dream of owning a home, I saved every dime, nickel, and penny that I earned. Literally. So I lived in my shoebox of an apartment in the worst part of town, never went out, and ate Top Ramen and tuna fish all the time.

Okay, maybe not all the time. Sometimes Safeway would have specials on Campbell's soup, or frozen dinners, and I'd stock up. And one of the benefits of living where I did was the inexpensive produce. I could buy oranges (avoiding scurvy was important) and lettuce in bulk for pretty cheap. Rice too—a twenty-pound bag of rice lasted forever.

Luc steered me expertly through the thick crowd. Every now and then someone would greet him. He never stopped but he always replied back warmly. I kept my eyes down so I wouldn't get overwhelmed.

"You need a glass of champagne," Luc said in my ear.

I shook my head. "You know I can't handle alcohol."

"One glass won't kill you. And you might loosen up enough to enjoy yourself."

I shook my head again. I didn't need to loosen up. It was unfair to put me in a foreign environment and expect me to be okay. I mean, you wouldn't expect that of a lion, would you?

Besides, the heat from his body was lulling me. I

didn't need champagne when Luc's warmth went straight to my head.

"Your list is due tomorrow," he reminded me. "If you loosen up, you'll be able to add at least a couple more names to it."

Good point. I wondered if they'd let me have the whole bottle instead of just a glass.

We made it across the room, and I took a deep breath. Over here it wasn't quite so crowded. It gave me a chance to study everyone. Most were dressed in black—the rich black of expensively dyed material. The amount of jewelry in the room could take care of the national debt of a large Third-World country.

Or help me buy a house.

Not that I'd go there. Really.

"Here." Luc shoved a glass in my hand.

I frowned at it. "Are you sure?"

"Only you would look at champagne like it's poison. Just take a sip."

I did—tentatively. It shot straight up my nose and made me choke.

At least Luc rubbed my back while he laughed. It made me less inclined to pulverize him.

"Luc! Good to see you, man."

A burly biker guy with a Fu Manchu walked up to us with a wide smile.

Hmm. Did a Fu Manchu count as a goatee?

"Gary, my man." Luc and Gary did that man handshake thing that mystifies me. They talked a little bit more but I didn't hear a word they said— I was distracted by Gary's laser blue eyes.

Wow. They were the bluest eyes I'd ever seen.

Even bluer than Luc's, and that was saying something. I absently took another sip of champagne. They had to make up for the fact that his goatee wasn't a goatee, right? I reached into my purse to drag out my handheld computer but stopped, knowing Luc wouldn't approve.

"—my best friend, Katherine. Kat, Gary is the artist exhibiting."

I jumped when Gary's humongous paw engulfed my free hand. "Pleased to meet you, Katherine. Luc's told me a lot about you."

"Oh." What did that mean? "Did you know Van Gogh didn't cut off his whole ear? He just cut the tip. But he did give it to a woman. A prostitute he frequented, actually."

I didn't have to look at Luc to know he was rolling his eyes.

Gary, on the other hand, looked rapt. He held my hand tighter. "I love this woman, Luc."

"Don't we all," Luc muttered.

I shot him an evil glare for the sarcastic comment and turned to smile brilliantly at Gary. He had the right color eyes, facial hair, was talented (I suppose—I hadn't looked at any of his work yet) and obviously quite intelligent. The perfect candidate for Lydia. "Are you married?"

Luc spewed the champagne he was drinking onto his friend, who didn't seem to mind. Gary swiped at his chest a couple times, a bemused look on his face. "No, I'm not married."

Yes! This was my lucky night.

"But that's my boyfriend over there."

I blinked and automatically glanced at the slight, pretty man he pointed out.

"Oh." Damn. And he would have been so perfect too.

I glared at Luc. Why did he insist I meet Gary? He had to know his friend was gay.

"Katherine"—Gary squeezed my hand—"promise me we'll chat later. I want to talk to you about a project."

I wrinkled my nose. "I don't know anything about art."

He grinned and patted the hand he held captive. He began to make me uncomfortable with his too-vivid gaze. "She's just fascinating, Luc. You were right. She's exactly what I'm looking for."

I gave Luc a questioning look, but he gave away nothing. Mona Lisa could have taken lessons from him, his smile was so enigmatic.

"Don't leave without finding me," Gary said, releasing my hand. He walked away, waving madly, before I could formulate a reply. "Lars! So glad you could make it."

I watched him shake hands with a tall, thin man who looked like he was going to cave under Gary's grip. "Luc, where'd you meet him?"

"Remember Jenny?"

I wrinkled my nose. I wished I could forget the last in Luc's long line of gorgeous, tall girlfriends. "Kind of."

"Well, she was into art."

Of course she was. I resisted the urge to gag by taking a swig of my champagne.

A horrifying thought occurred to me. "Tell me she's not going to be here tonight."

Luc laughed. He trailed a finger down my cheek. "The expression on your face is priceless, squirt."

Frowning, I batted his hand away. "Don't call me that."

I looked around. There was no way I was going to be able to approach any of the men here. I mean, they were perfect—exactly what Lydia would want: well off, intelligent, and cultured. But approaching them? My stomach cringed at the thought.

I wished I weren't here. I wished I'd never gotten this stupid assignment. I wished I'd never heard of Lydia Ashworth and her stupid company.

"I told you."

"What?" I wrinkled my nose at him. What was he talking about?

He pointed at my glass. "The champagne. I knew you'd like it."

I looked down. Oh wow. It was all gone.

"Can I get you more?"

Very tempting. Exceedingly tempting. "No, thank you."

Luc shrugged. "I see a friend over there. Want to come with me or do you want to look around at Gary's paintings?"

I looked to where he pointed. Ick—another tall blonde. Surprise, surprise. "I'll take a look around."

He squeezed my hand. "Calm down, squirt. If you relax you'll be fine."

Right. I tried to smile at him reassuringly but by the way he rolled his eyes I gathered I didn't succeed. He shook his head and walked off. I resisted the urge to grab his jacket and scream *don't leave me!*

I bit my lip. Yeah, maybe I'd take a look at Gary's work.

Turning around, I stared at the painting right behind me. It was an oil painting, eight feet by six feet (I read that on the little placard to its right). It was predominantly white but in the top left corner there was a giant red splotch.

I stepped closer. I stepped back. I squinted my eyes. Shaking my head, I murmured, "It looks like a big red blob on a white background."

Someone laughed right behind me. Someone masculine, judging by the sound. I grimaced. Did he hear my comment? He was probably laughing at someone else.

Whoever it was moved to my side. "I was just thinking the same thing. Except I called it a splatter."

Oh God. I can't believe someone heard me. I bit my lip. Maybe if I ignored him he'd go away.

No such luck. "A 'splatter' is a touch more accurate, don't you think?"

I wrinkled my nose and studied the painting again. "Actually, I think 'blob' is more fitting. It's—" I turned to him and everything I was about to say flew out of my mouth in the face of his two dimples and his eyes. "I never knew so many people in the world had blue eyes. Though I know blue is the most common eye color, followed by brown."

The corners of his eyes crinkled. "Is that so?"

"So help me." I held up two fingers like a good scout.

He laughed again. "I don't think I've ever seen you at an opening here."

The words popped out of my mouth without thought. "Do you come to all of them?"

"No, I guess I don't." His brows furrowed—not

in displeasure but in puzzlement—and he held his hand out. "I'm Joseph Bailey."

"Katherine Murphy."

His shake was firm, warm but not sweaty. He leaned closer to me. "Katherine Murphy, you're intriguing."

"Ha!" Oops—I clapped my hand over my mouth. That slipped out.

Joseph grinned. "I can't believe you're here alone."

"I'm not."

"Oh."

I pointed to Luc, who was listening raptly to the blonde (the bitch). "With my friend Luc."

"Oh!" He grinned. "Well, that's great."

I wrinkled my nose. "It is?"

"Yes. For me, at least." He took my elbow and moved closer to me to protect me from a couple who tried to run me down. "What made you come here tonight?"

I shrugged. "Luc said it was a good place to meet men."

His beautiful sea blue eyes widened.

I giggled—I couldn't help it. It was comical. I patted his arm. "And I found you, so it was worth the torture."

"It was torture?"

I nodded. "I can't stand crowds. In case you haven't been able to tell, I've got terrible social skills. Completely lacking, really. You're lucky I haven't quoted many facts at you yet." I sighed. "But give me some time."

Joseph threw his head back and laughed, long

and loud, attracting everyone's attention. The entire gallery went quiet for the span of two seconds and I felt my cheeks flush a deep red that matched the blouse I wore.

"Stop it." I slapped his arm. "You're making a spectacle."

"That's not all I'm making." He tightened his grip on my arm. I didn't care, not as long as he kept the laughing to a dull roar. "Why were you looking for a man?"

I sighed again. "It's a long story."

"The gallery doesn't close for another three hours. And if that's not enough time, I know a great place in Chinatown that's open twenty-four hours."

I stared up at Joseph's eyes. They looked so sparkling and clear and interested that I couldn't help spilling out the whole story.

It took fifteen minutes instead of all night. I didn't take a breath until I finished.

Silence.

Biting my lip, I studied his face. I thought it was indigestion I saw there, but it might have been incredulity.

Oh well. I looked around for another man I could attack.

"Katherine, you're full of surprises, aren't you?"

I glanced back at Joseph. "I am?"

He nodded. "You doubt it? You just told me you're looking for a sperm donor for your boss. I'd count that as mildly surprising."

I winced. "Is that bad?"

"Not bad, just . . . surprising."

What did that mean?

"I can't believe I'm going to say this." Staring at me, he swiped back his hair. "I'm game."

"Excuse me?"

"Count me in. Put me down as a potential sperm donor."

I wiggled a finger in my ear. Spending all that time in those clubs was obviously affecting my hearing. "What did you say?"

"I said I'd meet your boss." He shook his head. "I know I must be crazy, but I have this odd impulse to help you."

Joseph's words slowly sank in. I gasped and grabbed his arm. "Do you mean it? You aren't just cruelly stringing me along only to dash my hopes on the rocks, are you?"

"Rocks?" He grinned. "No rocks."

"Good." I grinned back. Then I surprised myself by throwing my arms around him, but I let go as soon as I realized what I'd just done.

"Oh shit. Oh God—I'm sorry." I smoothed the lapel of his coat (very luxurious wool, I noticed).

"It's okay, Katherine. I don't mind."

No, he didn't. His eyes sparkled with contained mirth.

I shrugged. Oh well—I'd rather he found me amusing than annoying.

"Hey, Kat. Everything okay here?"

I smiled over my shoulder at Luc. "Everything's absolutely wonderful now that I've met Joseph." My smile faded when I noticed the way Luc was scowling. "Is something wrong?"

"I don't know. You tell me." He might have been

talking to me, but his gaze never wavered from Joseph.

Joseph cleared his throat. "Maybe I should give you my phone number and we can discuss the details of our arrangement later."

"Great." I pulled out my handheld and carefully tapped in his cell, home, and work numbers (can't be too careful, you know). I saved the info and smiled at him. "You don't know it, but you've just made my dream a little more possible."

"Fantastic." He pushed back one of my dratted escaped curls. "Talk to you soon?"

"Of course." I only had two more weeks before my deadline.

With barely a glance at Luc, he squeezed my shoulder and walked away. I watched him stop to shake Gary's hand before he walked out the door.

"You've just made my dream more possible?" Luc said with unconcealed sarcasm. "What the hell did that mean?"

"Nothing. Just that he helped me in a big way." I frowned at him. "What's the problem? I thought you brought me here to meet men."

"I did. But for your boss, not for you."

I recoiled. "I didn't meet Joseph for me."

Luc snorted. "That's not what he thought."

"Sure it is. I told him everything."

"What?" He studied me for a few seconds before he groaned. "You told him? And he agreed to help you?"

"Of course." I pushed my glasses up on my nose and tried to look authoritative. "Why wouldn't he want to help? It's a perfectly valid mission."

Okay, I wasn't sure I bought that. After all, just

minutes ago I was cursing the fact that I'd ever met Lydia, but Luc didn't have to know that.

"It's insanity." He exhaled and scrubbed his face with his hand. "Kat, do you really think he offered to help because of the sheer joy of contributing some spunk for a good cause?"

I nodded. Why else would he volunteer?

"Shit." He shook his head. "I can't decide if you're really that innocent or really that stupid."

"*Stupid*?" I sounded shrill even to my own ears.

He winced. "I didn't mean stupid. I meant blind."

It didn't matter what he meant—he'd said stupid.

I pouted. I couldn't believe that's what my best friend thought of me. "If you don't want to help, you don't have to. I can do this on my own."

Right. I hoped I sounded like I believed it. Inside, I cringed at the thought of having to face this alone.

Still, I wouldn't show weakness. I turned on my heels and started to walk away.

Luc's hand on my shoulder stopped me. "Wait, Kat."

I glared at him. "Why should I?"

"Because I love you and I'm only interested in what's best for you."

"Ha!"

He sighed. "Come on, squirt. You know I didn't mean it like it sounded." He pulled me close and gave me a one-armed hug.

I inhaled his scent and felt the tension in my body melt away. Luc smelled the same as he did fifteen years ago, at least underneath the scented soap and shaving cream. It was comforting, like walking into a restaurant and smelling macaroni and cheese like your mom—or your dad in my case—used to make.

"Okay, fine." His jacket muffled my voice. "I'll forgive you if you take me to dinner. Italian."

He chuckled. I felt it vibrate through me more than I heard it.

"Don't even *think* about giving me a noogie." I glared and pulled out from under his arm.

He laughed and pulled me back. "Don't worry. I won't mess up your hair."

It wasn't my hair I was worried about—it was always a mess anyway. "So are you taking me to dinner?"

"Come on."

We headed out together. It wasn't until I was halfway into a fettuccine coma that I remembered I hadn't found Gary again. I mentally shrugged. It couldn't have been that important anyway.

Chapter Six

When Lydia called me into her office for our status meeting, I was armed and ready.

I sailed past Jessica with a breezy "Good morning."

She squinted at me. I wanted to tell her she should get glasses before she developed unsightly crow's feet but Lydia was waiting. Patting the manila folder, I straightened my shoulders and walked in.

Lydia sat on her throne, her back to me. I thought she was contemplating the sunny autumn San Francisco day through the wall-to-wall window until I heard her bark into the phone.

"I don't give a damn. I will *not* let this happen. Do you understand me?"

I bit my lip. The person on the other end of the line would have to be deaf not to understand her. I hesitated by the door. Maybe I should go back outside to give her privacy.

Before I could escape, she whirled around and

waved me into the chair across from her. Then she pounded her fist on her desk. "That's bullshit, Drake, and you know it."

Wow. I adjusted my glasses and sat down. I'd never seen Lydia so, um, impassioned. She was usually the epitome of cool. Now she had red splotches on her cheeks. And was that a strand of hair out of place?

She hit the table again. "Damn you."

I jumped. Yikes. I hoped she never got angry with me.

"The day I see that happen is the day I see you in hell." She slammed the phone down and glared at me.

Oh shit. I swallowed. Maybe now wasn't the best time for this meeting. "I can come back later . . ."

"Sit," she barked, getting up from her chair. I wanted to cringe as she came around her desk toward me. Fortunately I resisted the urge to scream *don't hit me*. Not that it mattered, because she continued on to her private bathroom.

Whew. I relaxed. That was close. At least now I knew that if Lydia ever got angry at me I should invest in a one-way ticket to Siberia and hope she didn't track me down.

When she reentered the office five minutes later there was no sign that she'd ever been upset. Her complexion was creamy again and her hair the shiny smooth cascade it always was.

"Give me your report," she said as she sat down and crossed her long, silk-encased legs.

I blinked a couple times. *Can we say schizo?* "I made great progress last week. While I don't have a long list, I believe the quality of the candidates makes up for the quantity."

"Let's see it." She held out an elegant hand that had a whopping sapphire on it.

Instead of thinking about the hefty down payment I could put on a house with that stone, I opened my folder and pulled out my spreadsheets. "I have a comprehensive report on each potential donor. Granted, they aren't as detailed as I'd like, but the initial information is accurate and gives a good picture of the positives and negatives for each one."

Lydia took the papers and flipped through them casually. I tried to read her expression for a sign of approval but I only saw frosty calculation.

I cleared my throat. "And I'm still amassing data, so this isn't the final gene pool to select from. Since I have another two weeks, I thought—"

"You have only one more week." Lydia handed the spreadsheets back to me. "I want to make my decision by the third week, which means you have until next Friday to amass your list. The last week I'll meet with the men you've lined up and make my decision."

I almost fell out of my chair. "Next Friday?" That was seven days away.

She arched a perfect blond eyebrow. "Is that a problem?"

Hell yeah, it was a problem. "No, not at all." I hoped I sounded confident instead of like I was going to throw up. "Next Friday is doable."

"Good." She opened her laptop and began clacking at an insane speed. I type fast but not that fast. Oh, the work I could get done if my fingers moved at the speed of light.

But even the lightning-quick tapping of Lydia's

digits didn't distract me from the burst of panic that shot through me.

Okay, I didn't have room for doubts. I needed to make more money, especially after the tidy sum I'd given my dad earlier this week. Earth was created in six days, right? Two weeks had to be long enough to find a sperm donor.

Besides, look at what I'd accomplished in one week. I didn't have a ton of names, but the ones I'd collected had potential. Especially Joseph—my gut told me he was the one.

Lydia glanced up. "Was there anything else, Katherine?"

"No." Silly me for not realizing I was dismissed. I gathered up my papers and arranged them in their proper order again. "I'll have the final list for you next week."

She gave me another cold look before returning to her work. I tiptoed out of her office so I wouldn't disturb her, easing the door closed behind me.

Jessica looked up and her eyes narrowed again.

I shook my head. "I can give you the number for my optometrist if you'd like. He's really excellent but inexpensive. Did you know about one and a half million Americans have glaucoma but don't know it? Tell you what—I'll e-mail it to you." I smiled at her and headed for my closet—um, I mean, office.

On my way down I made a mental list. First, I needed to call Luc and ask him to take me out again. Two more outings and I should be set.

Then I needed to start my expense report—going out was costly. Good thing I wasn't a social creature—I couldn't imagine where my savings would be if I went out all the time.

Being the queen of multitasking, I opened an expense sheet in Excel as I reached for the phone to call Luc. The phone rang four times before his answering machine clicked on.

"You've reached Healing Touch Massage Therapy. I'm sorry I missed your call, but if you leave . . ."

I was looking for a receipt in my handbag when the digital beep on Luc's machine sounded. "Luc, it's me. I was wondering if you'd like to go out. Maybe this weekend?" I smiled appealingly before I realized he wouldn't be able to see it. "Um, call me, okay?"

The second I hung up, my extension rang. "Research. This is Katherine Murphy speaking."

"Katherine, this is Gary. Luc introduced us at my gallery opening last night."

"Hello, Gary." I wrinkled my nose, momentarily giving up on the receipt. Why was he calling me?

"You're probably wondering why I'm calling you—"

Ha.

"—I saw you and knew you were just the person I was looking for, and I was wondering if you'd sit for me."

"Sit for you?" The first image that came to mind was of me in a leash, obediently heeling. "I don't know what Luc told you, but I'm not into kinky sex."

Gary roared so loudly I had to hold the receiver away from my ear to avoid going deaf from his laughter.

"God, you're hilarious. No kinky sex," he said,

gasping for breath. "I just want to paint your portrait."

"Why would you ever want to do that?" I mean, I wasn't chopped liver, but I wasn't the kind of woman poets wrote odes about. I did look really good in my DKNY suits, though.

"You have an amazingly interesting face. Your eyes—I can't wait to tackle the challenge of capturing the mix of innocence and imp reflected there."

"I don't know what Luc told you, but I don't have much time. Especially over the next few weeks." When Lydia gave me the VP spot I was going to be extremely busy.

"I don't need much of a time commitment from you. I just need to draw some initial sketches that I'll use as guides for the painting."

Remembering some of his artwork, I frowned. "I'm not going to be a big, frizzy blob on a white canvas, am I?"

He was still roaring with laughter when he hung up a couple of minutes later. I'd read that laughter could cure all manner of illness. Gary must be one of the healthiest people on earth.

I opened my calendar and typed in the time and place of our meeting. He was eager to get started, so I'd agreed to meet him Sunday morning at eleven.

As soon as I hit Save my phone rang again. I sighed mentally. "Research. Katherine Murphy speaking."

"Hey, squirt. What's up?"

I frowned. "Why can't I have a better nickname

than squirt? Why can't you call me Kat-woman or something? It sounds so much more heroic."

"Squirt seems appropriate. Especially given this assignment your boss gave you."

"Humph."

"This is a switch. Usually when you want something from me you don't complain."

Oh yeah. I forgot about that. "Have I told you lately how much I value your friendship?"

"You need more suckers for your list, don't you?"

"What if I just wanted the pleasure of your company?"

He snorted. "Kat, you haven't called me just to hang out in months."

Oh, the guilt. He was right. I was a shitty friend. I vowed right then that once this assignment was over and I had my raise, I'd do something really nice for Luc to show him how much he meant to me.

Now, I cleared my throat. "Does this mean you won't go out with me tonight?"

There was a pregnant pause before I heard him sigh. "No, I'll go. God knows you need someone to keep an eye on you."

"Oh, thank you, Luc." What a relief. "According to most religions, including Christianity, Islam, and paganism, your good deeds will be rewarded in the afterlife."

Luc grunted. "I should be so lucky. Meet me at Market and Octavia at eight. Bring your laundry."

"My laundry?" I wrinkled my nose.

"Do you trust me?"

Damn it, I hated it when he asked that. "Yes."

"Then just be there. Don't be late." He hung up before I could ask any additional questions.

Laundry? What was he planning on doing? Beating men into submission with my underthings?

Gross. I shook the image out of my mind and got back to the grind.

This side assignment of Lydia's was seriously infringing on my regular work, and I had a ton of research to catch up on. We'd just landed an account for a major chocolate manufacturer, and the marketing geniuses upstairs wanted the history of the Easter Bunny for some brilliant idea they had.

I was neck deep in pagan lore (I never knew Easter wasn't celebrated in the United States until after the Civil War) when a knock on my door disrupted me.

In this day of cellular technology and e-mail, no one knocks on my door. So when it happened, I didn't know what to do except to stare at it like the plywood had suddenly sprouted arms.

A head poked in. "Hi, Katherine. Are you busy?"

I frowned at Rebecca. I was at work—of course I was busy. "Did you need something?"

Rebecca slipped in and, since there was no place for her to sit, she closed the door and leaned against it. "How's it going?"

"Okay."

Rebecca was the slave—I mean assistant—for the VP of operations. She hardly ever talked to me, much less visited me in my closet/office. She's one of those women whose mouth wouldn't melt butter in the presence of men or other women more powerful than her—like Lydia—but who didn't give the time of day to those deemed lower than herself.

Ergo, me. The mere fact that she was here made me suspicious.

She smiled. "I heard you had a meeting with Lydia today."

I smiled back. "That's right."

"So." She adjusted her skirt, which was too short for the workplace, though I bet it got her a decent salary. "What did you guys talk about?"

"Some research she wants me to do for her," I answered cautiously. I was no dummy—Rebecca was on a fishing expedition. I just didn't know why. Why would anyone care if Lydia was jonesing for sperm?

"What kind of research?"

Did her skirt just ride up to show more of her legs?

I blinked my eyes a few times. And then I gasped mentally. She was flirting with me. First that bartender, and now Rebecca. What was it about me that suddenly had women coming on to me?

Maybe I was exuding some kind of pheromone. "Did you know the chemicals that attract us to other people are predominantly found in sweat?"

Her eyes widened. Uh-oh—I hoped she wasn't getting turned on even more by my intellect. It *was* one of my most alluring features.

I needed to nip this in the bud before she got the wrong idea about me. "Rebecca, I went to this club the other night. The bartender there was really nice. You should go meet her." I wrote down the name and address of the bar on a sticky note and handed it to her. "She's a doll—you'll love her."

She looked down at the note with a puzzled expression. I smiled encouragingly at her. It couldn't be easy being open about your sexuality, even in this day and age. People could be judgmental. I added what I hoped was an extra bit of compassion to my gaze.

She walked out of my office like she was astounded. Probably overwhelmed by my understanding.

I worked nonstop until after seven—not planned but because I lost track of time. And I still had to pick up some laundry before I met Luc.

I looked at my Timex. Expense a cab? I sighed and dashed out of the building to catch the Muni home.

Of course the bus was late, so I arrived at home with milliseconds before I was due to meet Luc a mile away. I grabbed all the laundry I could find and stuffed it into a large bag. I took the time to make sure my hair was under control and even touched up my gloss before I waddled out (my bag was heavy).

The bus stop was a couple of blocks away, and by the time I walked uphill to the corner where I was supposed to meet Luc I was breathless. And limping—my blister had flared up with a vengeance. Sweat made my glasses slip down my nose, which I hate, and the silk shell I wore under my suit stuck to my skin and bunched uncomfortably under my arms.

Luc stood on the corner unencumbered, looking cool and fresh. He dared smile at me—not trying to conceal his amusement at the spectacle I made.

The bastard.

I tried to remember that he was helping me, but

I was tired and hungry and grungy. So my greeting was like a growl. "Where's your laundry?"

He took the bag off my shoulder and I was suddenly much lighter. "At home. I have a washer and dryer, remember?"

"Then why do I have my laundry?" I could have met him at his loft and done it there.

"Because you need to meet more men." He walked up the street, shortening his stride so I could keep up.

"So this is a *wax on, wax off* kind of thing?"

He grinned. "Exactly." He pushed the door open. "After you, squirt."

I gave him a dirty look and walked into the laundromat. "What does doing laundry have to do with meeting—"

I adjusted my glasses and then blinked a couple times for good measure. Wow—the place was really crowded. I glanced at Luc. "But it's Friday night. I didn't think people did their laundry Friday nights."

"They do here. This is a great place to pick up people." He dumped my bag in front of a washer that had just opened up (I didn't miss the come-hither smile the woman who just finished using it gave him, or that he returned it) and stood back. "Get to it, squirt."

Glaring at him, I began stuffing the machine. I didn't have very many clothes to wash other than underwear (I have to dry-clean my suits and blouses), but I had linens like towels and sheets. I wrestled it all into the washer, slammed the door closed, and started the load.

"Done." I looked up but Luc wasn't there. It took me a moment to find him (yes, there were that many people). He sat on a plastic seat, talking to the woman who had just vacated our washing machine.

Hey! We were supposed to be finding men for me. I scowled at him. Fine. I could do this on my own. After all, I was the one who found Joseph.

I surveyed the scene, cruising for the perfect sperm donor. No, I wasn't sure what the perfect sperm donor looked like, but some men were easy to eliminate. Like the guy in the back left corner who wore the spiky dog collar and had a green Mohawk. Though the mood I was in tonight, I was tempted to go over and get the guy's info. Hey—if he had blue eyes and dimples he was viable.

But I decided to approach a man in the opposite corner of the room. I sighed, reminded myself of my dream, and straightened my skirt. Here went nothing.

I advanced upon my quarry, a smile pasted on my face. I felt disappointed when I saw he didn't have the right color eyes, but I stifled that and forged on. "Excuse me."

He raised both his eyebrows at me. "Yes?"

"Do you consider yourself ambitious?"

His face screwed up like he was giving the question serious thought. Great—he was introspective. That was excellent.

"I suppose," he answered slowly.

Hmm. He sounded unsure. I wasn't sure Lydia wanted an indecisive baby, so I had doubts about this one. Still, it couldn't hurt to ask him a few more questions just to be sure. "Have you ever had a run-in with the law?"

"No." He frowned at me. "Have you?"

"God no. I mean, other than that time in college when someone pulled the fire alarm and they questioned everyone in my dorm."

His eyes crossed, which had to mean he was especially genetically evolved, right?

I bit my lip, wondering what to ask him next. Then I remembered my conversation with Gary. "Are you into kinky sex?" I was sure Lydia wouldn't want a deviant for offspring.

His eyes widened. "Are you?"

I tipped my chin and thought about that. I wasn't sure, actually. I didn't think I was, but then I'd only ever had two sexual encounters. Both in college with the same guy, and both suboptimal. At least I think they were suboptimal—I had no basis for comparison.

"I'm not sure," I finally responded. "I suppose there's always a possibility."

His eyes widened more. Even though they weren't blue, they were a very pretty shade of gray. If he wore the right color shirt, I was sure his eyes would look blue enough for Lydia.

Yes, I could add him to the list. I dug in my purse for my handheld. "Could I get your name and number?"

"Sure!"

I loved his enthusiasm—that was just what we needed. I quickly jotted down all the info he gave me (he was quite thorough, giving me his home, cell, and work numbers in addition to two e-mail addresses), smiled at him genuinely this time, and went in search of the next candidate.

I bit my lip. A lot of men, but they all looked kind of young. I wondered if it was a bad thing.

Probably not, considering sperm was more vital the younger the guy was, right?

In fact, a younger guy might be just the thing. Variety was the spice of life, and the more choices Lydia had, the better.

I surveyed the crowd and found the perfect young specimen. He was clean cut, wore glasses (that was surely a sign of intelligence), and was reading the *Wall Street Journal*. It'd be a match made in heaven.

I made a beeline for him. He didn't look up as I approached. Apparently the article he was reading was fascinating, because I stood directly in front of him and he didn't notice me. Focus—that was a good thing. I took the opportunity to get closer and check out his eye color.

He glanced up, did a double take, and jumped back with a muffled shriek.

Hmm. He was a little jumpy. I wasn't sure Lydia would like that.

I smiled. "Hi. Are you a student?"

"Y-yes," he answered hesitantly.

He stuttered. Maybe I'd chosen the wrong guy.

But I decided to give him the benefit of the doubt and interrogate—er, interview—him a bit more. "Do you work?"

"Um, yes. Part time."

Industrious. He was looking better by the second. "Have you had any childhood diseases that could impair sperm production?"

He choked.

Odd. I frowned at him. He wasn't chewing anything. Did he choke on saliva? Did I want someone on Lydia's list who couldn't handle spit?

Don't think so. I smiled at him, said "I think I hear my friend calling me," and crossed the laundromat to rejoin Luc.

"What'd you say to that poor guy? He looked like he was going to hurl."

"Did you know when frogs vomit, they eject their whole stomach, clean it on the ground, and then swallow it again?"

Luc grinned. "Charming."

"Thanks."

"So that guy"—he jerked his chin at the boy I'd just questioned—"wasn't he a little young?"

I shrugged. "I thought there might be advantages to younger men."

"Right. They might be more malleable. And more horny."

"Please." I held out my hands. "I don't need details."

He laughed. I took a second to bask in the joy of it before I went to check on my laundry.

Time to throw it in the dryer. I grabbed a basket and began unloading.

Luc came over to help. "So how many more names do you need on your list?"

I shrugged, shaking out my sheets. "Five would do it, I think. It's hard to tell. I've got some candidates with great potential, though."

"Jesus, Kat—we've got to take you clothes shopping." He held up a pair of ratty bikinis.

"Hey!" I snatched them and glared at him. "Leave my underwear alone."

"Seriously, Kat, we should go shopping." He wheeled the cart over to the only available dryer.

"You need some casual clothes and obviously some lingerie."

"Lingerie?" I wrinkled my nose. "What do I need lingerie for?"

He rolled his eyes. "Don't tell me I need to draw you a picture."

I flushed. In high school, I heard some girls in the locker room giggling about sixty-nine. Like an idiot, I asked Luc what that meant. He drew me a picture. A very detailed one.

The way he gazed at me, I knew he was remembering the same incident. Except instead of the amused light I expected to see, he looked like he was considering something.

"I see a man over there I need to go meet." I gestured behind me, hoping there actually was someone. "Be back soon."

I rushed off, trying to calm myself. I wasn't sure what had just happened, but it felt significant. Something that felt like panic welled in me. I pushed it back and strode toward the first man I saw.

He wore a leather jacket and had an elaborate tribal tattoo down one side of his neck. His hair was long and tangled but at least it looked clean. I couldn't tell what color eyes he had because of the sunglasses perched on his long nose.

I was beyond caring about the criteria. I took a deep breath and stopped right in front of him. Smiling professionally, I asked, "Do you wash your whites separately, or do you throw everything in together?"

He slid his glasses down and stared at me from above the rims. I think I heard him growling too, but it might have been the hum of his dryer.

Not that I was taking chances. I backed away—very slowly. "Good boy. Down." I wished I had a treat to throw at him. I wondered if a box of dryer sheets would be an appropriate substitute.

I bet if I tossed him a pair of black lace panties he'd heel. Maybe that's what Luc was talking about. I made a mental note to buy a pair of black panties to keep in my purse. For emergency situations like this.

Chapter Seven

I met Gary at his flat Sunday morning, eleven o'clock sharp. I would have liked starting earlier, but in retrospect eleven was good. Spending the entire night out was wearying.

Okay, Luc and I weren't out the *entire* night. I guess not even half the night. But after a couple days in a row it seemed like all night.

Though last night was pretty mellow. We went to a reading at a bookstore.

Now—standing in front of Gary's door and reflecting on the night before with Luc—a happy, warm glow infused me. I was still smiling softly when Gary opened the door.

"Katherine! You're just in time." He grabbed my arm and yanked me in. "The light is absolutely perfect right now. Come, come."

He guided me through his house so quickly I barely had time to register the enormous canvases lining the walls, floor to ceiling. Or the plush white furniture and rugs. I glanced down at my shoes and hoped they weren't muddy.

"Nice place," I commented as Gary dragged me up a narrow staircase.

"Thanks. My parents left it to me when they passed on."

If only I had parents who left me a cottage in Sea Cliff. I wouldn't be able to afford a closet in this neighborhood, much less a house.

Jealous? *Me?* Never.

I craned my neck to look up where we were headed. "It's pretty big, isn't it?"

"Yeah, but I rent out the bottom floor. It affords the luxury of working on my art. And the whole house is too big for just me and Jeremy." He glanced back at me. "That's my boyfriend."

Right—the slight, bookish man at the gallery opening.

We reached the top of the stairs and Gary pulled me through a doorway into a room of light.

"Oh wow," I murmured reverently.

Gary laughed, the deep belly laugh I was beginning to recognize as part of who he was. "It is spectacular, isn't it?"

"Understatement." Half the roof was glass as well as one entire wall, letting light stream in unfiltered. He had canvases in various stages of production propped up all over, an easel standing in the middle of the room. In one corner, there was a long lounging couch. It made me want to go drape myself across it dramatically, like in a faint. "It's fabulous."

"Thanks." He grinned at me. "But we're wasting time."

"Okay." I couldn't help it. I went to the fainting couch, dropped my bag on the floor, and flopped across it. "Ready."

Gary laughed. "Perfect. Hold that pose." He rifled through a box and pulled out a huge pad and thick pencil.

Propping my chin on my fist, I watched him begin his maniacal sketching. He was a paradox. Just looking at him, I'd think he was more at home on a motorcycle than in an attic studio. Amazing that such big, hamlike hands could produce what they did.

"Tilt your head to the left. Not so much—yeah, just like that. Wait." He reached over and plucked my glasses away.

"Hey!" The world was suddenly sharply out of focus.

"Better," he muttered. He flipped a sheet of paper over and continued his crazy drawing.

I stared at him a while longer before I gave up trying to bring him into focus and let my mind wander to the night before. Unfortunately, I hadn't met any men to put on the list. I completely forgot that was what I was out to do. Once, I started toward a promising-looking guy, but Luc pulled me back and said, "I don't like all this attention you're giving other men. Be with just me tonight, Kat." I'd felt so guilty about being a lousy friend that I didn't give my assignment another thought all night.

At least, I think that feeling in the pit of my stomach was guilt.

Surprisingly, I didn't mind the lack of progress. I'd had fun. Luc was fun. I'd forgotten what it was like to have all his attention focused on me. It was like a sugar high without the inevitable crash.

"Whatever it is you're thinking, don't stop. No— don't move." More furious scribbling.

I froze in midmotion.

"Damn, you're not thinking it anymore," Gary mumbled under his breath. "I want that smile back on your face. I've never seen that smile on your face before."

I was going to point out that Gary hadn't exactly known me for long, but I decided to keep my mouth shut. Instead I shifted to get more comfortable and dreamed about the color of the tile I was going to put in the bathroom of the house I was going to buy after I got my promotion.

It was the change in the room's light quality that alerted me that quite a bit of time had passed. I listed in my mind everything I needed to do today, starting with finalizing my sperm donor list and the reports on each one. I tried not to fidget but I could feel the seconds tick by—each second I could be spending working toward my dream of owning a home.

Gary sighed and slapped the gigantic pad against his thigh. "You lost that look again."

"Sorry." I hoped I sounded sincere. Not that I wasn't—I just didn't really know what I was apologizing for.

"That's okay. I think I got what I wanted anyway."

I swung my feet down and sat up. "I can't believe you want to make a painting of me."

"You have such an interesting face. Urchin, with

these great eyes full of wise naïveté. It'll be a challenge conveying that on canvas."

Personally, I thought my lips were more of a selling point than my muddy green eyes, but I let him think what he wanted.

"Do you always wear suits?"

I looked up from straightening my clothes. "Excuse me?"

He shrugged and then stretched. "Just wondering. I've only ever seen you in suits."

What was it about this guy? You'd think he'd known me forever, the way he talked. I couldn't help pointing out our brief relationship this time. "This is only the second time we've met."

"But it's Sunday. No one wears suits on Sunday."

"Well, I do." Really, I had no choice. All I had were suits. They were easy and practical. And I didn't want to spend money on casual clothes when I didn't need them.

Gary walked me down to the main floor of his flat. To my surprise, Luc and Gary's boyfriend were chatting and having coffee.

I frowned, hands on hips. "What are you doing here?"

"That's what I love about you, squirt. You always make me feel so welcome."

Gary's chortle turned into a cough when I shot him my Lydia stare. "Katherine, have you met my boyfriend?"

Jeremy smiled at me. "Gary's been so excited to get started on your portrait."

"Oh." I glanced at Gary, who beamed proudly at his man. "Did you know the U.S. government won't allow portraits of living people on stamps?"

Luc snorted and stood up. "We should go."

"We should?" I wrinkled my nose at him.

"Yeah. We have things to do."

Oh—he was going to help me with my assignment again. I smiled at him, full and genuine. Luc was such a great friend.

He smiled back and took my hand. "Thanks for the chat, Jeremy. And the ideas."

"Anytime." Jeremy winked.

I stared at them. What was that about?

But I didn't have time to ponder it before Luc started dragging me out the door. (What is it about men manhandling me all the time?)

Normally, I would have been full of questions about where we were headed as well as cluing him in on my schedule, but today I was distracted by the way he held on to my hand, firm but not restricting, as we walked down the street.

Luc is touchy-feely. I know this. But holding my hand for so long was unprecedented, even for him. Usually he'll put an arm around me as we walk, sure, but this holding hands business was weird. Really weird. I began to feel uncomfortable, trying to discreetly pull away, but he held on tighter.

"Where are we headed?" I opted for an innocuous question.

"To my car."

I nodded. Sure. Of course we were. "Are you going with me to the park?"

He looked down at me and cocked an eyebrow. "The park?"

"I thought it'd be a good place to meet men." On Sundays, Golden Gate Park was closed off to car traffic and opened to rollerbladers, bicyclists, and pedestrians.

"You're going like that?"

I looked down at myself. "Like what?"

He shook his head. "Sometimes you're so clueless, Kat."

What the hell? I looked down again. I was wearing Donna Karan. My Ferragamos were polished, my suit ironed, and my nylons had no snags. I was no cover model, but I did really well in the clothes department, I thought, considering I had no female influence growing up. Not past the age of six anyway.

Besides, I remembered my mom to be dressed up most of the time. Heels, dresses, make-up—the whole works. So my dad would remember how attractive he found her and wouldn't be tempted to stray, I heard her tell a friend once.

It worked too well—he still hadn't forgotten.

Luc unlocked the car door and held it open for me.

A moment on his car. If he were ten years older, I'd think he was going through a middle-life crisis. Luc drives an *expensive* convertible Mercedes. He maintains that the car's older and that he got it for a steal, but I looked up the Blue Book value once (the Internet is a wonderful thing) and saw exactly what it was worth. Which wasn't taking into consideration that he kept it in mint condition and spent what I was sure was an obscene amount on upkeep.

I was strapped in and ready to get rolling by the time he climbed in. I was already mentally arranging the list of questions I was going to ask the men I met by the time he turned the key in the ignition.

I suppose it was because I was so focused on my questions that I didn't notice we were headed in the opposite direction from the park. "Where are we?"

"Union Street."

What the hell were we doing on Union Street? The only things there were expensive clothing stores and chichi restaurants. I never came to Union Street.

I was about to protest, but then I noticed all the men walking around on the street. I turned to Luc and smiled. I knew I could count on him. "Thank you so much."

He glanced at me. "We haven't done anything yet."

"But it's going to be fantastic. I just know it." I sat back and rearranged my questions again. Asking someone if he was prone to athlete's foot probably wasn't the place to start in a nonathletic setting.

Luc pulled into a parking spot right on Union Street. His parking karma is remarkable. If I a) had a car and b) were trying to park it, I was sure I'd have to go Timbuktu to find a spot.

As he locked up, I took the opportunity to look around. Where to start? "Do you think it'd be too abrupt if I just walk up to someone and ask them if they wear boxers or briefs? Briefs inhibit sperm production, you know."

Luc rolled his eyes and took my hand again. "Come on."

What was with the hand-holding?

But I didn't say anything since he was guiding

me with purpose. Obviously he had a plan, and when Luc has a plan there's no standing in his way.

I didn't notice where we headed because I was so distracted by all the successful preppy men strolling in the street. In fact, Luc had opened the door to the shop and was guiding me in before I snapped out of my reverie.

"What the—" I slapped my hand on the door frame to keep from being pulled in. "Where are you taking me?"

"Inside." He tugged on my hand. "We're buying you some clothes."

"The hell we are." I gripped the wooden frame with all my might.

"Come on. You need some casual clothes. You can't keep going out on Sundays dressed like that."

"Sure I can."

"No, you can't. Remember junior year when I convinced you to go to the winter formal?"

"I wish I could forget." I'd worn this glittery pantsuit I found at the thrift store and had stood out like a sore thumb. Who knew bell-bottoms were out? I winced, recalling the way the other kids had whispered and pointed. It would have been better if I'd been invisible like I was every day at school. At least Luc had been there, and having him at my side kept any *Carrie*-like situations from happening.

"If you'd been wearing something appropriate for the occasion, you'd have had a great time." He squeezed my hand. "That's all we're going to do. Get you some clothes so you have better success."

"Thoreau said to beware of all enterprises that require new clothes."

"It won't be so bad, Kat."

"Easy for you to say." My fingers slipped and I was in the store.

Finally I knew the location of hell on earth.

Shit.

I turned around to dash out but Luc wrapped his arm around my waist and pulled me back. He leaned down to speak softly into my ear. "You need some casual clothes. Don't worry. I'll help you. It won't be so bad."

His breath tickled me in a funny way I ignored. I had bigger fish to fry. "There's no way I'm wasting my money on casual clothes."

"You won't be wasting your money. Look at it as an investment."

I stared back at him suspiciously. "How do you mean?"

"You'll have better success collecting your list if you're a little less"—he cleared his throat—"up-tight looking. I mean, come on, Kat—how many people wear suits to the park on Sunday?"

Maybe he had a point. I pouted. "You think I'll be more successful?"

"Definitely."

Luc wouldn't lie to me, so I relaxed. A tiny bit. I wasn't happy that I'd have to waste money on clothes I didn't want. Maybe I could expense them?

Then I became conscious of the press of his front against my back and I flushed. Bright red, I'm sure.

I eased away. "Fine. Let's get this over with."

Luc smiled, full and bright, making me feel like a jerk for resisting when he was obviously so looking forward to outfitting me.

A saleswoman chose that moment to approach us. "What can I help you with today?"

I glanced at Luc and shrugged. This was his thing. I had no idea where to start.

Luc tapped his chin with one long finger. "Let's start with jeans."

Jeans. I felt excited despite myself. I hadn't owned a pair of jeans since college, and those I bought secondhand from the thrift store for a buck fifty. They gave me bubble butt.

"Of course." She smiled at him like she wanted to offer him a whole lot more than denim. I resisted scratching her eyes out. "Is there a style you had in mind?"

"What would you suggest?"

Luc and the woman stood back and eyed me up and down. I couldn't help fidgeting. "Did you know one bolt of denim weighs about a quarter of a ton?"

They ignored me, talking about me like I wasn't present.

"She has a very nice figure. I think." The woman frowned. "That suit doesn't do a thing for her. The skirt should be at least two inches shorter."

Gasping, I held my skirt in place. They weren't touching my suit. No way. DKNY was sacred. Sure, I'd got it cheap from an outlet because the lining on one sleeve was sewn wrong so it bunched in the armpit, but still.

Luc nodded. "Do you think you can do something with her?"

"It's a challenge, but I think we can manage." She didn't sound convinced. "Maybe some brighter colors too? The gray of her suit washes her out."

"Hmm." Luc nodded. "I especially like dark greens on her."

I huffed and crossed my arms. "Hey. Remember me? The guinea pig? I'm still here. No need to talk about me like I'm invisible."

They barely glanced at me before they moved to a rack and began rifling through clothes.

Hmm. Fine. I wrinkled my nose at them before attacking one of the racks myself. (Really, I wanted to stick my tongue out at them, but that would have been childish.) I'd show them, though—I'd pick out my own clothes.

I shoved some shirts aside to get to the pants hanging behind them. Green camo. Eew. But they had lots of pockets—the better to carry my hand-held, a notepad, and other necessities. I took it out and searched for the price tag.

Shit! I quickly put them back before I got my fingerprints on them and had to buy them.

Who paid that much money for a pair of pants? Even if they had lots of storage space.

I turned around to tell Luc I'd changed my mind, that I'd make do with the clothes I had (I could dress down my suits by wearing flatter heels), but I didn't get a chance. The saleswoman intercepted me, held my arm firmly, and guided me toward a set of doors in the back.

Somehow I knew that if I passed those doors I'd never make it out alive, so I began to struggle. "This isn't a good idea. I don't need jeans. I'm sorry to waste your time—"

"It's no trouble. I love helping moths metamorphose into butterflies."

I wanted to tell her it was caterpillars that

turned into butterflies, but I was too distracted by the doors looming on my horizon. I tugged my arm. "It's okay. Really. I don't mind being a moth."

Her grip tightened. Damn, she was strong. "You're a butterfly in moth's clothing."

Before I could scream for Luc, she shoved me into a dressing room and closed the door. I could be wrong, but I swear I heard a lock slide into place.

I looked around for a way out, but the walls were all the way to the ceiling. The only thing in there was a chair that'd look great in Lydia's office, a mirror, and a truckload of clothes hanging on a rack.

Shit.

The mirror. If I slammed the chair through it, I could use one of the shards to slit my wrists. Only then there'd be a big mess to clean up and, because I hate housekeeping so much myself, I couldn't put that burden on anyone else.

I sighed, glanced at the clothes, and admitted defeat. Just because they'd trapped me in here with all these clothes didn't mean I was obligated to buy anything. I'd just pick a T-shirt to assuage my guilt that the woman worked so hard and leave. And to appease Luc. After all, how expensive could a T-shirt be?

I picked one up and checked out the tag.

"Yikes!" I adjusted my glasses and looked again. No way—that had to be a typo, didn't it?

"How's it going in there?"

I jumped at Luc's voice. "Um. Okay."

"I want to see it all."

Great. I resolutely took off my clothes, grabbed

the first pair of pants, and crammed myself into them. Literally. I'd blow out the seat if I tried to sit down in them, they were so tight.

I turned to the mirror and frowned. My underwear poofed out of the low waistband of the pants, like tissue paper out of a gift bag. Was it supposed to do that?

"Probably not," I muttered. Unfortunately, stuffing them down so they wouldn't show was almost impossible, and they made the most unsightly bulges.

"Kat?"

I threw on the first shirt that I saw and cracked open the door. "I need a bigger size."

The woman stepped out from nowhere. "Let's see."

Gritting my teeth, I walked out. "It's tight."

"It's supposed to be tight," Satan's handmaiden replied.

Luc made a circle with his finger. "Turn around."

I glared at him but did as he commanded.

"Actually, I think it looks fantastic. What do you think, Leah?"

"It's perfect, Luc. It gives her shape. And it's stretchy, so it'll be comfortable."

Oh great—he was on first-name basis with the help. They'd cemented their united front. I was doomed.

I pouted. "It's not comfortable. I feel mummified."

Leah nodded. "And the shirt looks great on her, don't you think? The wraparound style is great for augmenting her figure."

Read: it makes her look like she has boobs.

Luc nodded. "Does it come in colors other than white?"

"We have pink as well."

"Great. We'll take them both. And the pants."

No, we wouldn't. I opened my mouth to tell them both that under no circumstances was I spending half my down payment on a pair of pants and two shirts, but they pushed me back into the room and told me to change into the next outfit.

In the interest of time, I cooperated. The sooner we finished this, the sooner I could get to the park and scope out the man situation. Enough time after the ordeal was over to tell them there was no way I was going to buy anything.

Unfortunately, as soon as I started to make a dent in the pile of clothing, Leah brought me more. And there was nothing I could do to get out of it.

Luc and Leah had a grand old time while I was locked in the airless changing room. I gritted my teeth against their laughter as I squished myself into the next outfit.

"Glad they're enjoying themselves so thoroughly," I murmured. I blew my hair back (it'd come completely undone) and shoved my underwear into submission. Knowing I must look like a madwoman, I swung the door open to find Luc lounging in a chair with a Coke, flirting with Leah.

I just about gagged.

They glanced up simultaneously.

Leah was the first to comment. "Those jeans look fabulous on her."

Luc nodded but didn't say anything, his eyes scrutinizing intensely.

"I have just the thing to top off that outfit." Leah

rushed off to a rack across the room, grabbed something off its hanger, and came back with her hands filled with red velvet. "Try this," she said as she stuffed me into what turned out to be a jacket.

I scowled at it before I scowled at her. But neither Luc nor Leah paid any attention to me.

"Fabulous." Leah nodded. "I knew it'd look fabulous on her."

"She looks good in red," Luc said, never taking his eyes off me, "and she loves velvet."

I wanted to protest but, in truth, *I* really liked the jacket too. Not that I'd admit it. So I said the only thing that came to mind. "Bees and bulls are attracted to red."

Luc's lips quirked. "Then it's good there aren't very many bulls in San Francisco."

It took another forty-five minutes before I got through all the clothes and was back into my own. I squared my shoulders and strode out of the dressing room to set Luc and Leah straight on fact that I was not spending a dime.

"Now—" I stopped abruptly. They weren't there.

I looked around and found them laughing by the register. There were three enormous bags by Luc's feet.

No way. I strode over and put my hands on my hips when I got to them. "I'm ready to go."

"Great." Luc smiled at Leah. "Thanks for your help. We appreciate it."

"It was fun." She smiled at him, that same smile women always gave him. I wanted to check his pockets to make sure she hadn't slipped him her apartment key.

Luc bent down, picked up the bags, and headed toward the door.

Frowning, I stared after him. To my credit, it only took me a couple of seconds to figure out what was going on.

"Wait!" I rushed after him.

"Just in time." He grinned. "You can open the door."

I did automatically. Ever helpful—that's me. But I rationalized that it'd be better talking out of Leah's hearing anyway. I hurried to his side and tugged on his sleeve. "Tell me you didn't buy those clothes for me."

He glanced down at me. "Well, I didn't buy them for myself. I'm not into cross-dressing."

"Ha ha." I scowled at him. "This is serious. I don't want those clothes."

"They looked great on you. You looked normal for a change."

"What the hell does that mean?"

"Just that you needed new clothes."

I shook my head. "I didn't. I don't. I can't afford to spend that much money. Especially since this week—" I shut my mouth before I said anything else.

Unfortunately, Luc caught my gaffe. He stopped in the middle of the sidewalk and frowned at me. "What do you mean, especially this week?"

"Nothing."

He stared at me and then let loose a string of swear words that had my ears burning. "Tell me you didn't give your dad more money."

I crossed my arms. "Fine."

"Damn it, Kat, when are you going to stop letting him use you?"

I didn't reply. I'd heard it all before. In my head, I even agreed with Luc, but in my heart I couldn't turn him away. I mean, he was my dad.

"Shit." He strode to the car and popped the trunk. I waited for him to unlock my door, which he yanked open, and then watched him walk around the car and get in.

"Shit," he said again, resting his hands on the steering wheel and staring out the window.

I decided to venture a question. "Can't we just return the clothes?"

"The clothes are not the issue, Katherine."

Uh-oh. I was in trouble. "What is the issue, then?"

He cranked the ignition and pulled out of the parking space with barely a look to see if it was clear. "The issue is you let your dad take advantage of you, which forces you to have to take ridiculous assignments at work to make up for it."

I couldn't deny that. "If we can't return the clothes, I'll just repay you." And then maybe I could sell them to a consignment store or something.

"Forget paying for the clothes. I took care of it."

I frowned at him. "What do you mean?"

"I mean screw the clothes. This was going to be my treat from the beginning. This is about that asshole you call your father."

"He is *not* an asshole." I didn't yell it, but it was close.

"What kind of guy hits his daughter up for money all the time? And not just for twenty bucks."

He glanced at me before darting around a stopped bus. "How much was it this time? A thousand? Two?"

I stared out the window and refused to answer.

"Shit," Luc spat savagely. He honked and swerved around a slow car.

Yikes. "Did you know one hundred fourteen people die each day in car accidents? In the U.S., that is."

"I don't get you." He shook his head. "You work so hard to save money, and then the second your dad comes around, you let him con you into giving it to him."

I started to make a clever retort, but Luc gunned it on a yellow light (which turned to red) so I clutched the door handle for dear life instead.

"What was it this time? Blackjack? Or is poker still his game of choice?"

I glared at him. "Are you finished?"

"No."

But he didn't say another word. Not as he tried to get us killed through the steep San Francisco streets, not when he pulled in front of my building, and not when he got out of the car to get my bags out of the trunk. He just handed them to me in angry silence and, before I was even done unlocking the first set of locks to the building, he'd torn off.

"Bastard," I muttered as I lugged my bags up the four flights of stairs. What right did he have lecturing me on my relationship with my dad? It wasn't like he had the most stellar track record with his. Did I ever lecture him? No.

Thankfully, Rainbow didn't poke out to say hello as I let myself into my apartment. I wasn't in the mood to deal with her excessive cheeriness and pleas for attention.

After I locked myself in, I went to my bedroom and dumped the contents of the bags on my bed. I organized everything into the proper piles. The count tallied to four pairs of pants, two skirts, nine tops (including two sweaters), and the red jacket.

I left everything where I'd folded them and put on the jacket.

Okay—I had to admit it. Even though I raised a fuss and didn't want to have the new clothes, underneath it all there was a tiny spark of excitement. I hadn't had anything new in so long.

Except for those pants that were so tight, I really liked the clothes. Luc chose well (as much as I hated to admit it)—most of the clothes were classic.

But the jacket . . . The jacket was perfect—the way it fit as well as how it looked on. Going into the bathroom, I examined my reflection in the old hazy mirror. The color made my skin and eyes glow.

Suddenly I remembered a dress I tried on for the prom—red velvet. I'd wanted it so badly. I'd gone to the store every week to make sure it was still there. I even took Luc there to show it to him. He'd offered to buy it for me but I wanted to earn it myself. I worked extra hours babysitting but I'd had to use the money to pay for our electricity instead. Not that it mattered—my date ended up canceling on me anyway.

Funny—I couldn't even dredge up my date's name. I frowned in thought. He was on the basketball team with Luc, that much I remembered. At the time, I had my suspicions that Luc had put him up to asking me out. After all, why would a popular boy choose to take *me* to the prom?

Luc came over after he found out I'd been stood up. He dismissed any question of what he did with his date (Jenny Sheridan, the head cheerleader—*that* I remembered in vivid detail) and hung out with me the rest of the evening. He said he should have taken me himself.

But Luc didn't count, because he was my friend before he was the most popular boy in school. Or maybe he counted more than anyone.

"Wonder if he remembers that dress," I mumbled to my reflection. I stroked my hands down the front of the jacket.

Somehow, I was sure he did.

Chapter Eight

Lydia was too busy to meet with me Monday morning, which was a relief, to tell the truth. I hadn't made a great amount of progress over the weekend. In fact, looking back, it'd been the most decadent weekend I'd had since I was seven and my dad took me to Las Vegas (we'd stayed at Circus Circus and I watched movies all weekend while he gambled away our rent for the next two months).

I closeted myself in my office and worked on finalizing the research on Easter for the chocolate account. I was tempted to lock the door—there was a lot of commotion going on this morning. But I didn't. No one ever visited me. Not unless they forgot the brooms were in a new location.

And I didn't want to talk to anyone anyway. I was still upset about the fight Luc and I had. I picked up the phone to call him a few times, but each time I set it back down. Once I even let it ring two times before I hung up.

I hated this people stuff. Facts were so much more straightforward. A fact was a fact. No guessing. No gray area. People were so complicated.

Around two o'clock, my phone buzzed, causing me to jump and knock my knees under the desk. I snatched it up before it made that obnoxious noise again. "Research. Kather—"

"There's a delivery for you," a voice interrupted. It sounded like an automated recording, but I knew it was the receptionist downstairs.

"A delivery?" I frowned. I hadn't ordered anything. "Are you sure—"

"Please come get it."

Dial tone.

I stared at the receiver. That was a little abrupt.

Resigned, I got up and headed down to get my so-called delivery. The last time I had a delivery, it was meant for Kathleen Murphy in accounting.

Taking the stairs (it's been proven that exercise reduces anxiety and depression), I got to the lobby a few minutes later. I wouldn't put it past the receptionist to decide to trash the package if I didn't arrive within five minutes.

I saw the flowers the second I stepped out of the stairwell and wished *they* could be for me. The white roses were plump and dewy and numerous. There had to be two dozen. But they wouldn't be mine—most likely Jupiter Communications had sent me some kind of promotional package.

"Hi." I smiled at the receptionist. "You called me."

She looked at me blankly. "And you are?"

I'd only worked here for almost eight years. You'd think she'd know me by now. "Katherine Murphy."

She nodded at the flowers. Then she turned a little and said, "Good morning, Ashworth Communications," into her headset.

I wrinkled my nose at the roses. They were gorgeous, but it was a mistake. No one sent me flowers. No one had ever even handed me flowers. I'd look at the card and end up having to take them to their real recipient.

In that case, might as well enjoy them while I could. I got on my tiptoes and took a deep breath. Wow, they smelled good. Like they'd been spritzed by perfume, because real flowers didn't smell that good.

Like I'd know.

I lifted the card out of the arrangement. Odd— it said *Katherine Murphy*.

That was me.

Frowning, I opened it and pulled out the tiny ivory card (heavy stock, expensive stationary). I blinked. It was in Luc's chicken scratch.

Don't be angry at me for caring about you.

I looked at the flowers and then the note, and then the flowers again.

Luc sent me roses.

I grabbed the vase and scurried for the elevator before someone popped up and said there was a mistake and they weren't really mine. I punched the elevator button for my floor until the doors closed and I was on my way back (fortunately there was no one in there to witness my insane behavior). I got to my office and closed the door, locking it this time. Setting the roses on my desk, I sat down and stared at them.

They were beautiful. So plump. That couldn't be natural, could it? I grabbed a pad of sticky notes and jotted down a reminder to research how roses were manufactured.

Luc sent me roses.

I smelled them again and felt guilty for being such a bitch. Luc was right—he was only being a good friend. I mean, he shouldn't have called my dad an asshole, even if my dad did take advantage of me. Still, he was just concerned about me.

And he bought me all those clothes and I just acted ungrateful.

I picked up the phone and dialed his home number.

"Hello?"

"I got the flowers."

Silence. I could practically hear him thinking. "And?" he finally said.

"I should be sending you roses. *I* was the one who was out of line."

"Yeah, you were a bitch, but I could have been more tactful."

"So, um"—I pushed up my glasses—"does this mean we're still friends?"

"Katherine Murphy, you'll never be able to get rid of me. So don't even try."

All the tension I'd been feeling drained away. "You're the best, Luc." When all of this was over and I had my promotion I was going to do something really really nice for him.

"Remember that in half an hour, okay?"

I frowned. "What does that mean?"

"Just promise."

Promise when I had a sneaking suspicion I wouldn't like whatever he had planned? I think not. "Tell me what you've done."

"No."

"Luc—"

"Promise, Kat. Remember the roses."

I gazed at them. I hated when he backed me into a corner. "Fine. I promise."

"Good." The delight in his voice set my teeth on edge. "Have dinner with me tomorrow."

"I don't know," I said, feeling disgruntled. "I have to pad my list for Lydia and I only have a few more days—"

"To hell with that for an evening. Just come have dinner with me." When I didn't reply, he said, "It's just one dinner. One evening is all I ask."

"Okay." I winced, thinking what a bad friend I was even though I'd resolved to be a better one.

"Wear a new outfit." He hung up.

I set the receiver down and touched a silky petal. I loved having dinner with Luc. It made the guilt over the fact that I wouldn't be working worth it.

But what was happening in half an hour?

I shuddered. Luc was capable of no end of mischief. There was one time in high school when he replaced all the formaldehyded frogs in biology with live ones. It still cracked me up thinking about how Jenny Sheridan, head cheerleader and class bitch, screamed when her frog ribbeted right as she was about to cut into it.

Somehow, I didn't think whatever Luc had

cooked up this time was going to crack me up. Instead of fretting the minutes away until whatever it was he did became apparent, I decided to immerse myself in work.

I didn't get very far before my phone buzzed. I startled—again—and hit my knees in the exact same spot. Rubbing them, I picked it up. "Research. Ka—"

"You have a delivery." Her voice was even more curt this time.

"Be—"

She hung up.

"—right down," I finished needlessly.

I ran down for the second time, alternating between feeling eager and reluctant. It was kind of exciting, even if it could potentially be a frog.

I burst into the lobby and walked to the front desk. "You said there was a delivery for me."

The receptionist looked at me. "And you are?"

Hello? Hadn't we been through this before? "Katherine Murphy."

She reached under the counter and pulled out a box. A big box. "Here." She pushed it toward me and turned her back to attend to something that was obviously more important.

Being dismissed didn't faze me this time. I had a package to deal with anyway.

More flowers? I shook it. Didn't seem like it. Nor did it feel like a frog.

I picked it up gingerly. Holding it out from my body (no telling what was in it, and if it was something gooey I didn't want it anywhere near my suit), I headed for the elevators.

A man stood there waiting. He eyed me and asked, "Going up?"

"Yes. Thank you."

He continued to stare, even when an elevator arrived. He held the door open for me before walking in. "What floor?"

"Twelve, please."

He grinned as he pressed the button. "The way you're holding that box I'd almost think it was a bomb."

I pursed my lips and studied the package. I wouldn't put it past Luc. "Could be."

Then I noticed his dimples. "Oh." I stepped closer to find out what color eyes he had.

Blue.

Yes!

I gave him a real smile. "Do you work here?"

"No. Just visiting a friend."

"A girl friend?"

"A guy friend."

I felt the elation melt from my face.

He chuckled. "Not that type of guy friend."

"Oh." But before I got my hopes up again I glanced at his ring finger.

Sans ring.

Yes!

I smiled again. "How do you feel about the act of procreation?"

He grinned and leaned toward me. "I'm all for it."

"Oh good," I said, relieved.

The elevator pinged its arrival.

I frowned. My floor. But I wasn't ready yet.

The doors slid open and I inched toward it. "Uh, I was, uh, wondering—"

"Let me give you my card." He reached into his suit coat, pulled out a card carrier, and slipped a business card under the ribbon tied around my box. "I hope you call me."

I had to be beaming as I backed out. "Oh, I will."

I love this package, I thought as I hurried to my office to record my impression of—I turned my head sideways to read the card—Pete Vondrigen. I loved Luc. If he hadn't sent this to me I'd still be sitting in my office and I would never have acquired another man for my list.

My mind occupied with thoughts of my spreadsheet, I absently pulled the ribbon on the box and opened it. Mentally reordering the list in order of greatest sperm potential, I clawed through fluffy tissue until my hand hit the contents.

And I froze.

What the hell?

I pulled out a tiny pair of briefs.

At least I think they were briefs. They didn't look like any Jockeys I'd ever seen. My underwear was white and functional. This was—well, brief.

"And see-through," I murmured, holding it up to the light.

I laid it on my desk and took out another fistful, each of them as lacy and lacking in fabric as the one before. I looked inside and saw matching bras that made my own Hanes Her Ways look like old-woman foundation garments.

Then I found a card.

To go with your new clothes.

I studied one of the panties again and the light clicked. Of course—they sat low on your hips so you didn't have to stuff your underwear into your pants. No bunching. Ingenious.

Another thought struck me. *Luc bought me underwear.*

No, not underwear—lingerie.

He'd picked out every single panty.

I lifted a bra out of the box. He'd touched this.

I shivered. A decidedly pleasant shiver.

My door burst open and one of the girls from the mail room barged in. "Hey," she said, tossing my mail on the desk in casual disregard like she did every day. The box caught her eye and she did a double take. "Holy shit! Did you get all that as a gift?"

"Yes, I did." I think I sounded as bewildered as she did.

"Holy shit." She shook her head. Then she noticed the roses. "Same guy?"

I nodded, feeling uncomfortable. I wanted to explain that it was just Luc, so it didn't mean anything. I mean, he was just being thoughtful.

"Hot damn," she said reverently. She picked up one of the panties. "I *love* Cosabella."

Who knew she was lesbian? I wondered if Cosabella worked for AshComm too. Maybe I should set her up with Rebecca, the secretary from operations.

"This guy *likes* you."

"Excuse me?" I pushed my glasses up to see her better.

She waved her hand over the box. "The guy who gave all this to you. He's into you in a big way."

"No, he's not."

"Yeah, he is. No guy buys a woman lingerie like this unless he's *really* into her. The only kind of lingerie I've ever gotten is tacky crotchless Frederick's of Hollywood shit." She picked up a bra. "This guy bought you tasteful, functional lingerie. You can deduce that he cares about your comfort—"

Okay, that was true.

"—but that he wants to see you in something sexy." She nodded. "Mm-hmm, he *really* cares about you."

"See me in it?" I began to hyperventilate.

"Well, yeah. No guy buys a woman lingerie without expecting to see it on her."

"They don't?" Spots appeared before my eyes. I dropped onto the corner of my desk, smashing the lid of the box.

"Hell no. And this guy is a smooth operator. Lucky you." She whirled around, her mailbag whacking my thigh, and walked out.

I looked down at the pile of new underwear. Sweat broke out on my forehead. I picked up one of the scarlet scraps and imagined modeling it for Luc.

Nope. Wasn't happening.

I stuffed everything back in the box, jammed the mashed-up lid on top, and shoved it under my desk. I sat down, ignoring how my feet kept knocking into it.

Only the scent of the roses kept distracting me. I debated putting them outside my office, but I'd never gotten flowers before and they really did smell nice.

White roses—red meant love. White, no doubt, meant friendship, right? I mean, Luc gave all this stuff to me because he knew I was stressed and he wanted to do something nice for me.

Yeah, that had to be it.

I opened a browser and Googled *roses colors meaning*. Clicking on the first site, I read down the list until I came to *white*. There were several meanings listed, but what caught my eyes were *you're heavenly* and *I'm worthy of you*.

Shit.

Wait a minute. I sat back. Luc probably didn't know what the colors meant. He probably didn't even pick them out.

Whew—what a relief. The tension melted from my shoulders.

Because the thought of me and Luc . . .

My breathing hitched and caught in my throat. Then I thought about his hands and the way they held mine and how the tips of his fingers were just a little bit rough and imagined how they'd feel trailing down my belly to push my new pants down to look at my new panties . . .

Holy cow.

I crossed my legs (which made my knees scrape against my desk—again) and fanned myself. Those were not thoughts I needed to have, especially about my best friend.

Focus. I needed to focus. Opening the file I'd been working on all day, I hunched and got busy. Only, instead of concentrating on the origin of the

Easter Bunny, all I could think of was Luc undressing me, his intense gaze devouring every inch of my body.

I managed to get through the day (barely), but by the time I got to my apartment I was in a state. Dropping my bag by the door, I paced back and forth in my apartment's entryway, holding the box of lingerie.

I needed to talk to someone. Usually I'd call Luc but—damn him—I obviously couldn't do that this time. Who else was there?

I stopped abruptly. I had no choice.

I headed back out the door, cursing Luc with every step for leaving me no other course of action. Propping the box under my arm, I took a deep breath and knocked.

In two seconds Rainbow swung open her door. Her face lit up like Times Square at night. "Kath! What a surprise."

"Can I come in?" I asked before I lost my nerve.

"Sure thing. I'll make us some tea."

At the mention of tea, I tripped over the pile of shoes by the door. "Um, great burglar alarm. If anyone breaks in, you'll hear them before they start burgling."

She grinned over her shoulder on her way to the kitchenette. "That's true. You're so clever."

I wish. Sometimes my intellect was right up there with an earthworm's.

Cautiously, to avoid breaking my neck on any other obstacles (though that would have solved all my problems—hmm . . .), I went into the living area. The futon was clear of clothing this time, so I set the box of lingerie on it and sat down.

Then I sniffed.

It smelled surprisingly good in here. Kind of fruity and sweet. I looked around for the source. Maybe she changed the kind of incense she used (thank God).

"I'm totally shocked you came over," Rainbow said, peeking out from the kitchen. "I wasn't sure you'd ever come over again."

"Why not?"

She shrugged. "You left so suddenly the last time. I thought maybe I did something to offend you."

Mental wince. "Um, I remembered something I had to do," I lied.

"Oh." She beamed. "Well, you're here now."

She disappeared again only to emerge a couple minutes later with two steaming mugs. She handed me one before sitting Indian-style on the floor.

"Thanks." I set it on top of the least precarious stack of magazines on the table. "Did you get new incense? It smells really good."

Her eyes lit up. "You think so?"

"Well, yes. I like it a lot. More than whatever you were burning the last time." Hint hint.

"It's a new combination I'm trying. I've been experimenting all week. I've had such a hard time coming up with the right ratio of citrus."

"Experimenting?" I almost groaned at the image of Rainbow playing mad scientist next door. I didn't have many possessions, but what I had I didn't want blown up.

"Yeah. I was thinking of expanding my aromatherapy line."

"Your aromatherapy line?"

She grinned sheepishly. "I kind of sell oils, incense, and lotions."

"Oh." Luc took me to Berkeley once and the streets were lined with people like Rainbow selling their wares. "Where do you sell them?"

"They get distributed to various stores on the West Coast."

"They do?" I knew my eyes had to be popping out of my head in surprise.

"Yeah. Well. It's groovy," she said modestly. "I earn money doing something I like, and I'm bringing pleasure to people in the process."

There was one thing I needed to wrap my head around. "How many stores on the West Coast?"

"Around three dozen or so. The business has really taken off the last couple years." She grinned. "My accountant's happy."

Rainbow—an aromatherapy mogul? What was she doing living here? I opened my mouth to ask her but I thought it might be rude, so I picked up my mug and drank some tea instead.

Yuck. At least the tea was the same. Not that I was complaining—I would have been really disillusioned if it hadn't been.

"What's in the box?"

I adjusted my glasses and focused on my neighbor. "What?"

"The box." As she pointed, her top lifted to reveal a belly button piercing. "Next to you."

I was torn between telling her belly button piercings took the longest of any to heal and asking her if she had any others. Though I wasn't sure if I really wanted to know where else she might be pierced (shudder).

"Hey, Kath." She waved a hand in front of my face. "You okay?"

"No, I'm not." I frowned. "If your best friend gave you underwear, what would you think?"

She wrinkled her nose. "Depends. Is my best friend male or female?"

"Male." Definitely very male.

"Is it my birthday?"

"No."

She tapped a finger against the stud in her nostril. "Long johns or G-strings?"

"G-strings."

"Oh." Her eyes widened.

I pulled the box onto my lap and opened it. "Luc sent me all this and I don't know what to think. I mean, I think he was being nice because he didn't want me to embarrass myself because my underwear didn't fit in under my new pants, but . . ." I shook my head.

Rainbow drew out a particularly frilly set and whistled.

I nodded. "I know."

"Well . . ." She shook her head and whistled again. "Is the box full of this stuff?"

"Yes," I said miserably. "And then a woman at work said that men only bought women underwear expecting to see them in it, and I don't know what to think."

"This stuff is gorgeous." She reverently held up another bra. "You know what I think?"

"What?" I leaned forward and held my breath for her words of wisdom.

"That he should pick out all *my* lingerie from now on."

Great. Some help she was.

By the time the next evening and—yikes!—dinner with Luc rolled around, I'd managed to work myself into quite a tizzy.

Luc had wanted to pick me up at home after work but I quickly vetoed that. Driving with Luc—small, enclosed space? The ultimate in awkward. What if he made a pass and I had to slap him back? What if he made a pass and I didn't slap him back?

For that matter, what if *I* made a pass?

No way. Better to meet him at the restaurant.

I got home with just enough time to take a quick shower, touch up my bun, and throw on some clothes. Yes, my new clothes. I was going to draw the line at the underwear, though—I was still weirded out by that—but then I spent ten minutes trying to tuck my old underwear down without having it bunch. I finally had to admit defeat and put on a pair of panties Luc had picked out. And since I did that, I figured I might as well wear the matching bra. The only justification was that they were so comfortable it was like wearing nothing. And the panties were thongs—who knew?

I was about this close to wearing my Ferragamos—they go with everything, after all—but Luc would have a fit. The only other type of shoes I owned was tennis shoes. They went with jeans, right? I shrugged and got into them.

Right before I slipped into my red jacket and left, I glanced at my reflection. On impulse I took down my hair and instantly regretted it, it looked so messy. But I was late, so I left it and ran out.

The Muni bus wasn't on time—surprise surprise. I considered catching a cab, but taxicabs didn't often just cruise around my neighborhood. So I got to the restaurant fifteen minutes late.

Luc was waiting for me at the outside entrance. He smiled wide when he saw me. "No way. You wore your new clothes."

I frowned. "You told me to."

"But I didn't expect you to listen." He scooped me up and hugged me.

God, he smelled good. "Did you know the nose can detect more than ten thousand different scents?"

He ignored me. Holding me at arm's length, he inspected me thoroughly. I blushed, wondering if he was trying to see if I was wearing the underwear too.

Finally he grinned. "You look damn good, even if I say so myself."

"Did you know we're born with three hundred fifty bones but only have two hundred six when we die?"

I wasn't sure what bones had to do with anything either, but it was the first thing that came to mind.

"Kat, I think you need food." Luc slung an arm over my shoulder. (Disappointed that he didn't take my hand? Not me.)

We walked into House, the restaurant Luc wanted to go to tonight. I'd checked it out on the Internet and it was fancier than I'd like. Well—it wasn't fancy so much as it was costly. I mean, why should you pay twenty-five bucks for a steak you can buy for a couple dollars at Safeway? But Luc was taking me out so I didn't complain.

I wanted to, though.

One thing about Luc: he's loose with his money. He's not a spendthrift per se, but he doesn't save like I do. I guess it's how he was raised. His family is loaded, so there was never anything he lacked. I, on the other hand, grew up in virtual poverty—virtual because we did okay despite our lack of funds. But whenever I had an extra penny I saved it for the day my dad would squander our rent or grocery money. Those pennies saved us more times than I can count.

Anyway, the host showed us to our table. Luc held my chair out for me (feminism be damned—I love that), waiting patiently while I took my jacket off. I dropped it on the back of the chair and sat down, ready for Luc to scoot my chair in.

Nothing.

I looked up with a frown. "Any day now."

He stared at me like he'd never seen me before. Or like I had a bird dropping in my hair.

My hand automatically went up to my fro. "I shouldn't have taken it down. Is it out of control? It's frizzing all over the place, isn't it?" Maybe I had a rubber band in my purse.

"No." He shook his head like he was trying to clear it of cobwebs. "No. It looks great. *You* look great."

He sat down across from me. Instead of opening his menu, he rested his chin in his hand and gazed at me with his bright blue eyes.

Which made me want to squirm. "What?"

He shook his head again. "After all these years, you'd think that I'd know you, but you continue to surprise me."

Whatever that meant. I was still the same old Katherine Murphy, even if I was in new clothes and had left my hair down. I decided the best course of action was to ignore him, so I opened the menu and looked for something to eat. Something easy to swallow because if he kept looking at me like he was now, I was going to have trouble.

The five minutes or so before the waiter came to take our order passed in excruciating silence. Fortunately, I had the menu to keep me occupied. When the waiter tried to take it from me, I gripped it tighter, which resulted in a momentary tug-of-war before he snatched it away from me with a triumphant lift of his brows.

Bastard. I wrinkled my nose at him. Then I pushed up my glasses and looked at Luc, who still looked shell-shocked.

It was up to me to strike up conversation. I wasn't as socially inept as I once was (look at the progress I was making on my assignment)—I could do it.

I adjusted up my glasses, smiled at him almost naturally, and said, "Did you know broccoli has twice as much vitamin C as an orange?"

He blinked a couple times. "Huh?"

"Really." I nodded. "And did you know a West German goes an average of seven days without washing his underwear?"

He looked completely baffled.

I wondered if maybe his hearing was going—we *had* been spending a lot of time in loud bars and clubs. I resolved to get him a gift certificate for Christmas to get his ears checked out.

In the meantime, I repeated what I said, only louder this time.

The conversation around us stopped for a breath. The way people gawked made my cheeks burn. But I lifted my head and told the people at the table right next to us, "Well, it's true. I know my facts."

I turned back to Luc, indignant that anyone would disbelieve my knowledge. I was a damn excellent researcher and I *never* got my facts wrong. Only Luc had his head in his hands and his shoulders were shaking.

"Oh Luc"—I reached across the table to pat his hand—"don't be upset. They just don't know any better."

He let loose a guffaw, throwing his head back.

The jerk wasn't crying—he was laughing. I pulled my hand back but he caught it and held it. Tight. And I almost forgave him for laughing. Almost.

"Oh, Kat." He swiped a tear that leaked from his eye. Lifting my hand, he kissed the knuckles. "You're hilarious."

I felt his laughter on my skin and my brain had a meltdown. I opened my mouth but I couldn't remember what I was going to say. Which is probably why my next comment slipped out. "Did you know there's no medical name for boogers?"

"God, I love you." He kissed my hand again, effectively shutting me up. "Especially the odd little facts you spout off when you're rattled."

My heart skipped. Because he loved my facts, I'm sure.

The waiter arrived with our salads, so I didn't

get a chance to reply. Good thing, because at that point I don't think I was capable of saying anything intelligible.

But that was okay. Luc kept up the conversation, drawing me in until we were talking just like normal. As if I weren't wearing panties he'd picked out for me.

If I thought about my underwear, I'd choke on my ribeye. In 1999, two hundred eighteen people choked to death on food. Fortunately, that was in the U.K., but I wasn't about to take any chances.

Chapter Nine

I've always been a diligent worker. In school
when a teacher assigned a project or report, I
started work on it right away, finishing it well before the due date.

In my job, I was the same way. I got an assignment with a deadline and I made sure I got it done
in plenty of time.

Lydia's special assignment completely threw me
off. Not only was I battling to get it accomplished,
but it was setting me behind in all my other work
(because I'd been leaving work earlier than my
usual 8:00 P.M. quitting time). And then there was
the wasted Sunday I'd spent with Gary and then
shopping, as well as all those dinners with Luc
where we hadn't done anything but hang out and
talk . . .

So I had to cram, not only on the chocolate account but also on compiling Lydia's list. I worked
late on Thursday, went out to a bar and collected a

couple more names (without Luc), and went home to tie everything up.

I hated it. Why people did this to themselves I didn't know. But I vowed never again. It wasn't worth the exhaustion I felt each morning.

But Friday I still got to work early to prep before my meeting with Lydia. She'd said she wanted daily status reports, but the past week she'd been too busy for me.

Over the last couple of days, I'd heard murmurings of a big deal going down, but there's always something big happening at AshComm, so I didn't pay much attention to the gossip.

I'd debated e-mailing her an update, but given the sensitive nature of my project I decided that wasn't a good idea. She'd just have to wait.

When Jessica, Lydia's assistant, called me at nine o'clock, I was ready. I had my spreadsheets (arranged by best match for her criteria) as well as fact sheets about reproduction. Like how men's sperm production was at each age and what factors affected it. Facts I'd want to know.

I hurried up to her office, taking the stairs of course, my manila folder under my arm. In the stairwell, I straightened my skirt and smoothed back my hair. I took a deep breath. This was it.

VP, here I come.

I marched into Lydia's front office, a professional smile plastered on my face. "Good morning, Jessica."

She didn't look away from her monitor. "Lydia's been waiting for you."

I looked at my watch. Only five minutes had

passed since Jessica called. Excuse me for not having a teleporter. "Shall I just go in, then?"

I interpreted her look as an affirmative. Squaring my shoulders, I knocked on the door and walked in.

Lydia sat furiously typing on her laptop. The usually flawless skin of her forehead furrowed. I think it was anger, but as thin as she was, it could have also been hunger.

"Sit," she barked, still tapping away.

Okay—anger.

As I took my usual chair across from her, I assured myself that it wasn't directed at me. I'd compiled a damn fine list (even if I said so myself) and my promotion was practically guaranteed.

Lydia slammed her laptop shut and glared at me. "Give me good news."

Gulp. "I have the list, just like you wanted. The men are ordered according to greatest compatibility to the, uh, features you requested." For the hundredth time I thanked God she hadn't asked for a specific penis size.

"Let's see it."

I pushed them across the glass-top desk. I held my breath, trying not to read anything into the casual way she flipped through the pages.

"Good," she finally pronounced. I practically fell to the floor and sobbed in relief.

The intercom buzzed. "Lydia, Mr. Drake is here for you."

She punched a button so viciously I felt sorry for the plastic. "He can goddamn wait."

Yikes. Whoever Mr. Drake was, I didn't envy him. She returned her icy gaze to me and pushed the report back. "Set up meetings with the top five candidates for late next week. Allot an hour for each."

She wanted *me* to make the dates? Rather than complain, I nodded, keeping a visual of the home I was going to buy firm in my mind. "Right."

"Arrange the meetings for the lobby of the Mark Hopkins Hotel."

I guessed that was so she could take whichever one she decided on up and get busy right away. I admired her take-charge attitude. "Of course. Anything else?"

The buzzer sounded again. "Lydia, Mr. Drake insists on seeing you right away."

Lydia turned off the volume to her phone. "Actually, Katherine, I've changed my mind."

I almost sighed in relief.

"Pick the ten best candidates. Set up four interviews on Tuesday, three Wednesday and Thursday, starting at seven."

I pushed my glasses up, counting to ten before I answered. I didn't trust myself not to squawk in protest. Tuesday was only a few days away. "That's somewhat sudden." Not bad. My tone had just the right amount of inquisitive without the stark outrage. "Are you sure?"

She cocked one perfect eyebrow.

Right. How silly of me to question her highness's mandate.

Before I could properly grovel at her feet, her door burst open and a man stalked in. A tall, very angry man by the look of him.

His eyes, a darker blue than Luc's, blazed in repressed fury. He wore his power as easily as he wore his expensive suit (handmade, I bet).

But wow was he attractive. In a dangerous, untamed way. Way too intense for me, but for Lydia . . .

Hmm. I appraised him a little closer. He even had a goatee. Maybe I could add him to the list. I wondered if insanity or any other debilitating illnesses ran in his family.

"Excuse me." Lydia's voice was ice cold, but fury raged in her eyes. "You can't barge into my office like that."

I pushed my glasses up, tempted to lean across the desk for a closer look. I couldn't help it—I'd never seen her gray eyes burn like that.

"I wouldn't have to if you'd honor your commitments."

Lydia's eyes narrowed to slits. Hands on the desk, she pushed herself up slowly.

Uh-oh. I shrank back a little in my chair and gazed longingly at the door. Maybe I could make it out before I got caught in the cross fire.

"*I* always honor my commitments," the ice queen said. I had the impression she was implying he didn't. "I'm in the middle of a meeting that's been scheduled for several weeks."

A little bit of an exaggeration, but I wasn't going to correct her. Not when she looked like she could take out an army with the pen clutched in her hand.

The man—Mr. Drake—glanced at me, minus about a thousand degrees of intensity. His lips tipped up in the barest smile. "Excuse me. I didn't realize."

Was that a hint of a dimple?

I smiled politely back at him, my eyes glued to his cheek. I wanted to tell him it was okay but I didn't think Lydia would agree, so I kept my mouth shut.

Mr. Drake turned back to Lydia, the cold fury banked. "I'll wait outside. But we *are* meeting. Don't think you can avoid me."

With a nod to me, he walked out as forcefully as he'd walked in. He shut the door behind him, softly, but somehow it seemed as forceful as when he'd slammed it open.

I glanced at Lydia. Red spots colored her cheeks. Under her couple-thousand-dollar suit her panties were in a wad, I bet.

Most disquieting. I cleared my throat, tried to stifle the frisson of unease, and got back to the matter at hand. "So you want me to pick the best candidates and set up dates?"

She blinked a few times. Why was seeing her unhinged so disturbing? "Yes. Set it up for next Tuesday."

She flipped open her laptop, clicked a few times, and then began typing manically.

I guessed I was dismissed. I gathered my reports and quietly tiptoed toward the door.

"Katherine."

I froze and looked over my shoulder.

"I'm sure I don't need to remind you that time is running out." Her steely gaze pierced straight through me. "Make good choices."

Right. Resisting the urge to salute, I nodded and smiled before I walked out. At least I think I smiled. As long as I didn't look like I wanted to throw up.

Mr. Drake paced in the waiting area outside.

Jessica had one panicked eye on him, like he was a caged animal that might maul her at any moment.

He did have that look, but underneath he looked like a fair man. Anyone with shoes so polished had to be somewhat civilized, right?

I gave him a slight smile as I walked through. I was almost to the hallway when I heard him call out.

"Excuse me, miss."

I turned around and, surprised to find him so close to me, jumped. "Uh, can I help you?"

"I think you may be able to." He took my arm and guided me down the hall to the elevators, away from Jessica's watchful eyes.

For some reason, I didn't mind his strong-arm techniques. I mean, I knew he was after something from me, but there was something about him I liked. Rainbow probably would have said he had a positive aura.

He waited until we were well out of earshot before he asked, "You work for Lydia?"

His use of my boss's first name surprised me. I was tempted to tell him I was employee eighty-seven out of two hundred thirty-six (sixty-two percent of which were women), but I pushed up my glasses and simply said, "Yes."

He studied me, his hand still holding my arm as if he thought I'd try to get away. "What's your name?"

"Katherine Murphy." I couldn't keep the suspicion out of my voice. After all, here was a guy who obviously had an adversarial relationship with my boss suddenly taking an interest in me. I might have thought Lydia was a demanding bitch (an upgrade from heinous bitch) but I still owed her my loyalty.

He smiled. It wasn't an effusive smile, but it was enough to show off his adorable dimple. "Katherine Murphy, a pleasure to meet you."

Somehow I could tell it really was. I relaxed, but just a tiny bit. I wasn't sure I trusted him yet.

Maybe I didn't hide my distrust of him as well as I thought, because he let go of my arm and cocked his head to the side. "You don't trust me, do you?"

I pursed my lips. "Does it matter? I don't even know who you are."

He watched me. Closely. I wanted to fidget—his gaze (did I mention it was blue?) unnerved me—but I stuck my chin out and stared right back.

The corner of his lips twitched.

Aha! A sign of discomfort. He wasn't as composed as he appeared.

Then he said, "Ms. Murphy, allow me to introduce myself." He held out his hand. "Viggo Drake."

"Mr. Drake." I expected his grip to be overbearing and crushing but it wasn't. It was firm but gentle, like he was concerned about me. Odd.

"Just Drake." He smiled at me again. "I've kept you long enough. I'm sure you have work to do, and I have a meeting with Lydia."

"Oh." I pushed my glasses up. That was it? He was letting me go? It was almost anticlimactic.

"I hope we get a chance to talk soon." His dimple flashed.

It was so little-boy cute it disarmed me. "Did you know there are three hundred thirty-six dimples on a regulation golf ball?"

He laughed, and it transformed him. "Let me guess. You're in research."

Wow. He was astute too.

"I can tell Lydia's lucky to have you on her team. Until the next time." He raised a hand in parting before striding back to Lydia's domain.

I watched him disappear into the office. He never told me who he was. Other than his name, that is. I wondered what type of man could whip my esteemed boss into such a frenzy.

Either a stupid one or one who was very cunning. And I doubted Viggo Drake was the former.

Chapter Ten

I was in the midst of a full-blown panic attack when Luc called me.

Let me set up the scene: it was Monday, the day before I was supposed to have the first set of dates lined up for Lydia.

Supposed to being the key words here.

That was the problem. It was Monday afternoon and I had nothing set up. And it wasn't for lack of trying. I started at the end of my list (with the least desirable of the bunch), methodically calling each candidate. At first, they sounded pleased to hear from me. It was when I told them what time they were supposed to meet Lydia that things would start to fall apart.

All the conversations went something like this:

ME: Hi. We met at _____ (fill in the blank) and you gave me your contact info.

HIM: Right. I didn't think you'd actually call me back.

ME: (frowning) I've always found unaccountability very unattractive.

HIM: Uh . . . yeah.

ME: I was wondering if you're free tomorrow.

HIM: For you, definitely.

ME: Great! Can you be at the Mark Hopkins at _____ (fill in the blank again)?

HIM: The Mark Hopkins? You don't waste time, do you?

ME: (murmuring) Time is a commodity I don't have.

HIM: What?

ME: Nothing.

HIM: So . . . Will you be wearing something sexy? I really liked that librarian look you had going.

ME: That's a DKNY suit, I'll have you know. Sure, I bought it at the outlet, but I doubt a librarian would be able to afford even that. Their wages are scandalous. Did you know septic-tank servicers earn higher salaries than librarians in California?

HIM: Uh . . .

ME: And besides, I won't be there.

HIM: Come again?

ME: I won't be at the meeting. (Thinking that maybe he's not as swift as originally thought.)

HIM: Then who will be?

ME: Lydia. My boss.

HIM: You're pimping for your boss?

It went downhill from there.

One or two, sure, I could understand that. But all of them? The odds that the 49ers would win the next Superbowl were greater. And I didn't understand why they thought they were meeting with me. No way was I ready to have a kid.

The only one who was amenable to the meeting was the college student from the laundromat. When he asked who he was meeting and I said Lydia, he paused for a second before asking, "Is *she* into kinky sex?"

Because I wouldn't have been surprised to find a whip or two in her closet, I replied, "Sure."

Then he asked, "Is she tall?"

"Yes." That one I could answer without hesitation.

Pause. "Does she have boots? Boots really turn me on."

I wracked my brain trying to remember if I'd ever seen Lydia wear boots. She had to have a pair, right? But I didn't know for certain. "Um, I'm sure she does."

Another pause. "You don't know?"

"Truthfully, no."

Apparently that was a deal breaker.

So there I was—Monday afternoon and no dates arranged. That's when Luc called.

"Hey, Kat. I'm calling in my marker."

"What?" I frowned at the receiver. What was he talking about?

"Remember when you asked me to help you with your little assignment?"

"Yes." That day would forever be etched in my brain as the day my life began its downward spiral.

"You promised me a boon."

"So?"

"I'm calling it in. I'll pick you up at five."

I sat up in my chair, completely focused on what he was saying this time. "Excuse me? At five?"

"You're going out with me tonight."

I shook my head. So vigorously I probably shook something loose. "No! No. I can't. I have to set up these meetings for tomorrow—"

"You gave me a boon. Are you going back on your word?"

He had me, damn him. "No." Sullen? Me?

"Good. Five o'clock." He hung up.

I banged my head on my desk. I didn't have time for this. I needed to focus. My promotion was at stake here and Luc wanted me to come out and play. What's worse, part of me wanted to ditch my assignment and have fun with Luc.

I flipped to the spreadsheet with Joseph's (the guy I met at Gary's show) information and dialed his cell. He answered on the third ring.

"Speaking."

I cringed at the cold tone. Oh well. Here goes nothing. "Joseph, it's Katherine. We met at that gallery opening—"

"Of course." His voice warmed. I could hear a note of laughter in it. "How are you?"

"Kind of in a bind, actually."

"How can I help?"

"Are you free tomorrow?"

"Is this for your, uh, project?"

"Yes." I held my breath. Say yes. Please say yes.

"Sure, I can do tomorrow. How about eight o'clock?"

"You know what? I love you."

He chuckled. "I don't think your boyfriend will like that."

"My boyfriend?" I frowned. "Oh—you mean Luc?"

"Is he the guy who wanted to tear my head off that night?"

"He didn't want to do that. Luc's a pacifist."

Joseph grunted. "That's not the impression I got."

I shrugged. Whatever. "Tomorrow. Eight o'clock sharp at the Mark Hopkins. You won't be able to miss Lydia. She's tall, blond, and beautiful."

"Katherine, will you give me your phone number? I'd like to call you."

Oh, how nice—he was going to call and let me know how things went. He was so thoughtful. I rattled it off and then decided to give him my home number too, in case he wanted to call me after meeting Lydia.

By the time I got off the phone with Joseph, the impending feeling of doom I'd had earlier had receded to a faint niggling sensation. Niggling I could deal with. I pushed it aside and concentrated on lining up more dates for the consecutive days.

Some time later a knock sounded at my door. I looked up to find Luc peering around the corner.

I pursed my lips. "It can't be five yet."

"I'm so happy to see you too. It's always such a treat."

I rolled my eyes, but I began shutting down my computer nevertheless. "You're only being punctual to drive me crazy."

"Driving you crazy is a distinct pleasure I look forward to."

I glanced at him, my gaze narrowed. I had the sneaking suspicion he meant something by that statement. If anyone else had said it, I'd know exactly what he was after, but Luc couldn't have meant it that way.

Could he?

Hmm.

Nah.

I shrugged and gathered up my papers to straighten my desk. I was probably being sensitive.

"Okay. I'm ready." I moved toward the door, looking over my shoulder longingly at my desk. I had so much work . . .

"Come on, squirt." Luc swung his arm over my shoulder and pulled me out the door. "We have a couple stops to make before heading back to my place."

"We're going to your loft?"

"Yep." He smiled at one of the research assistants who looked up from her desk. She gawked at Luc, blinked at me, and then gawked some more.

I shook my head. Luc was attractive, but could she be more obvious?

Turning my attention back to Luc, I asked, "You pulled in your marker to get me to go to your loft? That's it?"

He shrugged. "Actually, I thought of taking you to the opera, but I didn't think you were ready for that."

I frowned. I liked music. When I heard it. Like in the elevator and stuff. "Why wouldn't I be ready?"

"Because it would've involved shopping for clothes and I didn't think you'd be able to take any more of that so soon." He pressed the elevator button.

I didn't get it. "Why would going to the opera involve clothes shopping?"

The elevator doors opened. I nodded at the two women (they were from sales, I think) who were already in there.

Luc pressed the button for the lobby. "Because, Kat, I would have wanted to buy you an evening gown to wear."

I wrinkled my nose. "Why on earth would you want to do that?"

He leaned down until his nose was practically touching mine. "Because I want to see you in one."

The women behind us sighed and then tittered (until that moment, I didn't even know what a titter sounded like). I glared at them, which did nothing to stem their interest in us, before turning my glare on Luc. "I don't get it."

He smiled ruefully and tugged on one of the curls that had escaped from my bun. "I know."

Frowning, I tucked the curl back into submission. Why was it I always felt like I wasn't in on the joke?

Somehow Luc had managed to score a parking spot right in front of the building. Only Luc would be able to find the one parking space that wasn't a designated loading zone during work hours.

"We have a couple stops to make before we go home," he said again as he started the car and pulled away from the curb.

"Hmm." I wondered if Lydia was going to be pissed when she found out I only had one candidate lined up for her tomorrow.

"I thought we could have dinner at home. Would you like to order something in? Like pizza. Or we could pick up Italian—I know how much you love the fettuccine from Fior's."

"Hmm." Maybe I could spin Joseph off in a positive way. I was certain he was the best choice—maybe she'd buy it if I said I wanted to give her the most time with him first, to spare her having to spend time with less desirables. After all, her time *was* really valuable.

"Or I could make some pasta."

I grunted. That idea had merit. She'd thank me for my initiative and see that I'd make the best VP of research.

"Katherine."

I looked up to find Luc frowning at me instead of watching the road. "Watch where you're going! Did you know that most car accidents occur because a car is on the wrong side of the road?"

He cursed under his breath but, much to my relief, looked forward again. "Maybe this wasn't a good idea."

"What?"

"This." He waved in my general direction. "I should have known better than to think you could keep your mind here rather than in the office. I'll just take you home."

If I had a whip on me, I would have flogged myself right then. I was such a bitch. Here Luc was attempting to do something for me—I had no idea what, but all the same I should have made an effort to cooperate.

Then I remembered the time in high school when he wanted to take me to a special exhibit at the Steinhart Aquarium he thought I'd enjoy. I'd never forget the look on his face when I ditched on him at the last minute. Sure, I cancelled because my dad had been on a binge and I needed to do extra tutoring to make up the rent, but still.

I put my hand on his arm. "I'm sorry, Luc. I promised you a boon. I'll try. Really."

He glanced at me, long and unwavering (good thing we were at a light). Then he smiled. "Okay."

Just that simply, he forgave me. I didn't have time to feel like a jerk because we pulled into a red zone in front of a toy store.

"I'm going in to pick up supplies. If a cop comes by, drive around the block, okay?"

I barely nodded before he was out the door. I pushed my glasses up as I watched Luc dash through the doors of the store.

What kind of supplies did we need from a toy store? I doubted they had parmesan.

I was keeping a vigilant lookout for the authorities when Luc came back out. "That was fast."

He grinned at me as he buckled himself in. "I knew what I wanted."

"What'd you get?" I poked a finger at the plastic bag he'd set on the console between us.

"No looking." Luc grabbed the bag and set it behind my seat. "You'll see later."

Mystery. I wrinkled my nose at him. I didn't like being kept in the dark. Surprises meant you couldn't be prepared.

But I doubted Luc would spring anything horrendous on me (if he did, he'd live to regret it), so I sat back and relaxed. "Are we going to your loft now?"

"Nope. One more stop."

It turned out to be the grocery store.

This time he let me go in with him. "Where should we start?" Luc asked as he snagged a cart.

I surveyed the store to get the lay of the land. Though once you'd been in one grocery store, you

pretty much had seen them all. "We should stick to
the outside of the aisles and go around the store."

"Why?"

"Because all the necessary stuff is on the outside. The aisles contain the crap that's not necessary but that TV tells us we want. Like cereal."

Luc's eyes lit up. "Fruity Pebbles. I haven't had
those in years."

I grabbed his arm before junk food distracted
him. "Let's start with produce."

After some debate over what to have for dinner,
I prevailed with a salad and Luc's fettuccine (which
is to die for). We also got some ice cream for dessert
and a box of cereal for Luc. On our way to pay for
our groceries, we passed a display that smelled dis-
tinctly familiar.

I gasped. "No way."

Luc stopped the cart next to me. "What's up?"

Staring in disbelief, I pointed at the colorful display. "See these aromatherapy products?"

"Yeah." He picked up a bottle of massage lotion
and studied the label. "So?"

"My next-door neighbor makes them."

When Rainbow had told me about her enter-
prise, I imagined homey, crafts-fair kinds of products. These were glossy and professional. They were
colorful, elegant little bottles that made you want
to buy.

"Looks good." Luc tossed the bottle into the
cart. "We'll have to try it."

We?

He raced toward the checkout line. I rushed
after him to ask him what he meant, but he was al-

ready exchanging football commentary with the checker and laughing like they were old friends.

He probably just meant the royal *we*.

It was a short ride to Luc's from the store. I thought I'd get a chance to peek in the toy store bag as I helped him carry everything in, but he slapped my hand back and told me to behave.

Pout.

Luc fairly bounced the whole way up to his loft. He set his bags down and rustled in his pocket for the house keys.

I eyed him suspiciously. "You're awfully buoyant this evening."

He grinned over his shoulder as he unlocked the door. "I'm spending the evening with my most favorite person in the world. Of course I'm buoyant." He shoved the door open, scooped up his bags, and walked in, leaving the door open for me.

I could only stare at him disappearing into his loft. I shouldn't have been surprised to hear that. After all, Luc was my most favorite person too. But I couldn't help being shocked into muteness.

"Hey, squirt! Are you coming in or not?"

Okay, that snapped me out of it. "Don't call me squirt." I headed straight for the kitchen and set the bags on the counter. "I'm no squirt. I've totally outgrown that nickname."

Luc glanced at me from behind the freezer door. "You're the same size you were when we met."

"That's because women mature early."

The way he grinned made him resemble a wolf. "I remember."

Impossible. Ignoring him was the best course of action, so I began putting away what we'd bought.

"I'll take that." Luc snatched the cheese out of my hand. "You go change."

"Change? What for?"

"So you don't get your work clothes dirty. You're going to help me cook."

I wrinkled my nose. I don't cook, and Luc knows it. "I'm not sure that's a good idea."

"It's an excellent idea." He gave me a sly look. "Scared you can't do it?"

"Whatever."

He grinned. Damn him—he knew he struck a nerve. "Then hop to it."

"I have nothing to change into."

"Come on. I'll find you something." He led me up the spiral metal stairs to his bower (his word, not mine). After rifling through a drawer, he pulled out a T-shirt and handed it to me. "Wear this."

"Only?" I actually squeaked.

"It's longer than most skirts women wear."

I stared at it. "Not me."

"A pity, I know." He tugged the same dratted strand that'd escaped my bun again and left me to change.

"You're always trying to get me out of my suits," I grumbled as I took off my jacket.

"It's my purpose in life," he called up the stairs.

I made a face in his general direction and changed. He was right—drat him—the shirt came all the way down to my knees.

Still, there seemed something vaguely disconcerting about hanging around a man's house in only a T-shirt. The underwear I had on (yes, the new stuff Luc bought me) hardly counted as a layer. It was more like froth.

I blinked when I realized what I'd just thought. A man's house? Since when was Luc a man?

I mean, I've always been aware of his gender, but I've never really been *aware*. Kind of like how you're aware a Barbie doll is female, but at the same time it's not—because it's sexless.

Luc wasn't sexless anymore.

Okay—different train of thought.

My, his bed looked cushy. I poked a finger at the thick down comforter and thought how cozy it must be to sleep in there.

I flushed deep red as an image of Luc sprawled under there rooted in my mind and ran down to escape—I mean, help with dinner.

Luc's loft was minimal, which accentuated its hugeness. From the top of the stairs, the openness of the space was even more exaggerated. I could see the front entrance, the main living area, the kitchen toward the back, and the small alcovelike office he'd created to the other side.

I don't know how Luc did it, but his loft was so homey. His furniture was mostly off-white but there were flashes of warmth all over, from the large paintings on the walls to the pillows and knickknacks all over. He always gave me the furniture he was getting rid of but I could never recreate the atmosphere of Luc's place.

But having my own home was going to make all the difference.

"About time," Luc said when I walked into the kitchen. "Here."

I looked down at the pot he handed me. "You can't seriously want me to cook."

"Why not?" He took out a pan and set it on a low flame.

"Because—" I floundered a bit at the faith-filled way he looked at me. "I'm no Julia Child. I tax my knowledge of the kitchen by opening a can of tuna."

He laughed. "God, Kat, you're so funny."

"Did you know on average Americans eat eighteen acres of pizza every day? I think we should do our part to help." I set the pot down and reached to grab the phone off the wall.

Luc caught my hand before I picked it up. He pulled me closer to him and tipped my chin up with a finger. "I'm right here, helping you out. This is going to be easy. No big deal."

"Are you sure?"

"You'd think after all these years you'd trust me."

My heart cringed at the hurt in his voice. "I do trust you. Really."

"Then trust me when I say you can do this."

As I gazed into his cloudless eyes, I felt like he was talking about more than making the pasta, but my mind couldn't wrap itself around what that might be. He was standing so close and he smelled so right I could practically see his pheromones doing a snake charmer's dance to lure me. I swayed toward him, wondering if he'd taste as exciting as he smelled.

Shit.

I stepped back before I did something I'd regret forever. He couldn't help his pheromones any more than I could help mine with Rebecca and that bartender.

His gaze was shuttered, and I couldn't tell what

he was thinking. Just as well. My cheeks scorched as I imagined the thoughts that were probably running in his head.

I cleared my throat. "I could probably boil some water without ruining it."

"Do that," he said finally. "I'm going to change."

Oh great. Now he was mad at me. I grabbed the pot and banged it into the sink. I twisted the tap and frowned at the water.

Luc's arm slid around my waist and his chin rested on top of my head. "No worries, Kat. I love you."

I relaxed against his chest. "Even if I'm socially inept?"

"Especially because you're socially inept." I heard the laughter in his voice so I didn't pretend to take offense. He dropped a kiss on my temple and left to change his clothes.

Making dinner with Luc turned out to be lots of fun. He was right—I wasn't as bad a cook as I thought. In fact, dinner turned out great. Through dinner, Luc grinned each time I exclaimed how excellent it was. Every now and then he'd say something to allude to the fact that maybe one day I'd believe he always spoke the truth.

I knew that, though.

Luc cleaned up and I made myself a cup of tea, which I took into the living room. Curling onto the couch, I held my cup between my hands and studied the painting that took up most of the far wall.

I'd seen it lots of times. In fact, I remembered when Luc bought it (and the shock when I heard how much he'd spent). But staring at it now, I realized it looked familiar. The colors were bold and the shapes indistinct, though it seemed like if you stared at it long enough it might make a picture—like those optical illusion posters.

Luc padded into the room with a glass of water and the bag from the toy store.

"The painting"—I pointed at it—"is Gary's, isn't it?"

"Yeah. He's really talented." Luc sat on the floor in front of me, his back against the couch, and looked at it. "I like the honesty in his work. The way he cuts down to the essence of his subjects."

I scrunched my lips as I studied it. It looked like a bunch of splotches to me, but what did I know about art?

My attention was diverted from the painting when Luc started taking things out of the bag.

"Can I look now?" I leaned over his shoulder. "What is it?"

He lightly smacked my hand when I reached for one of the little containers. "Be a good girl and I'll let you play."

"I am a good girl," I protested.

He grinned up at me and then went back to arranging the little containers on his glass coffee table.

"Are those paints?" I got down on the floor next to him and picked one up. I raised my brows at him. "Finger paints? I haven't finger painted since—" I frowned. Actually, I couldn't remember ever doing it before.

"That's why I got them. You need some fun in your life." He took out a couple of pads of thick paper and set them on the table. "You're too serious."

"I am not." I crossed my arms. "I have fun all the time."

Luc gave me the shortest sidelong glance ever, but he still managed to convey his disbelief loud and clear.

"I do too have fun. All the time."

He cocked an eyebrow. "Like when?"

"Like at work."

"Kat." He said it gently, like he was breaking some seriously bad news to me. "Work is work. It's not entertainment."

My arms tightened across my chest. What was he talking about?

"Here." He handed a piece of paper. "Let loose. Humor me."

Fine. I scooted off the couch, knelt in front of the table, and snatched it from him. Opening the jar of red paint still in my hand, I dipped my finger in. Eew—I could feel it ooze under my nail.

I stabbed at the paper, not sure what to do. Then I had an inspiration. With an evil grin, I set to painting at a furious pace, mixing the other colors Luc had opened as well.

Within minutes I was done. I held my fists up in triumph. "Yes!"

Luc glanced at me from his painting. "Done already?"

"I'm not just done—I've created a masterpiece." I held it up for him to see.

He studied it, tilting his head to look at it from different angles. Finally he asked, "What is it?"

"It's you. See the horns?" I grinned maniacally when he narrowed his eyes at me. Take that.

"Cute, squirt." He drawled out the nickname only because he knew it'd drive me insane.

I'd show him. I grabbed a second piece of paper and began another portrait of him. I reached for the jar of green paint and scooped out a glob. The better to paint scales with.

Intent on drawing a snake with Luc's face, I didn't register the feeling of cold wetness tickling my leg until it was too late. I glanced down and gasped at the blue streak on my bare leg. "What the hell?"

Luc grinned, looking like a mischievous little boy. "It looked like it needed color."

"Luc! You're going to get paint all over your furniture." I held still, imagining streaks of color staining his expensive rug. And the couch . . .

Holding my gaze, Luc drew another deliberate line down my shin.

Fine. Two could play this game. I snatched the jar of red.

Luc's grin widened as he armed himself with not only the blue but the yellow too.

First strike was mine. I managed to get a streak of red down his cheek and his neck before he tapped a blue blob on my nose. I didn't waste any time swiping at it. Instead I armed my finger with more paint and smeared his arm.

"Have I ever told you you look great in blue?" he asked as he continued to dot my face.

I reached for another container of blue. "I think it might be your color more. Matches your eyes." I made a streak down the other side of his face.

I shrieked when he grabbed me and set me on his lap. I struggled but he held me firmly in place with one arm.

"My turn," he said gleefully. He tapped the yellow jar against my thigh until a good amount of paint oozed onto my skin. Holding my leg in place with his, he began to write on it.

I bent over to read what he was writing. *KM has cooties.* "Oh, really mature, Luc."

He continued to scribble things up my thigh as I squirmed to get free. I'd show him.

I don't know the exact moment it happened, but suddenly things changed. His fingers stroked rather than painted. I became aware of where I was and the feel of his puffs of breath on my neck and how my borrowed shirt had crept up. At the moment, whether Luc could see my underwear or not seemed the least of my worries.

I squirmed harder to get away but I felt something shift under me.

Oh shit.

I froze, my face burning. I wasn't very experienced, but even I could figure out that I felt Luc's package stirring to life.

Somehow I managed to look over my shoulder at Luc. He stared at me, his eyes blazing beneath half-closed lids.

I said the first thing that came to mind. "Peanuts are one of the ingredients in dynamite."

"Katherine."

I blinked at the way he breathed my name and I knew I was going to do something stupid. Like push my paint-coated fingers into his hair and pull him down so I could find out exactly what the girls were talking about in high school when they whispered how he had such an excellent mouth.

Which was exactly what I did. Only he fell over (probably from shock) and I landed on top of him.

I didn't care. I was in another world exploring his mouth. It was wondrous, warm and exciting. I probed it gently, unsure but dying of curiosity.

And Luc let me. He lay there under me, patiently letting me kiss him.

Letting me kiss him?

I pulled back, aghast. I couldn't believe I was taking advantage of him this way. I opened my mouth to beg his forgiveness but I didn't get a chance. His mouth closed over mine and what was merely exciting became electrifying.

Someone moaned. It took me several seconds before I realized it was me. I had an excuse—my hands had gotten inside Luc's shirt and the feel of his skin, the light peppering of hair on his chest, was distracting.

He nibbled down my neck and murmured against my skin. "Katherine."

I opened my eyes at my name, looked down, and saw Luc clasped against me.

Luc. My best friend.

I recoiled in horror and crawled back to push away from him, my fingers over my mouth. I didn't trust myself not to blurt out something I'd never be able to take back. Like a plea for him to take me up to his bed and ruin me for all other men.

Luc stared at me, his chest heaving under the force of his breath. "You're getting paint on your lips."

I lifted my fingers and stared at them. They'd been under my best friend's shirt, on his skin.

Gulp.

I jumped up. "Uh, um, I—"

Luc stood up, making my panic rise to an all-time high.

"Um, I have to go." I ran up the stairs like all the hounds of hell were on my heels. I changed back into my suit, not caring that I was getting finger paint all over it. I almost dropped the T-shirt Luc had lent me on his chair, but on second thought I stuffed it into my purse. To wash it, I told myself, but I knew I was keeping it as a reminder of one of the most wonderful and most horrible nights of my life.

Luc was standing at the foot of the stairs when I went back down. I squeezed by him, evading his hand as he tried to stop my flight.

"Kat, wait—"

"Gotta go. Work tomorrow, you know." I smiled brightly at him. I felt like my face was going to crack. "Thanks for dinner. It was great. I'll talk to you soon, okay?"

"Kat—"

I didn't wait to hear what he was going to say. I scurried out as quickly as I could, running down the hall and all the way out into the street and to the bus stop.

The Muni gods took pity on me. A bus arrived not long after I got there. I flashed my monthly pass and headed for the first available seat. I sat down primly, pulling my skirt over my knees. Noticing a long streak of blue paint on my calf, I gasped and rubbed at it. Only the paint had dried and it wasn't coming off except for a small chip every now and then.

The second I got home I jumped in the shower and scrubbed my body. I told myself I wanted to get rid of the paint, but underneath I couldn't deny I was doing it to erase the tingling feeling of Luc touching me.

But it didn't work. I could still feel the imprint of his lips on mine. I wasn't sure what was worse: the lingering feeling of hands where he caressed me or the aching of the parts he didn't touch.

Chapter Eleven

Wretched. That's how I felt.

My urges lost me my best friend.

And as if that wasn't bad enough, my dad showed up at my apartment after my shower.

"Katie girl!" he boomed when I opened the door. He threw his arms around me in a bear hug.

I tried not to recoil at the toxic smell of alcohol that seeped through his pores. "Dad, this is a surprise."

"Can't a man visit his only offspring?"

Shit. "How much, Dad?"

He looked mortally offended, putting a hand on his chest like his heart pained him. I couldn't help thinking he should have taken up acting. "I'm hurt."

I sighed and walked into the living room. I needed to sit down for this.

He followed me, blustering all the way. I waited till he'd worked up enough steam to begin his rant of what a faithless daughter he was blessed with.

"I've been blessed with a faithless daughter!" he bellowed.

This was bad. He didn't begin with shouting unless he owed a lot of money.

"What have I done to deserve this?" He shook his head and paced the narrow room. Good thing I didn't have much furniture to get in his way. "I come over just because she's in my thoughts and this is the thanks I get. Doesn't even offer me anything to drink."

I sighed. "Would you like some tea, Dad?"

He stopped in his tirade and smiled faintly. "No, thank you, honey. But do you have any bourbon?"

"Sorry." When have I ever stocked alcohol in my house? "I'm all out."

He heaved an enormous sigh. "Don't suppose I really need it."

I glanced at the time. "Dad, I'm sorry to rush you, but if you're done ranting can we get to why you're here? It's late and I have work tomorrow."

"To tell you the truth"—he shot me a sheepish look as he dropped onto the couch—"you were a wee bit right about why I was here."

No kidding. "Dad . . ."

"I know." He held up his hands to forestall my argument. "I know. But, Katie bug, I'd never had a hand like this one."

My blood chilled in my veins. I was afraid to ask, but I had to know. "How good was your hand?"

His hands fell to his sides. "It was *amazing*."

Shit. "How much, Dad?"

I tumbled off my chair when he told me. Literally.

He rushed to my side, pushing my head down between my knees. "Breathe, Katie bug. That's it."

When the blood flowed back into my head and I could utter more than incoherent gasps, I said, "*Are you insane?*"

My dad winced. "Now, Katie, it's not good for you to get so excited—"

"Damn it, Dad, what did you expect? That you could come in here and I'd roll over and just hand you the money without raising an eyebrow?"

Wait. Of course he'd expect that. It's what I always did.

I shook my head. "No more."

"Katie bug—" He adopted that kicked-puppy dog look he was so good at. "You have to help me. You know Ivan isn't a forgiving man—"

"Not Ivan again!" I held my head in my hands. "I thought I told you to stay away from him the last time."

His smile was feeble. "I had to try to win back the money you gave me last time."

All the fight drained out of me. "Dad . . ."

"I've learned my lesson. I swear it's my last time." He held up two fingers. "Scout's honor."

"You were never a scout," I mumbled as I reached for my purse.

He held his breath as I wrote out a check, not exhaling it until it was in his shaking hands. "Katie, you're an angel."

I snorted. No—an idiot maybe, but definitely not an angel. Angels didn't have the raging murderous thoughts I was having.

He kissed me on the cheek and patted my shoulder. "I promise I'm finished. No more poker for me."

It didn't occur to me that he didn't swear off

roulette, blackjack, and the horse races until after he left.

Like usual, the next morning I got up early, prepared myself for work, and arrived at the office before everyone. As my computer fired up, I propped my elbows on my desk and buried my head in my hands.

Not for the first time, tears filled my eyes. What was I going to do?

Well, there was one thing I could easily do right now: get my dad back on track before he cleaned me out.

Gambling wasn't the problem—he used to be a stockbroker, after all. Gambling was in his blood, and he'd been really good at it at one time. But when he coupled it with drinking, he lost control and made bad decisions that led to taking chances he wouldn't normally take.

So Alcoholics Anonymous it was. I opened a browser, searched for the site, and printed out the meeting info. Folding the page in thirds, I carefully tucked it in my purse. I might not be able to get my dad to go to the meetings, but I could try.

It was a step in the right direction, but it wasn't going to solve the fact that my savings were now seriously depleted or that I'd messed up my relationship with my best friend.

Maybe I could move to South America and start life over. I bet I could buy a house down there on what I had saved up. It'd be me and the drug lords.

I toyed with the cord on the phone. Maybe I should call Luc and apologize for coming on to him. I could blame it on the alcohol. Except we didn't drink anything but water, so I guess that excuse wouldn't fly.

My hand was on the receiver, about to pick it up (I swear) when it rang.

I shrieked and recoiled. Oh shit—that was Luc. My sixth sense told me so.

I let it ring and ring until it was on the verge of transferring to voicemail when I snatched it from the brink. I cleared my throat but my voice still sounded thick and clogged, kind of like how my heart felt. "Research. Katherine Murphy speaking."

"Katherine, it's Joseph."

I frowned. "Are you sure?" Joseph didn't croak like this person on the phone. I bet it was the tech guys in the basement making crank calls again.

"Of course I'm sure. I had a date with your boss tonight." He began coughing. Over the phone, it sounded like he was hacking up a lung.

The pit of my stomach clenched. *Did he use past tense?* Deciding it was just a grammatical mistake, I ignored it and forced a smile into my voice. "You sound like you have a little bug."

"A little bug?" he asked hoarsely. "I've been hit by the cold from hell."

Could my life get any worse? "Well, I'm sure Lydia won't mind a little snot—"

He sneezed so violently I could feel the vibrations on my end of the phone. "Katherine, I'm not going to make it. I'm going to knock myself out with cold medicine and die in the privacy of my own home."

Yes, my life could get worse. Panic welled up inside. I thought about the other dates I didn't have lined up and I began to hyperventilate. "You can't pull out now, Joseph."

"No choice. Sorry. I'll call you when I'm better and we'll set up something."

"That'll be too late because my life will be over as soon as Lydia sees I've failed." But I said that to the dial tone because Joseph had already hung up.

I dropped the phone into its cradle and dropped my head onto my desk. Then I lifted it and banged it a few more times. Maybe it'd jar an idea loose.

My door opened and one of the admins walked in. When she saw me bang my head on the desk, her eyes got huge and she took a step back, even as she was reaching out to hand me the papers she had in her hand.

I smiled thinly. "Did you know banging your head against a wall uses one hundred fifty calories an hour?"

Her expression was hard to decipher. I bet it was her breakfast coming back to haunt her. I didn't get a chance to ask, though—she dropped the papers on the edge of my desk and ran out.

"The closest restroom is down the hall to the left," I called out after her.

I shrugged. I didn't have time to care where an admin got sick. I needed to figure out what I was going to tell Lydia when I met with her in exactly—I looked at the display on the phone—seventy-three minutes.

The next fifty-eight of them I spent pacing, which is a feat in the tiny space of my office. I spent about four more in complete and utter hysterics. And then I did what I always did when I needed help.

The thought that I shouldn't call Luc crossed

my mind, but habit and sheer desperation over-
rode any doubts I had. My goal was at stake.

Luc answered on the first ring. "Kat?"

How did he know it was me? "Hi, Luc."

He exhaled. "I'm so glad you called. About
last—"

"Luc, I need your help," I interrupted him quickly.
I didn't think I could face what he was going to say
about last night—not with what happened with
Joseph this morning. I also didn't want to hear him
say what a mistake it was, that we were just friends.
That would be too embarrassing.

Because he knows me so well, he heard the
panic in my voice. "Are you okay, Kat?"

His concern brought tears to my eyes. I really
didn't deserve a friend like Luc. "I'm in so much
trouble."

Like it always did in a crisis situation, his voice
became calm and soothing. "Tell me what happened."

"Joseph cancelled and I have no other meetings
lined up for Lydia and she wants to start the interview process tonight and she's going to fire me
when she finds out I've failed and I won't be able
to buy my house," I wailed.

"Wait a minute. This is about your *project?*"

"Yes. Joseph got sick."

"The nerve of him."

I nodded. "I know."

"So what is it you want my help for? To go out
and meet more men?"

I wrinkled my nose at the sharp edge in his voice.
If he were a woman I would have accused him of
PMSing. But because it was in my own best inter-

est, I toned down my irritation. "I'm out of time for the meeting phase. She wants to have her choice made by the end of the week."

"So what is it you want from me?" he repeated.

I swallowed and blurted it out. "I need you to meet Lydia tonight."

Silence. A very charged, heavy silence.

"Excuse me?" he asked finally. "I thought I heard you say you wanted *me* to meet Lydia tonight."

"I did."

"What?"

I winced and held the phone away from my ear. Only I could still hear him ranting despite the space.

"Of all the insane, ludicrous, absurd ideas."

He felt kind of strongly about this, I saw. "Does that mean you won't do it?"

"Damn right I won't do it."

Uh-oh. Luc was really pissed—I could tell from his tone of voice. "It's not like it'd be a hardship. Just get together with her and flirt. You do it with every other woman you ever meet." Was that a trace of resentment in my voice?

"What are you talking about?"

"Oh, please, Luc. You know you flirt with everyone."

"I do not." He actually sounded incredulous.

"Remember when we went to that bar and you played pool? And that woman at the laundromat. And Leah from the clothing store, and—"

"Okay," he said, cutting me off. "I get the picture. But I wasn't flirting. Not with intent. I was just being friendly."

I snorted. "Any friendlier and you'd have to use a condom."

"Come on, Kat. I can't believe you'd think I was interested in those women."

"Fine." I was willing to concede if it meant he'd take Joseph's place tonight. "So does that mean you'll have drinks with Lydia?"

"No."

God, he could be stubborn. I needed to reconsider my strategy.

Time to bring out the heavy guns.

I took a calming breath, put a whimper in my voice, and batted my eyes. (Yes, I knew he wouldn't be able to see my eyes batting, but it made me feel my role more.) "Please, Luc, you have to help me. I just want you to meet with Lydia this once. Nothing more. Only for tonight. I'll have other candidates set up"—I hoped—"but I just need you to bail me out of tonight. Please please please."

"No."

"I'll never ask you for another favor ever again for as long as we live. Please, Luc." I put extra little-girl pleading in my voice.

"Kat . . ."

Yes! He was weakening. "Please. I'd do it for you."

"Great. I'll keep that in mind if I ever decide I want to pimp you out."

I ignored his sarcastic remark (as well as the pang I felt at the idea of him passing me off to another man) and waited quietly, willing him to say yes.

"I can't believe you want me to do this."

I wilted in relief. I knew it—he was going to do it. "Thank you so much, Luc. I'll make it up to you. Really."

He snorted.

"Meet Lydia at eight o'clock at the Mark Hopkins." I paused. Then I went ahead and asked, figuring it couldn't hurt. "Um, Luc. If I couriered it over to you, do you think you could glue on a goatee?"

"Kat—"

"Right," I said quickly. "Never mind. It was just an idea. Eight o'clock. Thanks, Luc. You're the best." I hung up before he could change his mind.

Opening Joseph's spreadsheet, I quickly reworked it with Luc's information. Fortunately, Luc had most of the criteria Lydia demanded. Minus the goatee.

I checked the time. Whew—that was close. I had a minute to spare.

Adjusting my skirt as I got up, I smoothed my hair and headed to let Lydia know about her schedule this evening.

Jessica manned her post with her usual *I'm too busy to deal with you* attitude. I knew she had to be competent for Lydia to keep her around, but each time I came up she seemed like she was in the midst of filing her nails or something. Today she was engrossed in whatever was displayed on her monitor. Probably Internet shopping.

I smiled at her. "Good morning."

She barely looked up. "You're late. Lydia's waiting for you."

I glanced at my watch. I was barely a minute late.

Whatever. Forcing another smile, I said "thank you" and walked into Lydia's office.

My boss was nowhere to be found (I even glanced under her desk to make sure she hadn't passed out because of a stress-related heart attack), so I sat down and waited for her to show up.

I was rehearsing my presentation when the door of her private bathroom opened and she strode out, heading directly for her throne. "What do you have for me, Katherine?"

Good morning to you too.

I took a deep breath, said a quick prayer for my promotion, and started on my pitch. "Lydia, given your need to have this assignment completed with the utmost haste, I decided to alter our strategy."

She coolly raised one brow and crossed her arms.

Gulp. "I picked the most eligible candidate out of the bunch and made an appointment for you at eight this evening. I truly believe"—I crossed my fingers surreptitiously—"this one will be the best choice for you. This seemed the most efficient way to go about the process. You won't have to squander your time with the other men who don't meet as many of your stipulations."

Lydia continued to study me. I met her gaze levelly even though on the inside I was squirming like a worm on a hook.

Finally she said, "Bold strategy. I like it." She picked up the spreadsheet I'd thrown together for Luc and glanced over it. "He looks good on paper. What happens if I decide he isn't the ideal candidate?"

I pushed my glasses up and lied. "I have other people lined up for Wednesday night, the way you indicated. At hour increments."

"Good." She slipped the spreadsheet into her briefcase. "I'll let you know how it goes tomorrow morning so you can cancel or confirm the other appointments as appropriate."

She actually went for it? I cleared my throat. "Great. Thank you." I stood up to leave before my luck ran out.

"Katherine?"

"Shoot," I mumbled, wincing. I turned around. "Yes?"

She smiled. Okay—it was the barest curve of the corners of her lips, but for Lydia it was like beaming. "Thank you. I'm very pleased with your work."

The world was coming to an end—I just knew it. "Um, thank you." I hightailed it out of there before she got the urge to throw her arms around me and give me a bear hug. At least it was a good sign for my promotion.

On my way back to my office, I tried to figure out what I was going to do next. I'd bought myself some time, but I still hadn't come up with any candidates for Lydia. Not any real ones anyway. When her "date" with Luc didn't work out, I'd need to have a passel of men lined up to meet with her.

How was I going to do that?

Drake's face flashed in my mind. He'd be perfect, except that he seemed too masterly. I wasn't sure he'd be willing to be used as a sperm donor, no matter what the incentive.

Not that I knew how to contact him anyway.

Maybe Joseph would be better by then.

Wincing, I remembered how sick he sounded. Even with my eternal optimism I couldn't make myself believe that.

As soon as I got back to my office, I began calling all those guys I'd accumulated over the past couple weeks. The victory with Lydia made me confident I could talk them into agreeing to meet with her. There had to be some way I could appeal to them, right?

Eight o'clock.

I looked at the time display on the phone and nervously tapped my pen against my desk.

Right at this moment, Luc was probably walking into the lobby of the Mark Hopkins and heading back to the bar to meet Lydia.

Even though I'd worked at AshComm forever (at least that's the way it seemed), Luc had never met my boss. The only thing he knew about her was what I'd told him—that she was a fair, hard-working woman who made my life a living hell. Okay, I might have intimated that she was also occasionally bitchy and colder than Santa's butt. A fairly accurate portrayal, actually.

I bit my lip, wondering how he'd react to seeing her. She was the kind of woman who made men walk into parking meters as she walked by on the street. Would Luc be as bedazzled?

I shook my head. Probably not. She wasn't his type, except for being tall. And blond. And utterly bewitching.

I stood up. I couldn't take it anymore. I thought I'd be able to get some serious work done this evening, but for the past half hour all I'd managed to do was worry about how Lydia's meeting with Luc would go. But I could do that just as easily at home, and I was hungry, so I called it a night. There was a can of tuna with my name written on it.

I'd shut down my workstation, cleared my desk, and was waiting for the elevator when I felt someone walk up behind me.

I stiffened, recalling all the stats on lone women being attacked at work after hours. Luc had made me take a self-defense class eons ago but the only thing I could remember was hitting the groin, which was a little difficult with your back to your attacker.

"We meet again."

"Oh." I practically dissolved in relief at the familiar gravelly voice. "You scared me," I said, turning around.

Drake smiled, his dimple flashing at me. "I'm sorry. I didn't mean to frighten you. I didn't expect to see anyone else here this time of night. Even Lydia's gone for the evening."

Tell me something I don't know. "I had a couple reports to finish up."

He gazed at me steadily, a blunt finger rubbing his five o'clock–shadowed cheek. "You work hard."

No kidding. About time *someone* noticed. "Well— you know."

The elevator arrived and Drake held the door open for me. He hit the button for the lobby once we were both in.

I wondered what it'd be like to be with a man who was so strong and confident. It was comforting in a way, but I imagined it'd get old fast.

No wonder Lydia just wanted a sperm donor. Most of the men of her ilk were probably like the man next to me. I grinned, thinking of Lydia with Drake. That'd be something I'd pay to see.

"You look cheerful."

I pushed my glasses up and glanced at Drake. "Excuse me?"

"You're smiling."

"I was just thinking how ironic it was that over twenty-five hundred left-handed people are killed each year from using products made for right-handed people," I lied.

"Yes, I can see how that would tickle you."

Did I detect faint sarcasm? I shrugged. Whatever. It wasn't like I worked for him.

Hey!

I frowned at him, hands on my hips. "What are you doing here so late? You don't work here."

The doors pinged open and he guided me out with a hand under my elbow. "You could say I was doing some research."

"Espionage! I knew it." I looked around for the security guard who was usually dozing in the lobby, but he was nowhere to be found. Shit—Drake had probably taken care of the poor man already.

He shook my arm. "Don't start imagining crazy scenarios. I'm a major shareholder in the company. The chief financial officer and I had some numbers to go over. You can ask your boss tomorrow when you see her."

A shareholder? Awfully convenient. Eyes narrowed, I glared at him. "You're not just saying that to lull me into a false sense of security before you take me out back and off me, are you?"

He threw his head back and laughed. "You, my dear, have been watching too many movies."

I sighed. "I haven't been to a movie in a really long time."

"You work hard," he said again. Only this time I thought I detected a hint of pity.

I tipped my chin up and adjusted my glasses. "I love my work."

"And you're one of the most loyal employees I've ever seen."

I wrinkled my nose. The way he said it sounded like he was noting it in my employee file. Was that why he was here? To check up on the staff?

No. He seemed too important. And frankly, I doubted Lydia would hire someone she obviously didn't like much to do a job like that for her.

Drake held the door open for me. "Are you headed home?"

"Yes."

"Do you need a lift?" he asked as a dark car pulled to the curb in front of us. It was one of those large town cars with the tinted windows that you see passing by on the streets and know some-one really important is inside.

I looked at it longingly, wondering what it'd be like to ride in it rather than a smelly Muni bus.

If I didn't take this opportunity, when else would I find out? I smiled politely. "Yes, thank you. That would be nice."

Drake opened the door before his driver made it around the car. "Katherine, meet Milton, my driver."

Milton walked quickly around the car to our side, ready. What he was ready for, I wasn't sure, but I had no doubt he could spring into action at a mo-ment's notice, even though he just stood there im-passively.

I gazed at him in wonder. He wore the typical

black suit and starched white shirt—both immaculate. How did he keep so crisp? "Hello, Milton."

He continued to stare impassively over my head. At least I think he was staring over my head—I couldn't really tell since he wore sunglasses. I wondered if I should tell him the sun had already set and that he didn't need them anymore.

Drake cleared his throat. "Milton, we're taking Ms. Murphy home this evening."

"Very good, sir," Milton said tonelessly.

Wow. Even his voice was expressionless. I wondered if that was something he worked at or if he was born with the talent.

I didn't have time to ask. Drake gestured me in, so I tumbled into the back seat. "Very smooth," I mumbled to myself.

"You okay?" Drake looked concerned as he climbed in after me.

"Fine. Thank you." I smiled at him stiffly as I rearranged my skirt. I hoped I didn't flash him. At least I had on another pair of my pretty new underwear.

The trip to my apartment was mercifully quick. Drake got a business call, so I didn't have to worry about making small talk. I wasn't comfortable around him. I mean, intuitively, I felt like he was okay. But I still felt like there was something I was missing. And then there was the fact that his power made me uncomfortable. Just like Lydia's did.

I had them drop me off a few blocks early, figuring anything to expend some of my excess energy had to be a good thing. I ran up the four flights of stairs to my apartment and even did a lap up and down the hall for good measure. But even still, as I was unlocking my door, my nerves jittered. I think it was with apprehension, but it might have been the five cups of coffee I had this evening.

Rainbow's door opened and she popped her head out, the heavy scent of burning perfume wafting. "Kath, are you just getting home from work?"

"Yes." Though you couldn't really call anything I'd done this evening work. Not unless *space cadet* was my title.

"You work too much." She shook her head. "When do you have time for fun?"

I pursed my lips. "Work's fun."

She lit up like a light bulb. "We should go out. Like, right now. Want to?"

"I don't know." Going out was really expensive, and I'd already spent too much money over the past few weeks. But I *was* going to expense those outings, and I was really strung out. I doubted I could do any of my usual nighttime activities, like working. Or reorganizing my closet.

Then I had an idea—a brilliant idea. I smiled at her. "Ever been to the Mark Hopkins?"

She scrunched her face. I barely even noticed how her nostril ring glinted in the fluorescent lighting. "Isn't that a hotel?"

"They have a bar. We could get a drink."

"Do they have organic beer? Because there's a place a couple blocks away that has great home brew that's organic."

Organic beer at the Mark Hopkins? "Uh, we won't know unless we go there."

Rainbow grinned brightly. "That's true. Let's do it."

"Great." I returned her grin and opened my door. "Come in while I change."

"Groovy."

I set my briefcase by my desk in the living room. "Make yourself comfortable. I'll be a second."

"Okay."

I glanced back at her before I went into my bedroom. She was looking around with a puzzled look on her face. I shrugged. Probably confused by the neatness and order of my apartment. No precarious towers of magazines or shoe mounds.

Hanging up my work clothes, I pulled out a pair of jeans and a black silk shirt. I debated wearing one of my new sweaters, but I wanted to be inconspicuous and a pink sweater didn't fit the bill. Though calling it a sweater was overstating its substance—it was more like spun candy than any sweater I'd ever owned.

"Hey, Kath!"

I turned around right as Rainbow walked into my room and flopped onto my bed.

"Oh!" I held the jeans in front of me. I wasn't used to having an audience while I changed.

"Is that the underwear your friend bought you?"

I looked down and blushed, clutching the pants closer. "Yes. Why?"

She whistled. "Wow."

I didn't know whether to ask her what she meant or how she did that with the silver stud in her tongue. I decided on the former.

She shrugged. "I've never had a friend who bought me stuff like that. Heck, I've never had a boyfriend who bought me anything that nice. He must *like* you."

The emphasis she put on *like* made my face burn hotter. I remembered last night, and how Luc sounded when I talked to him on the phone today, and frowned. Even if he had liked me before (and I still thought that was a stretch), he wouldn't now—not after what I did last night. "I don't think so."

She shrugged again. "If you say so," she said absently, looking around my room.

I waited for her to leave so I could put my clothes on, but it seemed like she'd settled in for the duration, so I took advantage of her inattention and quickly dressed.

I laced up my tennis shoes (maybe the next time I went to the outlet stores I'd buy a pair of boots—I could wear boots to work too, right?). "I'm ready."

Rainbow glanced at me and frowned. "Are you sure?"

"Yes." I frowned. "Why? Don't I look okay?"

"Your clothes look great. I had no idea you ever wore anything but those ugly suits—"

"Hey—"

She continued before I could protest that my suits were Donna Karan. "—but your hair could use some help."

My hand automatically flew up to my head. I had no idea what she meant. It felt in order.

"Come on." Rainbow bounced off the bed, grabbed my arm, and dragged me to the bathroom. Pushing me down on the toilet seat (thank God the lid was closed), she began pulling the pins from my bun.

"But, Rainbow, I don't think—"

"Shh." She was so forceful, she shushed me right up. "This'll just take a second."

I wrinkled my nose and let her do her thing, only because I figured I could put my hair back up after she was finished.

"Do you have hair spray or gel or anything?"

"In there." I pointed at the medicine cabinet.

She frowned at the tube of styling gel. "This company does animal testing."

I pictured a rat with its fur styled into spikes. But I resisted grinning—by the look on Rainbow's face, I didn't think she'd appreciate the humor.

"I'll use it this time, but it goes against my beliefs." Her face scrunched, she squeezed a little into her palm and tossed the bottle into the garbage.

"Hey!" I'd worked half an hour to pay for that gel.

She patted my head. "I'll bring you some better product. There. I'm done."

I'd avoided looking in the mirror as she worked, fearing the results. I mean, would you trust your hair to someone with frizzy dreads?

But I had no choice because she held my shoulders and made me look.

Hey.

I blinked my eyes, pushed my glasses up, and leaned closer. "It looks good."

She grinned. "I know."

My hair was in smooth waves, still on the curly side but softer looking. Tousled. "It looks—"

"Sexy," she said. "You should wear your hair this way more often. Do you have lipstick? You need some."

At this point, if she said I needed a piercing I

would have believed her. I glossed my lips and, at
Rainbow's pronouncement that I was ready, I
grabbed my coat (my dress coat, not the red one—
I didn't want to stand out), locked up, and waited
for her in the hallway.

She emerged from her apartment in an old army-
style coat and a knapsack made out of some faded
carpet material. "Let's go."

I wondered what they'd think at the Mark
Hopkins, but I was too eager to get there to worry
about it. It was already late. Chances were Luc and
Lydia were already gone, but I wanted to see. I had
to make sure everything went well. For the sake of
my promotion.

Really.

Because of the time, I sprang for a cab. I know—
I wouldn't be able to expense this. Sometimes you
just had to splurge.

Rainbow and I had to walk several blocks before
we caught a taxi (they just don't hang around our
neighborhood). But once we got a hold of one, it
was no time before we were at the hotel.

The Mark Hopkins overlooks downtown San
Francisco, at the top of Nob Hill. Nob Hill is where
San Francisco's Gold Rush and railroad million-
aires settled. The housing there is still stately and
expensive. Needless to say, I didn't have much cause
to go there often.

The doorman opened the door for us to enter.
He nodded at me and then Rainbow. Then he did
a double take and gaped at my neighbor.

I scowled at him. Rainbow might not have been
the traditional type of customer that frequented

the Mark Hopkins, but he didn't have to be so rude about it.

"Is there a problem?" I asked in my coldest Lydia voice.

"No, ma'am," he replied quickly.

I couldn't believe how well that worked. I almost clapped my hands in glee. Practicing in front of the mirror was paying off.

We stopped in the lobby. I looked around for the lounge area—that had to be where Luc and Lydia were meeting, right?

"The bar's back that way."

I looked to where Rainbow pointed. Excellent. I smiled at her. "Let's go."

But when we got closer I stopped. What if Luc saw me? I didn't want that.

Rainbow ran into my back. "What's wrong?"

I saw the worried look on Rainbow's face and grimaced. "I have something to tell you."

Her brow furrowed. Then she placed her hand on my shoulder. "You know, it's okay. I kinda wondered at first, but then there was your friend who bought you the underwear so I thought I was wrong, but I guess I was wrong about being wrong. But I don't mind. I mean, I don't do chicks—not that I haven't tried them—they just aren't my thing. But I'm very flattered. You know, I have one or two friends you might dig in a big way. Especially Dill— she's into the power suit, femme lipstick thing."

Pushing my glasses up, I wondered what she was talking about. I shrugged. She'd probably inhaled too much incense. "Um, thanks. I was just going to tell you that I brought you here under false pretenses."

"I get it." Rainbow smiled reassuringly and patted my arm. "It's okay. I can dig alternative lifestyles."

Maybe I needed to go clear out the incense from her apartment before she completely lost it. "Listen, you know my friend Luc? The one who gave me the underwear?"

"Yeah."

"He's supposed to be here tonight. With my boss."

Her forehead scrunched. "Don't tell me you have a thing for your boss. That can only end up bad. Trust me. I went out with the manager of the Wienerschnitzel where I worked in high school." She gagged. "Bad scene. I had to go work at Wendy's, and the fries weren't as good." She frowned. "That was before I became earth conscious."

"Um. Okay." I think I missed something somewhere along the way. "Here's the thing. I set up Luc and my boss because I want to buy a home."

Rainbow gawked at me with her big, round eyes. Then she took my arm and pulled me toward the lounge. "I think we need a drink."

"That's the thing." I dug in my heels. "I don't want Luc and Lydia to see me."

"Whatever you say." Then I heard her murmur under her breath, "I hope they have organic beer. I really need one."

The lounge was right out in the open but set back from the lobby. The only thing separating us from their view was the foliage in front of us.

Actually, Rainbow was really good at sneaking. She headed straight for one of the enormous potted plants, dragging me behind her.

She parted the branches an inch or two, just enough to peer through. "Okay—you see them?"

I snuck a look, my eyes zeroing in on Luc immediately. "Over there."

"Holy shit, Kath."

"What?" I asked, alarmed.

"He's hot." She whistled. "How can you be into women with him around?"

Into women? I frowned. "What are you talking about?"

"It's okay," she said distractedly, still staring at Luc. "To each his own."

I shook my head. "Focus, Rainbow. How are we going to get in there?"

"Come on." She took my hand and we skirted around the lounge, with a brief stop to snatch a couple of menus from the bar, until we were as far away from Luc and Lydia as we possibly could be. There was a table right there that we took.

Rainbow quickly opened a menu and handed it to me. "Hold this in front of your face."

She was brilliant. I peeked above the menu at her. "How'd you become so good at sneaking?"

"Subterfuge was my middle name in high school." She opened the menu and glanced through it. "Shoot. They don't have organic beer."

That was the least of my worries at the moment. I glanced around the menu at Luc. I couldn't believe they were still here. I checked my watch for the time—it was almost ten o'clock. Had they been here the whole two hours?

I pushed my glasses up, squinting to get a better look. They seemed like they were having a great time. I pursed my lips. Luc was leaning on the table, listening to Lydia speak. I knew firsthand how having him listening to you felt. It was an active thing—he did it with his whole body and you felt like you were the center of his world.

Then he laughed and squeezed her hand.

I scowled. He seemed awfully into the assignation for having been so reluctant.

"They seem cozy." Rainbow surreptitiously peeked over her shoulder. "They're obviously having a good time."

I grunted.

"Madams." The waiter nodded regally to us. "Can I get you something to drink?"

"Do you have organic beer?" Rainbow asked hopefully.

"Let me see what we can do." He turned to me and waited patiently.

I realized I'd lowered the menu, so I snapped it back up to cover my face. "A Coke, please." A Shirley Temple seemed too tawdry for the Mark Hopkins.

"Very good, madam." He nodded again and went to carry out our order.

"A *Coke*?" Rainbow shuddered. "Do you know how bad Coke is for you? They use that stuff to wash blood off the freeway after accidents where people get decapitated."

"Did you know Iceland consumes more Coke per capita than any other nation?"

"That doesn't mean *you* should drink it." She held up her hand. "But live and let live, I always say."

I looked around the menu again, keeping an eye on Luc and Lydia.

Really, it was very considerate of him to act so nice to my boss even though I knew he had to be suffering. I mean, what would Luc have in common with her? Poor guy, he was probably counting the milliseconds till he could go home. I owed him big for doing this for me. When I bought my home, I'd invite him over for dinner. Of course, he'd have to do the cooking.

"Did I mention how cool it was that you set up your boss with your friend?"

I wrinkled my nose over the top of my cover. "I didn't set them up. Well, not really. Luc's just doing this so I won't lose my job."

"Huh?" She dropped one of the napkins so she could bend down and peek behind. She spent so long down there that when she came back up her face was red from the blood that'd rushed to her head. "I don't get it."

I sighed and explained the whole situation to her—from the sperm project to how I'd failed setting up any dates for Lydia to what I had to do to set up the meetings for tomorrow (I winced when I thought of that one).

"You promised all those guys you'd organize their clothes if they got together with your boss?" She slapped her knee and guffawed. Loudly.

"Shh!" I snapped the menu, which I'd let slip down, back in front of my face. "They might hear you. And it seemed like good incentive at the time. Men are bad when it comes to keeping their closets in order." Luc couldn't even keep his shoes in neat pairs.

"I bet they can't wait till you take care of their Jockey shorts. Did they give you any special *han-*

dling instructions?" She roared, rocking with laughter.

"Rainbow," I hissed. "Shut *up*."

Fortunately, the waiter arrived with our drinks. He had a pinched expression on his face. I wondered if his feet hurt. I glanced down—those shoes he was wearing looked stiff. I'd probably grimace too if I had to walk in them for any length of time.

"An organic beer." He set Rainbow's bottle in front of her along with a chilled glass.

She beamed at him. "Thanks. I didn't think you had any."

"We went out and fetched some for you, madam." He put my Coke in front of me, made sure we didn't need anything else, and left us alone.

"They went out and *fetched* me my beer. How groovy is that?" Rainbow grinned and tapped her bottle against my glass before taking a swig.

I worried my straw as I shot furtive glances across the room from behind my cover.

"You know, you've got to come out from there eventually."

I frowned at her over the top of the menu. "No, I don't."

She shrugged. "So are you going to do it?"

"Do what?" Was he holding her hand now?

"Organize closets for those guys."

I grimaced. "I don't have much choice. I told Lydia this date would be the one. She's going to be really angry that it doesn't work out. I need to make sure I have alternatives lined up."

I didn't mention I wasn't sure how well those would turn out, but hopefully by then Joseph would be better and able to meet her. (I really did think Joseph was the one.)

Well, Joseph had to meet with her. Otherwise I was out a job and a dream.

Rainbow beat a tribal rhythm on her bottle. "You know, those guys are probably expecting more from you than just folding their laundry. You'll be in their boudoir. Don't you think they'll make a move?"

I shook my head even though she couldn't see me. "No, they know I'm only interested in them meeting my boss."

"Hmm."

Something caught my attention from the corner of my eye. I lowered the menu a fraction to see what was going on.

Luc stood and pulled Lydia's chair out so she could rise. Even from the distance I could hear his low, sexy laugh as she said something.

Not a big deal. I mean, he'd held out my chair for me hundreds of times. It was one of those polite things he did unconsciously. It wasn't anything special.

He held out Lydia's coat so she could slither into it. She smiled at him over her shoulder.

That look. I squinted at her. That happy look again. Creepy was the only word for it.

Luc's hands lingered on her shoulders even after she was in the coat. I waited for him to back away.

And I waited.

And waited.

But he didn't. He slid his hand down her arm until he held hers and walked out with her, their bodies close. Too close.

Luc was touchy-feely, though. That didn't mean anything. And he always helped me with my coat.

Wrinkling my nose, I tried to recall if his hands lingered on my shoulders. That'd be something I'd remember, right? They'd be warm and engulfing and would make me feel secure.

Yes, I'd definitely remember.

But I didn't.

I growled.

Rainbow leaned across the table, her eyebrows drawn together. "Are you okay?"

I smacked the menu down. "Wouldn't you remember if Luc's hands lingered on you?"

"Hell yeah." She grinned. "He's hot."

"That's what I thought." I pouted, trying not to panic that I'd opened Pandora's box when I made Luc meet Lydia.

I needed to calm down. I took a deep breath and thought about this rationally. Luc knew how important the promotion was to me—he was just doing his part in helping me secure it. He was pretending to be nice to Lydia. For me.

Of course.

But, somehow, that thought wasn't as reassuring as it should have been.

Chapter Twelve

Armed with a detailed schedule, I marched up to Lydia's office the next morning bent on saving my career, my future home, and my best friend.

I took no flack from Jessica. Breezing past her, I said, "I need to see Lydia." I didn't even wait for her reply. Of course, some of my confidence might have stemmed from the fact that Lydia had set up the meeting the day before.

The first inclination I had that something was wrong was after I knocked on the door and walked in. Instead of barking out orders on the phone or typing manically on her computer, she sat at her desk and stared out at her panoramic view. That in itself wouldn't have alarmed me overly much—what really panicked me was the dreamy look on her face.

Dreamy? Lydia didn't do dreamy.

My salutation died on my lips and I stood frozen in the doorway.

She looked up and smiled. "Come in, Katherine."

Right. I headed right for the chair I usually took and sat down. "Um. Are you okay, Lydia?"

"I'm perfect." She smiled. "You were absolutely right."

"I was?" I relaxed. Being right was a good thing.

"Yes. And I can't thank you enough."

"Um. Great." I smiled a confident, professional smile even though I felt anything but at the moment. Mostly I just wondered what I was right about.

"I knew my faith in your judgment wasn't misplaced." She tipped her head and looked at me consideringly. "Have you thought about how you'd like to decorate your new office?"

Yes!

My heart jumped into my throat. I knew Lydia would realize I'd set things right, even though Luc didn't work out. I barely stopped myself from falling to my knees and kissing the pointy tips of her Jimmy Choos.

Instead I cleared my throat. "I'm sure however it's decorated is fine." I wanted to ask if I got my own bathroom, but I thought that might be pushing it. Better to wait for tomorrow.

Because I knew she must have been waiting for it, I pulled out the schedule and handed it to her. "You'll need this."

"What is it?" Her forehead wrinkled as she looked at the schedule.

"Your schedule for tonight. I set up them up at hour increments."

She shook her head and handed it back to me. "I won't need this."

"You won't?"

"No." She smiled gently.

That should have been my first clue something was amiss. Lydia typically wasn't gentle about anything.

"Katherine, I think you misunderstood me. The assignment is complete."

"Oh." Oh. What a relief. She'd realized this idea was insane and she'd decided to drop the sperm search. I practically collapsed, I was so thankful.

"You did a great job. And you were right. To tell you the truth I had doubts, but I should have trusted you. Like I said before, you're impeccable in your research."

"Thank you." I didn't preen. I was just happy Lydia had come to her senses and realized this search for the perfect sperm was an asinine notion. And it didn't cost me my promotion.

Lydia leaned back in her chair and crossed her legs. "Luc is absolutely the perfect choice to father my baby."

I choked.

Lydia stood up partly. "Are you okay, Katherine?"

I managed a strangled "fine" in between the coughing. When I could breathe again, I asked, "You picked Luc?"

"Of course." She gazed at me through narrowed eyes. "Maybe you should take a couple days off. You've obviously been working hard."

"No. No—I'm fine." A month off wouldn't have

been enough to recover from the shock. All I heard in my head was *Luc* and *the father of my baby*.

She smiled a most un-Lydia-like smile. "You far surpassed my expectations, Katherine. Luc is different than the men I usually meet. So different that I might have to reconsider my initial plan."

"Reconsider?" The dreaminess of her expression made panic spike through my system.

"Yes. Luc just might restore my faith in the opposite sex." She flashed a wry smile.

I rubbed my eyes behind my lenses. I had to be seeing things. I was calling my optometrist for a checkup as soon as I returned to my office.

"I'll let you know how it goes. Luc and I have a date tomorrow night." She lifted her eyebrow suggestively and turned around to stare out the window again.

A *date?*

Stunned, I had to sit there for a few seconds before I trusted myself to get up without passing out.

I'm not sure how I did it, but I managed to get myself to my office, where I collapsed into my chair. Luc and *Lydia?*

Okay, Lydia was his type. He had a history of going out with tall blondes. But in spirit they were completely at odds. I mean, Lydia was a ruthless business tycoon while Luc was a massage therapist. He was sensitive and she was a heartless bitch (in the best possible way, of course).

It was just that when I thought of Luc settling down, I never imagined he'd do it with someone like Lydia. Actually, if I really thought about it, I never imagined who he would settle down with. I mean, I knew it would happen eventually, but I wasn't ready for it.

I leaned my head back, squeezed my eyes shut, and tried to picture hanging out for the holidays—me, Luc, and Lydia.

The Christmas tree and Luc were finally firmly in my mind and I was working on making Lydia materialize when I heard a knock on my door.

"Are you busy, Katherine?"

I opened my eyes to find Drake standing in the doorway.

Now, I could picture Drake and Lydia next to a Christmas tree without an effort. Lydia held her baby in her arms and she was smiling one of those freaky, happy smiles I'd never seen on her face before today.

"Katherine?"

I pushed my glasses up and focused on Drake. "Yes. I mean, no, I'm not busy. Come in."

He looked at me oddly but came in, closing the door behind him. "I noticed that you had another meeting with Lydia this morning."

"Yes." Unfortunately. It was one meeting I wish I'd never gone to.

"You have a lot of meetings with her."

I shrugged. "I work for her."

"You seem to know her well."

"I don't know." But if she and Luc hooked up, we'd practically be family.

Wait a minute.

A horrible thought popped into my head. Would I really be able to hang out with Luc if he and Lydia got together? I doubt she'd like that. She'd probably tell him he couldn't see me anymore.

I'd lose my best friend.

"Katherine?"

"Hm?" I frowned at Drake.

He frowned right back at me. "Are you okay?"

Why was everyone asking me that today? I smiled and hoped it wasn't as pale as it felt. "I'm fine."

He didn't look convinced but he dropped it. "So, how well do you know Lydia? Personally?"

"Personally?" I pursed my lips. I knew she was planning on putting moves on my best friend.

I gasped mentally. What if Luc didn't know she was planning on making a move? That must be it. I mean, Luc was kind of clueless sometimes. He was probably just being nice to her on my account (I *did* tell him my promotion rested on how well the meeting went). He probably had no idea what was going on.

I had to call to warn him.

"Katherine?"

The sharpness in Drake's voice made me snap to attention. "Yes, sir!"

He studied me, tapping a finger against his chin. "Are you sure you're okay?"

I gritted my teeth to make sure my smile didn't slip. "Of course."

He blinked but before I could assure him I really was okay, he said, "Tell me about Lydia."

She wants to be pregnant by next week and wants to steal my best friend away from me.

But out loud I said, "She's a fair employer."

"What can you tell me about her personal life?"

"She—" I scowled. "Why do you want to know about her personal life?"

He gazed at me steadily. "I wanted to get a feel for her."

"Why?" I wasn't sure why, but I was suddenly very suspicious.

"It's good to know who you're doing business with."

Of course. That's why he was around so much. Still. "You should ask her for a curriculum vitae."

He smiled and his one dimple winked at me. As intimidating as he looked—he was very imposing—he really was attractive when he smiled. Attractive in a gruff, manly kind of way. "I was hoping you'd be able to tell me something about her."

I shrugged. "She's very dedicated."

"Do you like your job?"

I blinked at the abrupt change in subject. "Yes," I answered cautiously.

He nodded. "What kind of projects are you working on?"

I gave him a brief rundown, minus Lydia's secret assignment (which, in reality, was taking up the bulk of my time).

Drake listened to me so attentively I really got into describing my work. Finding facts and doing research is a fine art. Not everyone is good at it, and certainly not everyone does it as thoroughly as it needs to be done. It's hard work, scouring the darkest corners of the Internet for obscure tidbits. You have to know how to finesse the information out of the ether, and not everyone can do that.

Usually when I talk about my work, something always interrupts the conversation. Like a pressing car detailing appointment.

The great thing about Drake was not only did he avidly listen but he asked questions. Intelligent questions. He got me so wrapped up in talking about my work that when he suggested we continue over a mocha and a bagel at the coffee bar on the corner I happily went along.

I didn't get back to work for an hour. At one time I would have really freaked out about that, but I felt too good to worry about it. I liked him. A lot. Drake got my mind off Lydia and Luc (shudder).

For a little while at least. I might have felt great when I got back to work, but within half an hour I was fretting again. Every time Luc came to mind (and Lydia, by default) my muscles clenched so tightly I felt like I was bound in a knot. I knew I had to call Luc to warn him, but I put it off for as long as I could.

Late in the afternoon, I decided I had to stop applying my Scarlett O'Hara philosophy to the Lydia situation and call Luc to caution him against her plans. He needed to know, and my promotion was out of danger, so there was no need for him to continue the charade.

He answered on the third ring. "Hello."

"Hi, Luc."

There was a long pause before he said anything. "Hey. How's it going?"

He sounded distant. Maybe he was in the middle of updating his schedule (he hated typing). "Pretty good."

"Good."

I frowned. Maybe he was bent out of shape because he had to spend so much time with Lydia last night. God knows, I'd be touchy. "I wanted to thank you for last night."

Silence.

Clearing my throat, I continued. "Right. Uh, it means a lot to me that you went, but I thought you should know—" How did I say this? That Lydia was like a black widow and she'd sighted him in her web and was going in for the kill?

But before I could finish my thought, Luc said, "I had a good time."

Blink. "You did?"

"Yes. Is that so hard to believe? You yourself said that your boss was attractive and intelligent. Why wouldn't I enjoy her company?"

"Uh—" Because she's a heinous bitch? "Good point," I replied weakly.

"I had such a good time I asked her to go out again tomorrow night."

"*You* asked her out again?" I almost toppled out of my chair.

"You were the one who wanted me to meet her."

Yeah, but I didn't want you to be interested in her. "Luc, I should tell you I think Lydia has ulterior motives."

"Like?"

I pushed my glasses up, gulped, and said, "I think she wants you to be her sperm donor."

Silence.

I knew it—I'd stunned him into speechlessness. I hoped he hadn't passed out from shock. "Luc? Are you still there?"

"Yeah. I'm waiting for you to tell me Lydia's ulterior motives."

I frowned. "I just did."

He snorted. "I knew what she was after when I went into this. Remember? You told me yourself what she was after."

"But—"

"What's the problem, Katherine? I'm doing what you wanted. You're going to get a promotion out of this, right?"

Luc sounded so unlike himself—so bitter—the only thing I could say was "yes."

"Great," he spat out. "I'm glad that's working out for you. I have a client arriving and I need to prep my studio. Talk to you sometime."

Sometime?

I opened my mouth to say something (I wasn't sure what) but the dial tone buzzed in my ear. I stared at the receiver for a long moment before I set it back in its cradle.

Images flashed through my mind. Luc and Lydia holding hands. Luc kissing Lydia. Lydia holding a baby with bright blue eyes like Luc's.

That's it. I pounded my desk with my fist.

Ow. I shook out my hand. That hurt.

Once the throbbing in my hand stopped and I could concentrate again, I tried to think logically. Luc might have asked Lydia out of his own accord, but after spending more time with her he'd see she wasn't the one for him. He wouldn't give her a baby. He'd told me many, many times how he'd never be able to give up a child of his.

And Luc and Lydia in a long-term relationship was unacceptable. It wouldn't happen. It couldn't.

Chapter Thirteen

"What can I get you?"

I startled and looked at the bartender. Instead of asking for a drink, I heard "Did you know Coca-Cola was originally green?" come out of my mouth.

His forehead wrinkled. "So, you want a Coke?"

I smiled. Finally a person who understood me.

I turned around from my spot at the bar and looked at the club. It was dark, lit with blue lights, and very modern. The people matched the décor—sleek and stylish. It was just the kind of place I'd expect Lydia to frequent. It didn't surprise me that she'd pick this place for a date.

I cringed at the word *date*. It was simply disgusting thinking of Luc going out with my boss. Kind of like thinking of your parents having sex.

Okay—I realized I was the one who set them up, but I never expected it to carry over into a second meeting. If I knew that, I would have gone out and dragged someone off the street instead of calling Luc to save me.

"Here you go." The bartender slid my Coke toward me. I almost fell off the bar stool when he told me how much I owed. I pulled out a bill and handed it to him, telling myself this was for a good cause.

I sipped my drink and looked out into the thin crowd. I guessed it was still early because the club wasn't full. A few people gyrated on the dance floor to what I supposed was music (it was more like an incessant thumping if you asked me).

No sign of Luc and Lydia.

There was a small booth in the back where it was dark. It looked out on the whole establishment without being noticeable—it was the perfect place to set up surveillance. I'd just slid off the stool and picked up my drink to go claim it when I heard a dark voice behind me.

"Fancy seeing you here."

I whirled around, spilling Coke over my hand, only to find Drake. He was dressed casually in a bloodred shirt (like dried blood really) and black slacks, but he looked as powerful as he did in his suits.

I frowned, set my drink down, and wiped my hand with a napkin. At least I didn't spill on my new clothes (yes, the ones Luc bought me)—the pants were dry-clean only. "What are you doing here?"

He cocked a brow. "I could ask you the same question since I don't see this place as your kind of hangout."

Asking *why not?* was on the tip of my tongue. But I didn't. Instead I repeated, "So why are you here?"

"Probably the same reason you're here. To see Lydia." He grinned at my wrinkled nose. "Can I get you another drink? What are you having?"

I looked at my drink and cringed. I could imagine the amused look in Drake's eyes when he found out a Coke was all I could handle.

So I squared my shoulders, tossed my head back, and acted like one of the actresses in the old movies Luc liked to make me watch. "I'll have whatever you're having."

He eyed my drink but didn't say anything. Signaling the bartender (who came over immediately, I noticed), he said, "A Bombay Sapphire martini and a cosmopolitan, please."

The bartender nodded and set to making our drinks. I wondered which one was mine—they both sounded exotic.

The bartender set the drinks in front of us. Drake tossed a bill (I had to cover my mouth not to gasp out loud at the large denomination) and handed me a pretty pink drink.

"To a successful evening." He clinked his glass against mine and took a sip.

I took a sip too. A cautious one—I didn't drink alcohol. Oh my. I pushed my glasses up and looked at it closer. It was refreshing and tasty. I smiled at Drake. "I like it."

The corner of his mouth twitched. "I thought you might."

I drank a little more. Really tasty. And it matched the wraparound top Luc had bought me that I was wearing.

"Let's go sit at that booth back there."

I looked to where he gestured—the same booth I'd been heading for before he accosted me. "Okay."

He escorted me through the club with a hand on the small of my back. As I slid into the booth, I tried not to think about what kind of activity usually took place back here or what I might be sitting in.

Drake slid in next to me and set his drink on the table. "A perfect view of the room, isn't it?"

Looking up at him, I wrinkled my nose in thought. "How did you know Lydia was going to be here?"

"I asked her secretary. How did you know?"

"I asked Lydia." I tried not to preen at his impressed look.

"Enterprising." He calmly sipped his beverage. "But that doesn't explain your interest in Lydia's life."

I drank as I tried to figure out how much I could tell him. I was a little surprised when I realized my glass was empty.

"Another drink?" he asked, lifting his hand to signal a waitress.

Drake didn't press me to answer his question until after the waitress brought over another drink for me. Then he swept in for the kill.

Leaning back in a deceptively casual pose, he stared at me with his disturbingly frank gaze. "Did Lydia ask you to meet her here?"

"No!" I shuddered to think what would happen if Lydia—and Luc—found out I was here. I picked up my pink drink and downed half of it in one gulp.

"Then why are you here?"

Why was he interrogating me? I scowled at him. "I could ask you the same question. Why are *you* here?"

"To spy on Lydia."

I pushed my glasses up. "That was a straightforward answer."

He shrugged. "No reason in beating around the bush. Now why don't you tell me why you're here."

Did I dare confess? I threw back the rest of my beverage for courage and set the glass down a little too hard on the table. "I'm here to spy on Lydia too. She's going out with my best friend."

"Ah. I see."

He did see, I could tell. I relaxed in the corner of the booth, at ease for the first time all evening. Everything was all hazy, and I felt good. Damn good. "They went out Tuesday night, just like I wanted them to. Only they weren't supposed to go out again."

"I see."

It was so nice to have someone understand you.

Another pink drink appeared in front of me. I leaned down to squint at the glass. "What are these anyway?"

"Cosmopolitans. Vodka, cranberry, and a touch of lime."

Cranberry juice was very good for you. "Did you know ten percent of the Russian government's income comes from the sale of vodka?"

"I didn't know that."

I narrowed my eyes at him. "Are you amused? You sound amused."

"I'm merely enjoying your company."

Suspicious. I kept a wary eye on him as I sipped my cosmopolitan. I felt so worldly drinking it.

Then something occurred to me. "Why are you spying on Lydia?"

"I found out about her date and wanted to see for myself." He gazed at me over the rim of his glass.

I got distracted by how manly he looked—a contradiction with the delicate glass in his hand.

Had to shake my head to clear it. The room tipped over a little bit. "Whoa."

"Are you okay?"

"Why is everyone asking me that lately? Don't I look like I'm okay?" I held my hands out and glanced down. I didn't just look okay—I looked smokin' tonight (I'd heard that expression in the mail room one day when I was delivering a package). In addition to the wraparound shirt (pink, just like my cosmopolitan—could I have planned that better?) I had on a pair of super-tight bell-bottoms on with lots of zippers—who knew bell-bottoms were in? And to top it all off, I left my hair down. It didn't look as nice as the other night when Rainbow styled it, but it was decent.

"You look wonderful," Drake assured me.

His mouth quirked again—I was sure of it. I leaned closer to him. "Did your mouth just twitch? I swear I saw your mouth twitch."

"I doubt that."

"There it is again. Definitely twitching." As I pointed at his lips, I almost tipped over into his lap. "Oops!"

"Careful." He righted me, holding my arm overly long.

I glanced down at it with a frown. "Are you making a pass at me? Because I don't think you should make a pass at me. I like you and I'd hate to have to slap your cheek."

This time he really did grin. "Then I'll make sure I control myself."

"Do that." I picked up my drink and swigged. "I *love* lime."

"I'm glad, but maybe you should ease up on the cosmos."

Cosmos! Such a cute nickname. I tipped the glass up, sucking every last drop. "I love this drink. You know what?"

"What?"

"I bet you Rainbow would love cosmos too." I gasped. "Is vodka organic?"

But Luc and Lydia walked in, so Drake didn't get a chance to reply. Or if he did I didn't hear him. My vision narrowed to the circle of light that haloed the couple.

I wrinkled my nose in their direction. They really did look like a couple. Luc was holding her hand, and Lydia was leaning into him.

"She's leaning." I pointed, catching my balance on Drake's thigh as I almost fell over. "Do you see that? She's leaning."

"Yes, she is."

I stared up at him, frowning. He sounded irate. I kind of thought he might have been thoughtful, but he sounded royally ticked.

Squinting, I leaned closer to get a better look at him. Yep—he was definitely ticked. I could see the tightness around his eyes and his jaw. "I knew it."

"Hmm?" He glanced at me for a second before returning to his study of Luc and Lydia.

"You care."

He gave me his full attention. "Excuse me?"

"You care." I grinned triumphantly at him.

"I think we should order some water and maybe a cup of coffee."

"Did you know a Saudi Arabian woman can get a divorce if her husband doesn't give her coffee in the morning? That's hard core."

He patted my arm and smiled at me. "You're really a cute drunk."

Oh my. I pushed my glasses up and stretched up to get a better look at his dimple. I reached up with a finger to poke its center.

"Katherine."

I pushed my glasses up again and blinked. "Luc?" Setting my elbows on the table, I rested my chin in my hands and grinned. "Fancy meeting you here."

"Who's your friend?"

I looked to where he pointed. That's when I realized I was practically sitting on top of Drake. Funny! I giggled. "Oops—I'm on your lap."

Lydia growled. "Viggo Drake."

Luc raised his brow. "You know him?"

She nodded. "Unfortunately."

Drake just smiled, but it was a pale smile compared to the one he gave me. I knew because his dimple didn't come out to play. "Lydia. I trust you're having a good evening."

Lydia growled again.

I looked at Luc, only there were suddenly two of him standing there. I took my glasses off and rubbed my eyes. "There's something wrong with my vision. I need new glasses."

Both Lucs scowled. "Have you been drinking?"

"Like a fish." I grinned. "Drake got me this really scrumptious drink called a cosmonaut and I *loved* it."

"A cosmopolitan," Drake corrected gently.

"Thanks." I beamed at Luc. "I really love this guy."

I think something happened to the lighting in the club, because the faces of both Lucs got really dark.

Drake cleared his throat. "Would you like to join us?"

"No," Lydia snapped. She tightened her grip on the Lucs' hands and pulled. (Somehow she was holding both Lucs with the same hand.) "Let's go, Luc."

The Lucs nodded. "I'll talk to you tomorrow, Katherine."

I watched them disappear into the growing crowd. "That sounded ominous. He never calls me Katherine, and that's at least twice today." I gazed up at Drake. "What do you think that means?"

"I think it means I should take you home."

"Oh." I bit my lip. "But I can't go home with you

because my work clothes are in my closet and I need them for tomorrow."

He grinned again. "Your Luc is a lucky guy."

"He's not my Luc." I pouted. "Either one of them."

"Come on, Ms. Murphy." He got up and held out a hand. "Your carriage awaits."

I followed him, but when I stepped out of the booth the ground wasn't where it normally was. "Someone moved the floor."

Drake slipped his arm around my waist. "You really are a lightweight, aren't you?"

I nodded. "I only weigh a hundred and ten pounds."

He laughed and pulled me closer.

I sniffed. "You smell really good. But not as good as Luc. Luc smells good even when he's sweating." I frowned. "But maybe that's just pheromones. Sweat is chock full of pheromones, you know."

"I do now."

As we worked our way through the club, dodging waitresses and weaving through people, the club began to rotate in clockwise circles.

I looked around. "That's really interesting. How do you think they make the room spin like that?"

Drake groaned. "Tell me if you start to feel sick."

"I never feel sick. I'm as healthy as a horse." As soon as I said that I felt my stomach roil. "Usually."

I made it outside before I threw up dinner and every drop of the cosmos (tuna fish and vodka apparently didn't go well together). Drake held my hair and soothed my back. The world stopped spinning—mostly—and my head cleared a little. "Do you think that potted plant will be okay?"

"The potted plant is the least of our worries at the moment. Think you can make it to the car now?"

I lifted my head from where it rested on Drake's chest to look at where he pointed. I shook my head. "Don't think I can make it all the way down there."

"It's only ten feet away. Lean on me."

I shook my head again and winced. "I think I need to visit the plant once more before we go."

Lurching toward the foliage, I was vaguely aware of Drake holding me again. I would have commented on it but I was too busy trying to keep my innards from coming up.

Something white flapped in my face. I whacked it away but it was persistent.

"Go away." I pushed it again, forcefully, feeling myself fall forward after it.

"Easy there." Drake's hold on me tightened. "I'm just trying to wipe your mouth."

"Oh." Might as well be cooperative. I pursed my lips and waited.

"Think you can make it to the car now?" he asked, patting my face with the handkerchief.

I peered around his arm. "All the way over there? Too far."

"Come on. I'll help you."

He must have had too much to drink because we stumbled an awful lot on the way to the car. I wiggled my finger at him. "You should take it easy on those drinks the next time."

"I'll try. Milton, I think I need a hand."

I looked up and grinned. "Milton!" Then I frowned. "It's dark out. Why are you wearing your sunglasses? They're prudent to wear during the day considering the damage the sun can do with UV rays, but you're safe at night." I tried patting his shoulder to reassure him but his body kept undulating so I missed.

"In you go, Katherine," Drake said, and suddenly I was facedown in dark leather, my butt in the air.

I rolled over to sit up and fell onto the floor. "Oof."

"Up you go." Drake hoisted me up.

I fell into his lap again. I pushed at him with a grin. "Are you getting fresh again?"

What happened next is all a blur. I must have given Drake my apartment number because the next thing I was conscious of was being dragged up the stairs of my building. At least I think it was my building—everything was fuzzy.

I tried to straighten my glasses so I could see better but they weren't on my nose. "Oh no!"

Drake glanced at me as he hefted me up a couple more steps. Or I think he did. "What is it?"

"The plant took my glasses."

I knew he grinned because I caught the white flash of his teeth in the semidarkness of the hallway. "I made the plant give them back. They're in my pocket."

"Oh good." Glasses weren't cheap, and I had to save all my pennies. "I'm going to buy a house, you know."

"Really?"

"Mm-hmm." I kept my head still, remembering what had happened the last time I tried to move my head. "A cozy house. After I get the promotion."

"Promotion?"

"Mm-hmm. I'm VP material, you know. Linda sees that now that I've found her sperm."

"What?"

I nodded. Bad idea. I tried to still the throbbing in my head with my hand.

Drake held me up against a wall, tilting my face up to his. "What's this about sperm?"

"Linda's—"

"Lydia."

"Oh." Right. "Lydia's clock is ticking and she really needs sperm bad. So I gave her Luc—" Tears filled my eyes. "I didn't mean to, though. Now I've lost my best friend."

The door next to us opened. I turned my head and glared at Rainbow. "Where were you? I knocked and knocked and knocked but you didn't answer. I wanted to ashk—" I frowned. There was something wrong with my mouth. First my eyes, now this. Good thing I still had control of my mind. "—*ask* you to go with me."

"I was on a date." She frowned at me, which I kind of noted even though I was entranced by her dreads, which rippled in sinuous waves.

Maybe she was Medusa undercover, like Bruce Wayne to Batman. I nodded sympathetically. "If I were Medusa, I'd keep it under wraps too."

"Do you think you could help me find her key? I think Katherine needs to lie down."

Rainbow nodded and came out to us. "I'll look in her pocket."

I giggled when I felt her touch. "You're tickling me."

"You smell like a distillery," she mumbled as she poked through my jacket. "You don't drink."

"But Drake got me this really great drink with lime called cosmetology and it was great." I frowned. "But I don't know if it was organic."

"Got it." Rainbow held up something that looked very familiar.

I squinted. "That looks like my key."

Then my door was open and Drake followed Rainbow in, pulling me along with him.

Drake grunted. "Her bedroom?"

"Through here." She turned on the light in my room and we all went in there.

"Can we have a slumber party?" I pouted. "Please? I've never had one."

Rainbow and Drake must have decided this was a great idea because they put me on the bed and undressed me.

I frowned. "I'm in my underwear. I'm not sure Drake should see me like this. But aren't the little panties Luc bought me cute? Look—they're low waisted so they fit under the pants. Isn't that ingenious?"

He grunted and yanked the covers over me.

"I have an extra T-shirt you can wear to sleep in." My voice was muffled from the blanket, and I had to bat at it a few times before it got out of my way.

"Thanks." Drake ran a hand over my brow and pushed my hair back. "Close your eyes now and sleep it off."

"I'm not sleepy." Still, I shut my eyes like he said.

I didn't think many people dared go against him. Besides, I was entranced by the way the darkness behind my eyelids spun in loping circles.

The light clicked off, and I heard him and Rainbow whispering. But their voices grew more and more distant . . .

I opened my eyes and felt a million rays of light try to use my brain as a pincushion.

Groaning, I pulled the covers over my head.

"Are you awake?"

I cracked one eye open. Tentatively.

Rainbow grinned from the doorway.

"What are you doing here?"

Her grin widened. "Making sure you made it through the night."

I'd never noticed how painfully bright her teeth were. I shielded my eyes from the glare. "Who let the sun in?"

She laughed. "Wait here. I'll be right back."

I didn't think I could move my carcass if I wanted to and, right now, that was the last thing on my mind.

"Here. Drink this."

I peeked from behind the covers at the greenish-red looking liquid in the glass that filled my vision. "What is that?"

"Your savior. Trust me. It's my guaranteed hangover cure. One of my ex-boyfriends still calls me all the time to beg for the recipe."

I couldn't come up with a good reason not to drink it—except that it looked like vomit—so I took a careful sip.

And gagged.

"No." Rainbow shook her head, making her dreads bob up and down. "You need to down it quickly."

She looked implacable, standing over me as she was. Or maybe I was distracted by the way my stomach flopped and my head pounded. In any case, I did what she told me to do. I still gagged, but at least I'd finished her witch's brew.

"Good." She eyed me closely.

I frowned. "What?"

"I'm just making sure it stays down."

Gross. I ducked my head under again. "Go away and let me die in peace."

"Get up." She jerked the covers off me. Completely. "You'll feel better after a shower."

Pulling covers off a person like that was evil under the best of circumstances. I glared at her. "You're the devil's spawn, aren't you?"

"Don't you have to go to work today?"

I blinked and looked at my alarm clock. Only the numbers were a blur (where were my glasses?), so I leaned over to get closer and fell out of bed.

But I did catch the time. "Oh, shit."

Rainbow threw her hands in the air. "That's what I've been trying to tell you."

I crawled to the bathroom (I wasn't sure my legs would work). Fortunately, Rainbow went ahead of me and turned on the shower, taking pity on me and helping me in.

The tepid water (the water in our building didn't even aspire to hot) went a long way toward restoring me. By the time I'd rinsed I felt well enough to nibble on the toast Rainbow made for me. She'd even placed my glasses next to the plate.

She was waiting for me in my living room after I got dressed and wound my hair into a bun. "You look like the living dead."

I wrinkled my nose. "Thanks."

"Let's go." She headed for the door before I could blink.

My only course of action was to follow her. "Where are you going?" I asked as I locked the door.

She dangled a set of keys in front of my face. "I'm taking you to work."

"You have a car?"

"Calling it a car is a stretch, but I like it." She grinned, linked her arm through mine, and pulled me toward the stairs.

Frowning, I stopped in my tracks, more because of confusion than the uneasiness of my stomach. "I don't deserve your niceness."

"Sure you do."

"Why?" I just didn't get it.

She frowned. "Because we're friends. Friends do this for each other. You'd take care of me if I were hungover and crotchety."

I shook my head. A week ago, I wouldn't have cared at all. "I'm crotchety?"

She grinned and tugged my arm. "Let's go."

Rainbow led me to an old Alfa Romeo parked on the street a couple of blocks away—not a convertible but the little sporty sedans they used to make. As far as I could tell, it was rust colored, but when she turned the ignition it sounded robust and healthy. Not what I would have expected.

But nothing about Rainbow was turning out as I expected, so I don't know why I was surprised.

We had a mad ride through the City, one that

would have rivaled the most insane taxi ride. But I
arrived at work in record time.

Clearing my throat and adjusting my glasses, I
turned to Rainbow. "Um, thanks. For everything."

"No prob, babe. Go get 'em." She smiled and
gave me a hug.

What should I do? I wasn't used to spontaneous
hugs. Sure, Luc gave them all the time, but he didn't
clutch me like Rainbow was.

So I did the only thing I could—I hugged her
back. And (I'm surprised to admit this) it felt good.

I didn't realize until I'd gotten out of the car
and she'd driven away that for once I didn't notice
her piercings.

I sneaked through the lobby and caught the elevator up to my office. I slunk down the hallway,
hoping no one would notice I was two and a half
hours late.

Didn't it make sense that I wasn't so lucky? When
I checked my messages, I cringed to find out I had
several from Lydia—via Jessica—to go up and see
her immediately.

Sighing, I rummaged through my desk for ibupro-
fen or aspirin. Anything to dull the throbbing in
my head. I took four tablets, smoothed my hair, and
headed up.

Jessica scowled at me the second I walked in the
door. "You certainly took your time."

"I just got in. I wasn't feeling well this morning."
I hated that I felt like I had to justify myself to her.

"Lydia isn't happy with you." She said it with a
little too much glee.

I resolved right then and there that if I ever ran
the company, Jessica was out. I bared my teeth at

her (in a smile—I swear) and tiptoed into Lydia's office.

She was furiously typing on her laptop. I mean *furiously*. I was surprised her keyboard didn't snap in two.

"Sit," she barked.

I did just that—promptly. I gripped the cold metal armrests of the chair to stop my hands from shaking (I think it was from my hangover, but it could have been sheer terror).

Lydia slammed her laptop shut and glared at me.

I smiled weakly. "You wanted to see me?"

Did she growl? I think she growled.

Gulp.

She leaned back and stared me with her frigid, slitted gaze. "I was surprised to see you at Indigo last night."

Her even tone chilled my heart. I tried to recall what Indigo was. Oh right—that club.

Should I sound casual or feign ignorance? I decided just to shrug and keep quiet.

Her gaze narrowed even more. "It doesn't seem like the kind of place you'd frequent."

Didn't Drake say almost the exact same thing to me? I just shrugged again.

"But what surprised me most was to see you with Viggo Drake."

Straightening my glasses, I remained silent and waited to see where this was going. I couldn't help thinking that maybe I should move to Maine. There were no poisonous snakes in Maine, and suddenly it seemed like I was dealing with a very cunning asp.

"I was so surprised because I thought you were loyal to me, Katherine."

I frowned. That wasn't something I could just let pass without comment. "I am loyal."

She leaned across her desk and slammed her fist on the glass top, her voice almost shrill. "Then why were you with Drake?"

I replied slowly, "I'm not sure I understand what that has to do with my loyalty to you."

Lydia laughed. (Personally, I wouldn't have called it a laugh because it was more like a cross between an evil cackle and a snort, but I didn't know what else to call it.) "Associating with the person trying to overtake my company has everything to do with loyalty."

"What?" The bottom fell out of my stomach, but after last night it barely registered.

"Don't play innocent, Katherine." She stood up and stalked toward me. "I see exactly what you're up to."

Swallowing the rising nausea, I whispered, "I'm not up to anything."

"Bullshit."

I cringed.

"Don't think I don't know how chummy you and Drake have become. He's been hovering around you. Don't try to deny it." Her cheeks flushed and, for a moment, I was certain she was going to pop. "He's vying to take over Ashworth Communications. I couldn't figure out how he was receiving the confidential information he was obviously getting, but now we know, don't we?

"I should have figured it out sooner. He does

have a history of seducing trade secrets out of women," she said with a bitter sneer.

Shit. I'd wondered what Drake was up to, but he'd been so nice to me I forgot my misgivings. The bastard.

I cleared my throat. "I'm not denying anything except knowledge of Drake's intent. He never told me anything about wanting to take over the company."

"You expect me to believe that?" she asked coldly, towering over me.

"Yes." I hoped I sounded strong. Any weakness and I knew she'd pounce. "I never told Drake anything about you or the company."

She stared at me, her arms crossed. I think she was waiting for me to break down and confess (I expected someone to shine a bright light in my eyes at any second), but I had nothing to confess, so I just stared right back.

When she realized I wasn't going to break under her scrutiny, she strode back to her desk, opened her laptop, and jabbed a couple of keys. "You do understand that I can no longer offer you the promotion. I need people I can trust on my team and, frankly, I don't believe you qualify any longer."

My heart stopped. No promotion? Tears filled my eyes and I quickly blinked them back. "But, Lydia—"

"I believe I'm being generous allowing you to continue working here," the ice queen said. "Not that you'll have a job if Drake is successful in his bid to take over."

Pushing my glasses up, I opened my mouth.

But she cut me off. "You have Luc to thank for

your job. I couldn't very well fire the friend of the man I'm involved with, could I?"

Involved with? What did that mean?

"That's right. Luc and I are going away for a romantic weekend together."

I think if I'd been in my right mind I would have noted that Lydia didn't sound exactly thrilled about it. But the only thing resonating in my head was the word *involved*.

Lydia began banging away at her laptop. "You're dismissed."

I nodded and stood up, hesitating for a second to make sure my legs would support me. Vaguely aware of Jessica's smug look (I wouldn't have put it past her to be listening at the door), I walked out in a trance all the way down the several floors to my office, where I sank into my chair. My head hit the desk with a thunk.

The first thought resonating in my aching head was that Drake was planning to take over AshComm. Hostilely, by the way Lydia talked about it. I remembered every prying question he'd asked me about Lydia and the company and felt like a fool. And betrayed. I'd thought Drake was my friend.

Then I heard Lydia telling me I'd lost my promotion, and my heart just shattered. I *needed* that raise.

I groaned. My dream of owning a home seemed more unattainable than ever.

Maybe I could still pull it off. If I was a little more frugal, I could probably afford to buy a house out someplace remote where housing was less expensive than the Bay Area. Like Lodi. Or Fresno.

"It'd make the commute hell," I mumbled into the plywood of my desk.

But I felt a little less doomed. Not much, but enough that I was no longer tempted to slit my wrists.

Until I started thinking about Luc. On a romantic weekend with Lydia.

My stomach churned.

The phone rang.

Luc. I grabbed it. "I was just—"

"Katherine," a masculine voice boomed.

"Yes?" I asked with a frown.

"It's Gary. I just wanted to let you know I finished your portrait and have already delivered it to Luc. It's magnificent, even if I say so myself."

My portrait? Who cared about that at the moment? "Um, thanks, Gary."

"I have another showing next month. Different gallery and a bigger show. You'll have to come. Luc promised I could have your painting back to display."

"Sure, Gary." Anything to get him off the phone so I could call Luc. I needed to tell him he didn't have to go out with Lydia anymore.

"You sound busy, so I'll let you go. You'll have to come over sometime soon. With Luc. Ta-ta!"

I didn't wait for the dial tone before I hung up and punched in Luc's number.

His machine clicked on after four rings. I didn't want to talk to it, but I didn't have any choice. I had to stop him from going away with Lydia. "Luc, it's me. Uh, Katherine. Listen, I wanted to thank you for everything you've done—it was beyond the call of duty, really"—I gave a pale chuckle—"but—"

The phone clicked. "Kat?"

I sighed in relief. "Luc! You're there."

"What do you want, Kat? I'm kind of busy."

I bristled. "I know. That's why I'm calling."

Silence.

Okay, so he wasn't going to make this easy for me. "I just wanted to tell you that you don't have to go away with Lydia anymore. It's okay. Thanks, though."

When he spoke, his voice was as cold as Lydia's. "What happened to your promotion?"

I swallowed the ashes of my broken dream. "She decided not to give it to me."

"If the promotion were still on, would you be making this call?"

That was an excellent question. I wish I had an answer for it.

Luc grunted. "I see. Well, thanks for calling, Katherine."

"Wait!" I felt him slipping away and nothing I did to stop it seemed to make a difference. Panic made my heart beat so loudly it resonated in my aching head. "Maybe we could have dinner or something this weekend."

"Can't. I'm going out of town."

"Still?" My voice broke with disbelief.

"I love you, Katherine, but I'm tired of waiting for you to get it."

Get what?

"I understand your need to succeed, but your priorities are out of whack. I just can't do it anymore. And Lydia's a warm, intelligent woman who's interested in more than just working."

I shook my head. "Oh, no, she's not." *That* I was certain of.

"You're hardly the perfect judge, are you, Katherine?"

Ouch.

He sighed. I could see him rubbing his neck, like he'd always done when he was really tense. "I've got to go, Kat. I have a lot to do before leaving this afternoon. Take care."

I listened to the dial tone in disbelief. Luc was leaving me.

I dropped my head onto my desk, beating it on the surface a couple of times for good measure. Maybe I could knock an idea of how to fix my quickly disintegrating life into it.

"How are you feeling, Katherine?"

I scowled at Drake's voice and lifted my head. "You bastard."

Amusement lit his eyes but he looked solemn. "Not too well, I see. You were quite knocked out last night."

"You got me drunk on purpose, didn't you? To wheedle secrets out of me." I fervently hoped I hadn't said anything damaging to the company. It was all a little fuzzy. "I thought it was strange that you showed up there, but you'd planned it, didn't you? You probably followed me."

Then I remembered he'd said he was there to spy. I glared at him. "You bastard."

He stepped in and closed the door behind him. He wasn't extremely tall, but his presence was huge and filled my closet of an office to the brim. I scooted back involuntarily.

He sat on the edge of my desk, studying me in

silence. Finally he spoke. "I suppose you've found out that I'm trying to take over Ashworth Communications."

I lifted my chin. "Lydia will never let you do it. In fact, I don't know why Lydia hasn't banned you from the building."

His lips twisted in a wry smile. "Lydia doesn't have much choice in the matter at this point."

He said it so matter-of-factly I couldn't help but believe him. I made a mental note to dust off my résumé.

"And you can't ban a major shareholder. But I'm starting to reconsider my . . . agenda."

I looked up. "You are?"

He nodded. "If you'll give me some information."

Ha! "What kind of idiot do you take me for? Don't underestimate women. We're responsible for inventing fire escapes, bulletproof vests, and laser printers, you know. Not to mention windshield wipers."

His lips twitched. "I'd never presume to underestimate you, Katherine. I have great respect for you. But the information I want isn't about the company. It's about Lydia."

If I were intelligent, I would've given Drake anything he wanted and made him promise to give me a job when he took control of AshComm. Only I couldn't. I just couldn't. "No."

"You're still loyal even after the tongue-lashing Lydia must have given you this morning," he said in wonder.

I winced at the reminder. Then I shrugged. "I'm sure it's a habit I'll break myself of. Eventually."

"I'm not so sure," he murmured, tapping a finger against his chin. He studied me quietly.

I lifted my head, pursed my lips, and studied him right back. I didn't want him to think he could intimidate me into giving him what he wanted.

How long our staring match went on, I have no idea. But finally he spoke. "I owe you an apology, Katherine."

"Excuse me?" I knew I had to be gaping. Drake didn't seem like the type of man who apologized. Ever.

He nodded. "I'm sure you understand that I couldn't have divulged anything before, given the circumstances, but I should have been straightforward with you last night."

I didn't say anything (stunned into speechlessness really), so he continued.

"Lydia and I used to be involved." He ran an impatient hand through his hair. "We were more than involved—I was going to ask Lydia to be my wife."

My mouth fell open. "*What?*"

He didn't hear me. At least, I don't think he did, because he kept on his train of thought. "I realize we were young, but I was committed and she wasn't. Not as committed as she was to her career and the drive to prove her father wrong by succeeding without his help." He smiled but it was unamused. "She was just as driven back then as she is now. Maybe more so."

Now that I couldn't imagine. It was too scary.

"Passionate. She was so passionate, talking about what she was going to accomplish. That was one of the reasons I loved her."

I cleared my throat. "What went wrong?"

He stiffened. I almost felt bad for asking, but I really wanted to know. (Curiosity is a great asset in fact-finding but a detriment in a lot of other facets of life.)

"I'd just started my first company. Lydia worked for a competitor, but it was never a problem." His expression grew colder. "I never thought it was a problem. Not until Lydia sold me out."

Gulp. Lydia had to be very brave to cross him. Or stupid. I knew *I* never wanted to be on his bad side. I was scared shitless watching him, and none of his anger was directed at me. "What did she do?"

"She gave her boss crucial information about my company—information they used to crush my business." He sat back, appearing to be calm. I knew better. "It was quite brilliant on her part. It got her a promotion. It was the first step toward starting her own company. I just should have realized she would have gone to any means to secure her position there."

Ouch. I winced. Sounded kind of familiar. I reheard everything Luc had yelled at me earlier.

"It's funny," Drake said, his thoughts distant. "Now I can't decide if I admire her for it more than I resent her."

Swallowing, I pushed up my glasses. "So I guess you broke up."

His grin was wry. "Yes, we did. I swore I'd rebuild my company and that I'd give her a taste of her own medicine. I swore I'd crush her just like she crushed me. Retribution." He smirked and shook his head. "Only she has more sway over me than I realized, because I can't do it. I still love her."

That had to suck. But I still didn't get it. "Taking over her company isn't the best way to get into a woman's good graces."

He chuckled. "True. You're very wise, Katherine. That's why I'm having second thoughts about the takeover. In fact, I think I have a better idea—a merger. Both in business and in life."

"I'm not sure Lydia will go for that." If there was one thing I knew about my boss, it was that her independence and need for control ran deep. I mean, look at this whole sperm-donor mess. There was no way she was going to surrender not only her company but also herself to a man as strong as Drake.

"I can convince her." He said it so confidently I was inclined to believe him. "But I need your help."

I bit my lip. "I don't know. If she finds out—"

"Katherine, don't you want your man back?"

"My man?"

"The one Lydia was with."

Luc. I opened my mouth to automatically protest that he was just my best friend.

But then I remembered the way he had kissed me that one night and the feel of his strong hands on me and the tone of his voice when he said he loved me after he chewed me out.

I flushed. Did he mean it in *that* way?

What if he did?

Closing my eyes, I pictured being with him. I would have thought it'd be weird to think of Luc in *that* way—he was my best friend, after all. But it wasn't. It felt right, like a missing piece of a puzzle

I'd been working on for years had suddenly fallen into place.

I imagined waking up with him. Laughing with him in the mornings with my head resting on his chest. Helping him make dinner at night and curling up on the couch watching a movie together afterward. His hand in mine for the rest of our lives.

My heart sank. I'd blown it big-time. Luc was going away with Lydia *right now*.

I gazed at Drake. Did he mean everything he was saying? "How can I trust you?"

He leaned forward, his eyes never leaving mine. "I give you my word."

Call me an idiot, but I believed him. "Okay. What do we do?"

Chapter Fourteen

"I don't know if this is a good idea."

"It's a brilliant idea." Drake pushed me ahead of him.

"No—really. We should reconsider." I dug my heels in, but on the slick floor of the hallway I slid ahead. "Did you know burglary has dropped thirty-eight percent over the past five years in San Francisco?"

"Don't you want to find out where they went?"

I pushed my glasses and sighed. There was that.

"Great." He took my sigh as a capitulation, I guess. "We're going to use your key to get into the apartment—"

"Loft," I corrected.

He didn't pay attention to me. "—and then we're going to sleuth out where Lydia and your friend might have gone."

By *sleuth out* he meant snoop around. The thought of invading Luc's privacy didn't settle well with me.

Drake prodded my back again.

Okay, let's think about this logically. Did I really want Luc and Lydia to end up together? No. What if they got together (in every euphemistic sense of the phrase) and it resulted in a little Luc—or worse, a little Lydia? (Shudder!)

Right. I took out my key. We were going in.

I wasn't really breaking in—I *was* using a key, after all. And I was doing this for him—to stop him from making the biggest mistake of his life.

The way the key slipped in and opened the door gave me a twinge of guilt. It seemed like a metaphor for Luc's trust, that it would let me in so easily.

Drake walked in before me. "He doesn't have an alarm system, does he?"

"Luc?" I wrinkled my nose. "No way."

He shook his head as he looked around. "He should. His art collection alone is worth a small fortune."

Gary's squiggles of paint? Right. Because I doubted Drake would take well to being corrected, I didn't bother to tell him he was mistaken about the worth of the paintings.

"Does he have an office?"

"Oh—right." Our mission. "This way." I led him to the partitioned workstation.

He flipped through some of the papers littering the top of the desk. "Do you know the password on his computer?"

I did, but I wasn't ready to admit that. "Let's look around a little first."

Drake leveled a look at me. "You aren't getting cold feet again, are you?"

"No." I really did want to stop Luc from ruining

his life on my account. But looking at someone's computer files seemed so intimate. "I just doubt he would have input it on his computer. He hates typing."

We did a thorough search of his office space, including the trash can (I never knew he ate so many Snickers bars—I thought Milky Way was his candy of choice).

We divided up the rest of the loft. Drake took the living room and kitchen, I took Luc's bedroom.

Big mistake. It smelled like Luc, even from where I stood on the top step of the circular stairs that led up there. A pang of sadness shot through my heart and I felt the futility of this. Even if we found them, I had the feeling my relationship with him would never be the same.

That made me depressed. More so than losing my promotion. I think.

Still, I had to try. I steeled my spine and stepped into his bower.

And froze.

Over his bed was a colorful painting I'd never seen before. I searched the bottom, looking for a signature even though in my heart I knew.

Yes—Gary's.

I looked at the painting again. It took my breath away. Swirls of dark red and hot pink paint around the hazy portrait of a woman with sultry eyes.

Me.

Only I didn't have sultry eyes. Did I?

Frowning, I raced to the mirror on the wardrobe door. I took my glasses off, leaned close (so I could actually see), and squinted at my reflection.

Nope. But I could see the beginning of crow's feet.

"My life as I know it is ending," I muttered, "and on top of it all I'm getting wrinkles."

"Find anything?"

I started at Drake's voice calling up from the bottom of the stairs. "Not yet."

"Need help?"

"*No.*" I gulped. "I'm fine, thank you."

Okay, Katherine—look around quickly and then get out.

Right. I got to business because, frankly, Drake seeing the painting made me uncomfortable. It wasn't me. Gary must have been smoking illegal substances when he created it. (I'd have to tell him how he was killing his brain cells each time he polluted his body with narcotics.)

I picked up a pad of paper by the phone of the nightstand, not expecting to find anything of value on it. But there it was—the location of Luc and Lydia's rendezvous.

I blinked. Wow. I didn't think we were actually going to find anything. I hurried down to show Drake.

He wasn't as pleased with my discovery as I thought he was going to be. In fact, my ears burned as he swore.

I did learn some excellent curses, though.

"You aren't happy?" I asked cautiously.

He glared at me. "I'm thrilled you found it."

If he were any more thrilled, I had a feeling I'd be a bloody mass on the floor. "Are you sure?"

He grunted. "Let's go."

I made sure to lock the door before following him to the waiting car. I had to jog to keep up with him. Ferragamos are *not* made for running.

"Um, Drake?"

He glanced over his shoulder at me.

"Have you ever tried yoga? I've read that the meditative aspects are excellent for calming one's system."

He yanked open the car door before his driver could get out. "Get in."

Gulp. Bad idea, but given the look on his face I decided it'd be more stupid to argue. I stumbled in, keeping a wary eye on him.

I relaxed when I heard him order his driver to my apartment. I smiled in genuine relief. Good that we weren't rushing off after the errant couple—not while Drake was in this homicidal-maniac state.

"How fast do you think you can be ready to go?"

"Ready to go where?" I asked, keeping an eye on the road to make sure the driver didn't miss my building. Not that it was easy to miss—it was the tallest penitentiary-looking structure on the block.

"To Harmony by the Sea Bed and Breakfast."

I almost fell off the seat. I'm sure it was the sudden way the car came to a halt, though. "Excuse me?"

He frowned at me. "What did you think we were going to do?"

Well, I hadn't thought that far. The plan had been to find out where they were going and then to play it by ear. "I hadn't expected—"

"Katherine, do you know how long they've been gone and what they could be doing *right now*?"

An image of Luc and Lydia playing pop goes the weasel materialized in my mind.

Eew.

"Just give me a minute," I said, jumping out of the car and running toward the building.

I ran up the stairs and got a couple of changes of clothes together in record time. I was locking up my apartment when Rainbow poked her head out of her door.

"Hey, Kath!"

"Hi, Rainbow." I frowned, jimmying my key so it'd click into place.

"Going somewhere?"

There—it locked. I faced her. "Yes, actually." I felt like I should ask her to watch my cat or something, only I didn't have one.

She smiled. "Want to come over when you get back?"

"Sure." I nodded. "I'd really like that."

She beamed at me, and I felt good. Then she surprised me by grabbing me in a bear hug. "Take care," she whispered. "Good luck."

I pushed my glasses up and blinked away moisture. She was so sweet to be so nice to me.

She smiled as she drew away. "Be happy."

I resolved then and there when I got back I was going to do something nice for her. Something special. Not because I expected anything in return but because I wanted *her* to be happy.

What was happening to me?

I decided as I flew back down the flights of stairs that whatever it was, I liked it.

Milton was waiting outside the car to let me in

when I burst out from the front door. He relieved me of my little bag and opened the door for me.

I thanked him and tumbled headlong into Drake's lap.

With a grimace, I looked up at him. "Sorry."

He didn't smile, but I think I saw amusement light his eyes. A little. Either that or he had gas. "I've never had a woman throw herself at me quite like that."

"I find that hard to believe," I murmured as I righted myself and sat next to him.

"What was that?"

"Nothing." I strapped myself in with the seat belt.

Fortunately, the inn was outside of Half Moon Bay—only about a half-hour drive—so the fact that we spent most of the trip in silence wasn't that big a deal.

But the closer we got, the stiller Drake became. It was unnerving.

So I did the only thing I could. I recited facts.

"Did you know last year the largest pumpkin at the Half Moon Bay Pumpkin Weigh-off was one thousand two hundred twenty-nine pounds?"

He barely glanced at me.

I looked out the window and saw a distant boat on the ocean. "Did you know ocean water has to reach eighty-two degrees for a hurricane to form?"

He blinked.

"Did you know the human eye blinks an average of 4.2 million times a year?"

"Katherine."

Right. I gulped and shut up.

Five minutes later he finally turned to me. "We need to go over our plan."

"Okay." I was greatly relieved to find out we had one.

"Our objective is to drive Lydia and your friend apart this weekend. Based on what I saw the other night at the club—"

I winced. I remembered just enough of that night to be mortified.

"—I think we should use jealousy to pull them apart."

"Jealousy?" My laugh sounded strangled even to my ears. "Lydia is never going to be jealous of me."

Drake frowned at me. "What do you mean? You're very attractive, Katherine."

I wasn't chopped liver, but I didn't delude myself to believe I was in the same class as Lydia. Not yet. Her shoes were better.

"We'll work on that," he said. "But mostly I was talking about your friend being jealous of me."

I shook my head. "There's only one problem with that."

"What?"

"Luc has to want *me* in order to be jealous of *you.*"

He grinned. "Oh, he wants you. Trust me."

I was really beginning to hate it when people said that.

"We just have to turn up the heat under him." Drake rubbed his hands together. In that moment, he looked so much like what I'd always imagined Satan to look like I had to rub my eyes.

But maybe he was right. I flashed back on Gary's painting hanging over Luc's bed. He wouldn't have hung it there if he didn't like me, right? I'd just have to figure out how much he liked me.

Though even if he didn't want me in that way, getting him away from Lydia would be enough.

It would, I repeated mentally, dismissing the sad pang from my heart at the thought that he might not want me.

Drake told me to let him do the talking when we got to the inn. I was happy to let him do it too, being uncertain as to how he was going to get us rooms at this late time. Didn't inns require advance notice?

Somehow he got hold of the innkeeper. I listened halfheartedly to their conversation as I looked up the stairs wondering which room Luc and Lydia were staying in.

Then I heard him tell the innkeeper we just needed one room.

"Drake." I knocked on his back.

He glanced at me and kept charming the woman.

"*Drake.*" I tugged on his sleeve.

He scowled. "Yes, Katherine?"

I lowered my voice and pulled his face down so the woman wouldn't hear us. "Do you think that's a good idea?"

"What?" he whispered back.

"One room."

He nodded and his stubble rasped against my cheek. "It won't be believable otherwise. Trust me."

Grr.

But then something amazing happened. Luc and Lydia walked in from a side door (one that went outside to the gardens and the beach, I assumed).

They froze when they saw us.

"Kat?" Luc asked. His voice was colored with disbelief and something subtle I couldn't identify.

I blushed and jumped back from Drake. "Luc. Um, hi." I smiled as brightly as I could. "Fancy meeting you here."

"Yes, it is a surprise, isn't it?" Lydia said coldly, glaring at Drake.

I shot tentative looks back and forth between Lydia and Drake. There were definitely still sparks between them, so potent you could feel the energy. I just hoped I wouldn't be zapped in the cross fire.

Drake took my arm. "Let's go up to our room, Katherine."

"Your *room?*" Luc's eyes bugged out.

Gulp. "Did you know cows have oval pupils?"

Drake tugged my arm. His grasp was so firm I had no choice but to follow him up the stairs.

When we got to our room (up the stairs and at the end of the hall) and closed the door, Drake grinned and grabbed me in a hug. "That was fantastic."

"It was?" I'd thought it was pretty wretched myself. I'd almost thrown up, I'd been so nervous.

"Did you see the way they looked at us? This is going to take less time than I originally thought." He hugged me again before heading for the wet bar and pouring himself some whiskey (at least, that's what I think it was).

"Drake."

"Hmm?" He glanced at me over his shoulder.

"Why was Lydia so upset?"

He shrugged and sipped his drink.

"Drake?"

"Well, if you want to know the truth, this is where Lydia and I came when I proposed to her."

"You actually *proposed* to her? *Here?*" I'd never known my voice could squeak that high.

He gave me a sidelong look before going to the mantle I hadn't noticed and turning a knob.

Instant raging fire.

He sprawled on a cushy-looking chair. "I told you I meant to marry her."

"Yes, but . . ." He actually proposed to her. *Here.*

Shit. I grabbed my purse, which I'd dropped inside the door when we walked in, and rifled through it for my handheld.

"Katherine, have a seat. Enjoy the room for the night."

"Can't." Aha. Here it was. "I need to get my résumé together right away since I'm not going to have a job come Monday morning."

He chuckled, stood up, and walked to me. He gently pried the device out of my hands and guided me to a couch. "Sit down and relax."

Dropping my head in my hands, I groaned. How did my life rage out of control so completely?

Drake pushed a glass in my hand and I absently sipped it, trying to come up with a strategy to get everything back on track.

Then I choked as it lit a fire down my throat.

"What is this?" I managed to gasp.

"Scotch."

I sniffed it and choked again on the fumes. Tempting to lose myself in an alcohol haze again . . .

No.

I set the glass firmly on the coffee table in front of me. That'd make me no better than my father.

"Relax, Katherine. Everything will work out."
He patted my shoulder. "I'll have my driver pick
up some food and you can watch a movie if you
want."

Luc forced me to watch movies every now and
then, saying I needed it to be able to understand
popular culture. I always told him it was a waste of
money.

Secretly I loved them. The sappier the better.

I noticed the large TV in the corner. Which
made me take stock of the rest of the room. It was
lavish—more so than I had expected. Dark wood
furniture, some of it antique looking. Paintings of
the coast. Pretty vases filled with autumn-colored
flowers. And a four-poster bed covered in lace and
pillows.

It was huge.

I swallowed, unable to tear my eyes from it. "Uh,
Drake?"

"Hmm?"

"What are the sleeping arrangements?"

"You get the bed, of course. Though it's big
enough."

"Oh." I wilted in relief. "Okay."

I poked around the room while he talked to his
driver on his cell phone. The room really was impressive. But I'd never been to an inn before. The
last time I'd been in a hotel was the first time I'd
had sex, and that was a Motel 8. I'd always wondered if Motel 8 rented by the hour, because Kevin,
the guy I was dating, was done and ready to go in
record time. The second time I didn't even rate
that—we did it in his car.

No wonder I'd never tried sex again, huh?

The evening turned out better than I could have hoped. Drake had his driver bring us steaks and baked potatoes from a local restaurant, and I gorged out in front of the TV while I warmed my feet with the fireplace. *And* there was cheesecake.

The only way it could have been better was if Luc was there with me instead of Drake.

I frowned at my dessert, thinking about him. And Lydia. And what they were probably doing right now.

Drake must have sensed my thoughts because he looked up from the paperwork he was doing (also in front of the fireplace). "It's okay. They're too disturbed by the thought of us being here to do anything tonight. Right now, they're wondering what we're doing." He grinned. "We have the honeymoon suite, after all."

I was only slightly reassured by his confidence. I still had trouble believing anyone could be with a woman like Lydia and not want to get it on. I mean, hell, *I'd* want to get it on if I were with her.

That wasn't something I needed to think about. I concentrated on finishing my cheesecake while the movie on TV came to its conclusion. But as soon as it was over I brushed my teeth, washed my face, and got into bed.

It felt strange to be in bed while there was another person moving around the room. I couldn't fall asleep, listening instead to all the little noises Drake made.

It amazed me what you could learn from a person just by listening to him. For instance, Drake was a compulsive multitasker. He couldn't even just brush his teeth without doing something else simultaneously. Listening to the whisking sound of his toothbrush against his teeth as he moved stealthily around the room, I got so curious I had to turn around and look.

With my unmagnified vision, it looked like he was going through a contract. And brushing.

"Did you know that every year there are over one hundred thousand toothbrush accidents reported in emergency rooms?"

He glanced over at me.

I nodded. "All attributed to people walking or running while brushing."

I thought he rolled his eyes but decided it must have been a trick of the lighting. That just didn't seem like something he'd do.

He *did* go back to the bathroom and finish up, though. At least he had sense. I wasn't sure what to do if he suddenly tripped and had a toothbrush puncture his palate. I turned around and punched my pillow a couple times to settle in.

I heard the lights click off and the slight rustling as he got into the covers I'd laid out for him on the couch. Then I heard him turn over. And turn over. And turn over again.

I sighed. This was ridiculous.

I flopped over. "Why don't you just sleep here? There's enough room." The king-size bed was at least twice as big as the full in my apartment.

There was a pause in the darkness. Then he asked, "Are you sure?"

"Yes." Even if he encroached on my side, there'd still be a couple of feet of space between us, that's how big the bed was.

"Thank you. The couch leaves a little to be desired as a bed."

More rustling and then I felt the covers lift and the bed shifted. I held my breath—this was the first time I'd ever slept with anyone. I mean, except for when I used to climb in bed with my parents when I was a little girl.

I stayed tense, listening to Drake's breathing. Soon, it evened out and I could tell he'd fallen asleep. I relaxed.

Actually, it was kind of soothing having his presence there. I cuddled into my pillow and let the rhythm lull me to sleep.

A knocking on the door jerked me upright. I blinked a few times, squinting at the room around me. Where was I?

I almost shrieked when the covers next to me lifted. Then it all came back to me. Luc, the inn, honeymoon suite, Drake. By the way the pale coastal sunlight illuminated the room, I gathered it was morning.

Drake swung his feet out of bed, muttering the whole time. I grinned—he wasn't a morning person. Who would have thought it?

He wore only his boxer shorts, and I took a moment to admire his body. He had to be in his late thirties or early forties. I don't know what I expected, but I should have known it would be as hard and chiseled as his personality.

He stalked to the door and yanked it open. "Yes?"

I fumbled for my glasses—didn't I put them on

the nightstand next to me? Yes—there they were. I slipped them on and got up on my knees to see who was there. Maybe it was room service with a delectable breakfast of French toast and strawberries. Did they have room service in this type of inn?

But it wasn't room service, I saw to my dismay. It was Luc.

I tried to gauge whether Luc looked satiated in that *just had incredible sex for the past eight hours* kind of way. I didn't think he did—more like he'd had curdled milk—but I wasn't exactly an expert on ecstasy.

Luc gave Drake and his boxer shorts (cringe) a quick perusal and then looked toward the bed. I saw his every expression as he took in the messy covers. Then his gaze lit on me.

I looked down. Shit. My T-shirt had ridden up, giving the guys full view of my underwear—another new pair from Luc. I wondered if he recognized it.

I pulled the shirt down over my knees and huddled, giving him a faint smile. "Hi, Luc."

For a second I was afraid he was going to explode. I mean, his ears went red and everything. I wasn't sure I'd ever seen him that angry. He'd been angry when he found out I hocked the calculator he gave me, but compared to now that was like mild irritation. Even when his father forbade him to go to massage school he didn't appear so livid.

Then he said to me through gritted teeth, "I'd like to speak to you. Later." He nodded at Drake and walked out.

Drake closed the door and turned around with a big grin on his face. "This is fantastic."

"This is terrible," I said at the same time, dropping my head onto my knees.

"No, it's fantastic. At this rate, our mission will be accomplished by this afternoon."

Drake was wrong. Didn't he see the expression on Luc's face? At this rate I was never going to have my best friend back.

Thing of it was, I wasn't sure I wanted Luc as just a best friend anymore.

"Hey."

The bed dipped as Drake sat down. I flinched the first time I felt his hand pat my head.

"It's going to be okay," he reassured me. "Everything will work out. It'll all be in perspective after a shower and some breakfast."

I nodded unenthusiastically, cursing the day Lydia gave me the secret assignment and ended my life as I knew it.

"You take a shower, I'll take care of the food." He nudged me. The way I was perched with my legs folded under my nightshirt, I toppled right over.

Drake chuckled.

I glared at him as I untangled myself. Glad someone was having a good morning.

I huffed out of bed, slamming the bathroom door. God, that was satisfying.

During my shower I realized what a simpering coward I'd been. Here Drake was willing to help me regain Luc's friendship and I was acting like a wimp. I needed to buck up and go for what I wanted—Luc. With the same tenacity that I'd pursued my dream of owning a home. Hey—I needed a new goal anyway, considering my home was a long shot in the foreseeable future.

Because it was a bathroom to luxuriate in, I took my time getting ready. This was the kind of bathroom I'd always dreamed of—airy and clean, with a big claw-foot tub. As I dried off, I decided before we left I'd take at least one long bath. I couldn't remember the last time I took one. My apartment only had a shower.

I emerged with a renewed purpose. To top it off, French toast was waiting for me. I wasn't sure life could get much better. (I mean, except for having Luc here instead of Drake. And having my own home. And still having a job I loved.)

"You look much improved."

I smiled at Drake, who sat at the little dining table sipping coffee. "I am. Sorry about earlier—"

He shrugged. "It's been a stressful time."

"Well, I'm over it." I sat down and tried not to drool over the luscious food.

Panic didn't hit me until Drake was in the shower and I was left alone to contemplate meeting with Luc. I wondered what later meant. I recalled the fury on his face and winced. Next year sounded good to me.

But I didn't have long to fret. The phone rang. Guess who.

"I want to talk to you, Kat. Now."

I glanced at the bathroom door. The shower was still going. Not that Drake would mind. In fact, he'd probably push me out the door. "Um. Okay."

"Meet me downstairs."

He hung up before I could ask about Lydia and

if she'd mind. Somehow I didn't think she was the type of woman who liked to share.

He was waiting for me on a couch in the lobby. He stood up when he saw me come down the stairs, rubbing his hands on his jeans. "Hi."

God, he looked good. Kind of wild. His hair was in its usual slightly unkempt look and he hadn't shaved this morning.

I never knew I was into wild.

He frowned at me, and I realized I hadn't said anything so I nodded. "Hi."

He opened his mouth to say something but closed it abruptly, frowning harder as he looked me up and down.

What? I looked down. I was wearing the clothes he had bought me. And I was positive they went together—I had brought the black pants with all the pockets and a couple of the T-shirts.

I knew it—the T-shirt was too small. That had to be it. It bared half my midriff, after all.

I tugged on it. "I told you it was too small."

He shook his head. "Let's go for a walk on the beach."

I shrugged. Then I nodded, thinking if he was going to yell at me it'd be better if we were out of hearing of other people. Like Lydia.

He took my arm and guided me out the side door, which I now knew led straight onto the beach.

Even though I'd lived in the Bay Area all my life, I'd never spent much time at the beach. Needless to say, I hadn't been sure what to bring, not sure what the weather would be like, and I forgot my red coat in the room.

Luc, on the other hand, being a windsurfer, was

decked out appropriately in a thick, off-white sweater and a windbreaker.

I looked longingly at it as I hugged myself to protect against a particularly brisk breeze.

He shook his head, took off his jacket, and draped it over my shoulders. "Where's your coat?"

"I didn't know I'd need it." His jacket was still warm from his body and smelled familiar, just like him. It went a long way in settling my nerves.

"For someone so smart, sometimes you're an idiot, you know."

I glanced at him, pursing my lips. "Is that a loving 'you're an idiot' or an angry one?"

He sighed. "What do you think, Kat?"

I just didn't know anymore. "I think I blew it."

He grunted and continued to lead me.

For a while I concentrated on the way my shoes sank into the sand and the sound of the waves lapping at the shore. I wondered how cold the water would be. Then I wondered if Luc and Lydia planned on taking a stroll down here tonight.

That was it. I had to ask. "How's Lydia? Are you guys having a good time?"

Luc's face closed up. "She's fine."

Hmm. Not exactly a fount of information. This was a switch—he usually wasn't so closed mouthed about his relationships.

Maybe he really liked her.

Chilling thought. I pulled the jacket closer.

How could he like her when she was only out for his sperm? Was this one of those temporary sex things men were always after? Not that I knew a whole lot about men. Except that they produced one to two teaspoons of sperm during ejaculation (I was up on all the current sperm data).

I cleared my throat. "So how is Lydia's project coming along?"

"She's changed her mind."

"What?" My spirits lifted.

"She wants us to have a relationship. To get married."

I stumbled and would have fallen face first if Luc hadn't steadied me. When I was on solid ground again, I stopped walking and faced him. "Are you going to?"

He stared down at me. "I don't know, Kat."

Gulp. "You sound like you're considering it."

"Why shouldn't I consider it? She's a beautiful, intelligent woman who wants me."

I tried to think of a reason why he shouldn't consider it, but he was right. Lydia was perfect (except for her bitchy streak).

I hoped my smile looked genuine and that I wouldn't choke on what I was about to say. "Well, I'm happy for you."

He just gazed at me, his hand under my elbow. It tightened, and then he dropped it, sliding it into his pocket. "Let's head back."

The walk back to the inn was painfully silent. I opened my mouth to make a comment a couple of times, but things had changed.

It wasn't until that moment that I realized what I'd lost.

I wiped at the couple of tears that leaked from my eyes.

Luc frowned at me.

"It's the wind," I lied.

Chapter Fifteen

I slammed the door to the honeymoon suite and almost fainted with relief when I saw Drake was still there. "We have to do something. Quick."

He turned around from the window with a frown. "Did you go out without a jacket?"

Hello. Didn't he hear me? "We need to do something *now.*"

He crossed the room and took my hands in his, his brow furrowing. "Your hands are ice. What were you trying to do, catch pneumonia?"

I tried to pull out of his grasp but, since he was stronger and had about seventy pounds on me, I got dragged toward our faux fireplace.

"Sit," he ordered.

We didn't have time for this. The situation was urgent.

He cocked an eyebrow.

Sitting now.

Drake perched on the end of the couch and

folded his arms across his chest. "Now what's this all about?"

"Lydia wants to keep Luc."

Silence.

I waved my hand. "Don't you see? This is serious! It's more than just for sperm."

He grunted.

God, did I have to spell everything out for people? I spoke slowly, enunciating each syllable. "Lydia wants to have a relationship with Luc."

"Evidently."

I scowled. No, it wasn't so evident.

"But while you were out walking with your friend, I did reconnaissance."

"You did?"

"Yes. Do you want to know what I found out?"

"Of course." I pushed my glasses up and automatically reached for a pad to take notes. Since there wasn't one handy, I settled for a cocktail napkin.

"I talked to Mrs. Lingham—"

"One *m* or two?" I asked as I scribbled the name down.

"One."

Because he sounded confused, I glanced up and gave him a cue. "And Mrs. Lingham is . . . ?"

"The innkeeper." He glanced at my napkin before shaking his head and continuing (I know—sometimes my efficiency amazes even me). "She told me Lydia and your friend—"

"Luc," I supplied as I scratched his name.

"Excuse me. Lydia and *Luc* are staying in separate rooms."

I stopped taking notes to look up. "Separate rooms? It's hard to get pregnant that way."

Drake grinned. "Yes, it is. And Mrs. Lingham also told me where they are going out to dinner tonight." He took my hand. "How do you feel about going out on a date with me?"

I gasped. "No."

"Oh yes, my dear Katherine."

"You aren't thinking—"

"It's not only what I'm thinking but what I've planned. Come now." He pulled me to my feet. "We have some shopping to do."

I wrinkled my nose. "Shopping?"

"You're going to look smashing tonight. Luc will be gnawing off a leg to get to you." He grabbed my jacket and nudged me toward the door.

I dug my feet in. "I can't—"

"I'm paying for this. Consider yourself on my payroll for tonight."

"Men are supposed to hate buying clothes," I mumbled as we headed down to his waiting car. Why was it all the men in my life wanted to take me shopping?

"Ah, but we love seeing our women dressed up. Hence the pleasure."

I couldn't decide if shopping with Drake was more uncomfortable than shopping with Luc or not, but one thing was for sure: it was easier. We walked into a store (on Mrs. Lingham's recommendation) and the shopkeeper swooped down and did Drake's bidding. I wondered if it got tiring having people grovel at your feet all the time.

She had two viable options: a black dress and a red one. I thought the black was perfect. It hit below my knees and had long sleeves (it was colder than I expected here on the coast). But Drake wanted to see the red one on—one should check out all possibilities, he said.

So like a good soldier, I put it on.

No way.

I shook my head at the reflection in the dressing room. Too tight. It showed *everything*—from my butt to my nipples (I'd had to take my bra off because the cut of the dress didn't allow for one). I blushed just thinking of Drake seeing me like this. And Luc . . .

No way. I wasn't even going to step outside in this one.

But I did poke my head out. "I think the black one was better."

Drake looked up from the business magazine he was reading. "Let's see it."

I tugged at the fabric behind me. "It doesn't fit."

"Let me be the judge of that."

"I really think the black—"

"Katherine."

I winced and reluctantly stepped out, my eyes squeezed shut so I couldn't see his reaction.

He whistled, loud and long.

I cracked one eye open to make sure it was him (I don't know—a construction worker could have wandered in, and they'll whistle at anything female that shows signs of life).

It *was* Drake. He stood in front of me, lips pursed, eyes wide like he was in shock.

Because the dress is so tight, I thought, pulling at the neckline.

"You look—" He shook his head.

Shit. He was struck speechless by the horror. I whirled to go take it off.

He grabbed my hand before I could escape and tugged me close to him. "Katherine," he said softly, "you look absolutely stunning."

I frowned. "I do?"

"Yes."

"Are you sure?" I looked down. It was awfully tight. And didn't provide much coverage in the front. Or the back, for that matter. "I think I need a size bigger. Or a few sizes bigger."

"No." He took my hand and drew me toward the three-way mirror. "You look fabulous."

Yikes. Seeing myself from all angles was the stuff of nightmares. Was my butt really that big?

"I'll never understand why women are so quick to criticize their bodies." He turned to the hovering shopkeeper. "We'll take this. Do you have a wrap to go with it? Preferably something warm. And if you could direct us to a store where we can find shoes."

While the woman jumped to fulfill his commands, I did something I shouldn't have done—I peeked at the price tag.

Oh my God. I thought for sure I'd faint. I would have sat down but the dress was so tight I was afraid the seams would rip. And then we'd have to buy an incredibly expensive dress that I wouldn't be able to wear.

"Drake." He'd gone back to reading his magazine, so I tugged on his sleeve. "You really don't need to do this—"

"Yes, I do, Katherine." He rolled up the magazine and lowered his head, staring directly into my eyes. "We've been through this already. We agreed that this was the best course of action."

That was before I knew he was going to buy me a dress that cost as much as a small foreign car. "Then I want to pay you back—"

"Nonsense. This is a business expense." He grinned wolfishly. "I fully intend on writing it off."

Oh. Well, that made all the difference in the world.

As it turned out, the woman who owned the store also carried shoes. In no time I was decked out in a cape (with a hood—I felt very gothic), shoes, and jewelry. Antique-looking rhinestone earrings and a matching choker. Thank God there wasn't a Tiffany's nearby—if there were, I had no doubt we'd be over there picking out diamonds to cover me in.

While Drake paid for the loot, I collapsed on a nearby chair. I needed a nap.

The woman handed Drake a large bag, which he promptly pawned off on me.

"Great," I said, visualizing the bed back at the inn and how warm and cozy the down comforter would be when I was tucked in. I followed Drake like an obedient puppy eager for its treat.

He glanced at his watch. "Geri made an appointment for you next door."

"Geri? Next door?" I looked up and groaned. "A beauty salon?"

Drake chuckled, grabbed my arm before I could escape. "I've never known a woman like you, Katherine. Most would love to be treated to all this."

"All this?" I asked weakly as he drew me into the salon.

"A trim and style, manicure and pedicure, and other services."

"Other services?"

"Waxing," he replied.

Gulp. "Did you know in ancient Egypt, priests plucked every hair from their bodies? Even their eyelashes."

"Interesting." He smiled at the woman manning the front desk. "Geri called to make an appointment for Katherine Murphy."

"Oh, yes." The way she smiled at me chilled my heart.

I backed up a step. "Uh, Drake . . . I don't think—"

But before I could talk him out of the *other services* part, the women who worked in the shop quite efficiently whisked me off for my torture—er, treatments.

The waxing was the most painful ordeal I'd ever endured—from my eyebrows to my legs and a couple of places in between. By the time we were done, I felt like a plucked chicken.

But my hair looked amazing. They'd cut it to just past my shoulders and somehow straightened it so it fell in a shiny, soft cascade. I kept touching it, it felt so luxurious. I'd gladly go through the waxing again if it meant I could have hair like this too.

The second we got back to the inn, I ran up to our room, impatiently waiting for Drake to open the door so I could look in a mirror to make sure it was real and not a trick of the lighting in the salon.

It wasn't. I looked damn good.

Drake laughed at the euphoric look on my face

as I emerged from the bathroom. "I take it you're pleased."

Pleased didn't even begin to describe what I was feeling. I was tempted to get down on my knees and pledge my everlasting devotion to him, but I settled on squeezing his hand. "I feel like Cinderella."

He grinned and squeezed back. "Then it was worth it."

It was. And as I got ready that evening for our pseudodate, instead of cursing every second of the primping (I'm more of a no-nonsense kind of girl—slap on some gloss and call myself ready) I reveled in it. I took my time and actually applied eyeliner and mascara (Drake had sent out his driver to stock up on make-up while I was being tormented by the aestheticians). I'd never spent that much time getting ready for anything—not even my first interview at AshComm.

Okay, I have to admit that partly it took so long because I don't know the first thing about make-up. So I messed up the eyeliner and had to start fresh (and it was a bitch to wash off). I found myself wishing Rainbow were around. Despite appearances, she was much better at the girl thing than I was.

Anyway, I was finally ready—powdered, lotioned, and dressed—impatiently waiting for Drake in the living area of our room when stage fright hit me.

Maybe the dress wasn't the right thing to wear. It *was* awfully revealing. It'd look cheap next to Lydia's cool elegance.

What if Luc saw me and didn't like it? Or worse—what if he was indifferent?

I groaned. I wouldn't be able to bear it.

This wasn't going to work.

Drake walked out, took one look at my face, and headed straight to the bar. He poured some of the dark amber liquor he'd been drinking the night before into a glass and pressed it to my lips. "Drink it. All of it."

I obeyed him without thought. And choked as it burned a hole in my stomach lining.

He whacked my back as I wheezed. When I finally caught my breath, I sputtered, "What did you do that for?"

"To loosen you up. You were choking up on me." He held my shoulder and stared into my eyes. "There's no need to worry. You're a beautiful, sexy woman, Katherine. If this doesn't work, you'll have other options. Besides, you have one thing going for you."

"What's that?" I asked, though I was pretty certain he meant my skill at ferreting out information. I was a maniac with facts.

"Your friend is in love with you."

I snorted. I wanted to tell Drake doing drugs would seriously affect his brain functionality, but I just grabbed my cape and followed him out the door.

Whatever the vile stuff was that he forced me to drink, it worked. By the time we were on the road and heading off for our assignation, I was relaxed. Very relaxed.

I looked out the window and was struck with a brilliant idea. "Let's go for a swim later."

"The inn doesn't have a pool."

"No—in the ocean."

He raised his brow. "Do you know what the temperature of the Pacific is?"

"Approximately fifty-six degrees."

"Let's wait and see how we feel," he said.

I settled back in my seat, happy with the compromise.

One time during senior year in high school, Luc convinced me to cut school and go to the beach with him. I went, but all I did was sit on the sand and study for my calculus final.

Now I wished I'd seized that opportunity. I hoped I'd have the chance again one day.

It didn't take long to reach the restaurant. After we pulled up to the front door, Milton came around and opened my side, holding his hand out.

I frowned at it, gave him five, and promptly tripped out of the car. "Oops!"

As he helped me right myself I swear I saw his lips twitch. To make sure, I got up on tiptoes and leaned closer to look. "Are you smiling?"

"No, ma'am."

Another twitch.

I wagged my finger at him. "I'm not so sure."

"Katherine, stop accosting my driver." Drake took my arm and propelled me toward the restaurant.

Turning, I looked at Milton over my shoulder. "I'm on to you. Don't think I haven't figured you out."

Drake sighed and muttered something.

I shrugged indignantly. "He's a wily one."

"Oh—one more thing." He stopped suddenly and plucked the glasses off my nose.

"Hey!" I protested as the world went hazy.

"Much better. Let's go."

The outside of the restaurant wasn't impressive at all (especially through my limited eyesight), but once we stepped inside it was warm, cozy, and quietly elegant.

And it smelled great. I inhaled deeply and my stomach rumbled.

The hostess greeted us with a smile. She and Drake conferred, heads bent together, and then she motioned us to follow her.

The dining room was large and overcrowded with tables, most of them full. The buzz of people enjoying dinner filled the room. I eagerly squinted around, trying to see what people were eating. I would have stopped to quiz a man about the particularly delicious-looking plate he was gorging on, but Drake prodded me toward our table, which was right in the middle of the room.

Good. That way I'd be able to at least try to see what people were having for dessert.

"Could I take your coat?"

"Cape," I corrected the hostess as I slipped it off my shoulders and handed it to her.

There was a momentary hush in the room. I looked around with a frown, wondering what the deal was. Maybe someone farted.

Then I saw Luc.

I know—I didn't have my glasses on. But he felt like Luc, and for some reason I could see his bright piercing blue eyes without any trouble whatsoever.

He was seated to one side and stared right at me. I lifted my hand and gave him a jaunty wave.

That was before I saw the golden blob sitting across from him.

Drake pulled out my chair and I sank down gratefully. Why did I think I could pull this off again?

"Do you need another drink?"

I shuddered, gaping at my dinner companion in disbelief. "Do you want to pour me back into the car?"

He chuckled and opened his menu.

Surprisingly, we had a great time. Drake was an entertaining date. It helped that I couldn't see, so I wasn't overly concerned about the glares we were drawing from Luc and Lydia.

Um. Okay—maybe I was a little concerned. Anyone would be with that kind of animosity directed toward her. But I concentrated on my food (absolutely scrumptious) and the company.

By dessert, I had to say it. I waved a fork at Drake. "You're really a great guy."

He grinned. "You don't have to sound so surprised."

I shrugged and took another bite of cake. (I love cake.) "It's just, what would such a great guy want with Lydia? She's a barracuda." I clapped a hand over my mouth. "Um, I meant that in all the best ways."

He laughed. "I'm sure you did."

"But really. Why Lydia?"

He sipped his espresso (I found it amazing that a man could look so virile delicately drinking from a tiny cup, but Drake managed it). "You can't help who you love. And Lydia used to be different. More open."

I wrinkled my nose, trying to imagine it.

Nope. I shook my head. Impossible.

"She still has that in her. I catch it in her eyes sometimes."

He had a faraway, determined look in his eyes that made me sigh. I wished someone loved me that strongly.

"Surprising seeing you here, Kat."

I looked up to find Luc and Lydia towering over us. Luc nodded to Drake, but Lydia just glared. At Drake—I think I was beneath her notice. Though I shouldn't have been in my dynamite red dress.

Squinting, I studied Luc while he was staring Drake down, trying to figure out if he was angry because we'd invaded their private dinner or because, like Drake believed, he was upset I was here with another man. I shook my head. I couldn't tell—it looked like his stomach was upset from all the rich food.

So I smiled wide. At least the whiskey and the good food had mellowed me enough that it felt kind of genuine. "Hi, you guys."

Luc transferred his dark look to me, and I gritted my teeth to keep my smile in place.

"Enjoy your dinner?" Drake asked. "I haven't been here in—it must be fifteen years, wouldn't you say, Lydia? I was surprised to find it as good as I remembered."

The narrow gaze she gave him would have frozen the most fiery pit of hell.

"But that might be due to the company." He rested his hand on mine, caressing the space between two of my knuckles with the tip of his finger.

My face flamed. I started to pull my hand away,

conscious of Luc's gaze, but Drake kept it tightly in his.

For a moment I thought Lydia was going to strike me dead right then and there. But she drew herself up, slipped an arm through Luc's, and pulled him closer. "You may be right about that."

"Kat, could I talk to you a moment?"

"Again?" I frowned at Luc. He'd wanted to talk that morning, and in the end he hadn't said anything.

Drake let me go and stood up to pull my chair out. "I don't mind. I'll keep Lydia company."

In other words, get lost, kid.

I could take a hint. I got up and walked out of the dining room to the entryway, conscious of Luc's gaze on my back. (I was very proud that I resisted the urge to tug at my dress. I even managed to shimmy my hips a little as I walked. I think.)

When we got to the foyer, Luc took my arm and led me to a dark corner, close to the hallway leading to the restrooms.

I turned around, my lips pursed. "So what's—"

He pushed me against the wall with his body and kissed me.

Only it wasn't a kiss. It was like being completely ravaged. His mouth ate at mine like he hadn't had a bite of dinner, and his fingers bit into my flesh. He palmed his way up my butt, my hips, my midriff, until he reached my breasts. He squeezed the tips, surprisingly gentle, and I just about fainted.

He swallowed my gasp in his mouth and pressed himself against me so I felt the hardness of him rubbing my belly.

Did I do that?

My heart lifted. Maybe Drake was right. Maybe Luc did like me—more than just as a friend. I wrapped my arms around his waist and kissed him with everything I had.

He groaned. "Katherine."

I started to protest when he left my lips, but he nipped my neck and every thought of complaining dissipated. All I was aware of were the sparks shooting through my system.

He quickly nibbled his way down my neck and chest, pushing my dress aside just enough to clamp his mouth on one aching nipple.

Stars burst behind my eyelids. I would have sunk to the floor if he hadn't been holding me. I tangled my fingers in his hair, holding on for dear life.

Then he stepped back, glaring at me so frigidly my blood, which had been heated to boiling point, immediately turned to ice.

Cold air made my nipples contract even more. I looked down and flushed, putting my dress back in place. "Uh . . . Um—"

"Shit," he said succinctly.

At the moment, I was in total agreement. But I cleared my throat and said, "What was that for?"

Luc gaped at me in disbelief. "Excuse me?"

I wanted him to say that he wasn't choosing Lydia. That it was, in fact, me he was in love with and wanted to marry. Me that he wanted to finger paint for life. I wanted to ask him why he stopped kissing me and beg him to do it all over again.

Instead I heard myself say, "Won't Lydia mind?"

His brow furrowed. Then he shook his head,

swiped his hand through his hair, and took another step back.

Then another.

And then he turned around and walked straight into the men's room. He shoved the swinging door open so hard it crashed against the wall and then slammed shut. I jumped at the sound, a horrible bang that felt like a death knell in my heart.

I touched my lips. I felt like they didn't belong to me anymore. I traced their shape, trying to get to know them again. To wipe away the tingling left behind from Luc's brand.

Somehow I doubted they'd ever feel the same again.

Chapter Sixteen

I dreaded going to work Monday morning. Dreaded with a capital *D*.

For one, I was tired. Drake and I had gotten back fairly early the previous afternoon, but I hadn't slept well at the inn. I chalked it up to being in a foreign bed, but I didn't sleep any better in my own last night. Blame it on Luc's sizzling kiss, because it haunted my every dream (or nightmare, depending on how you looked at it).

Two, I wasn't sure I still had a job. If Lydia's attitude last weekend was any indication, I was history. In fact, I expected to be escorted out of the building as soon as I got there.

To cap it all off, my dad knocked on the door as I was squeezing into my nylons. I knew who it was by the jaunty rapping.

"As if I need this now," I muttered as I rushed to get the nylons up. Big mistake, because in my haste I punctured the right side with my fingernail.

I growled, kicked them off, and stomped barefoot to answer the door.

"Katie bug!" He grinned and threw his arms open wide.

I narrowed my eyes. "What are you doing here, Dad?"

His brows furrowed and his lips pursed indignantly. "Does a man need a reason to visit his only flesh and blood?"

Hadn't we had this conversation before? But instead of saying anything, I moved aside and waved him in. Better to take care of this inside rather than telegraphing our problems to everyone else on the floor.

I watched him stumble to the couch and drop down onto it. Drunk. Typical. Crossing my arms, I counted to ten to control the anger rising and then said, "What is it this time?"

"I don't know where you get your suspicious nature. It certainly wasn't from me." He shook his head. Then he winced and put a hand on top, as if to hold it in.

I recognized the symptoms of a hangover, having recently gone through one myself. I just glared at him. I had no sympathy.

He cracked open an eye and sighed. "Okay. Okay. You got me. I need your help."

Of course. I knew that, but part of me still wilted at the admission. Why couldn't he come over to comfort me for a change? Why couldn't he be a real dad, like he used to be when my mom was alive, and ask me how I was doing? Maybe even ask me if *I* needed *his* help?

But he went on, oblivious that my world was collapsing around me. "I ran into Leon last night and we had a couple drinks—"

I groaned.

"Now, hear me out, Katie. It's not as bad as all that—"

As if I hadn't heard *that* before. "How much, Dad?"

"I was winning and then—"

"*How much?*"

He cleared his throat, told me, and gazed at me intently, probably to gauge my reaction.

I nodded, totally calm. He was right—it wasn't as bad as his last loss with Ivan.

Exclaiming in relief, he grinned at me. "I knew you'd come through for me, Katie bug."

"No."

He blinked in surprise. "Excuse me?"

To tell the truth, I shocked myself. "No," I repeated tentatively. Because it felt so good saying it, I straightened and said it again with more conviction. "No. I'm not helping you out of this one."

He gaped at me for a full minute before he flashed his charming smile at me and chuckled. "You had me going there for a second, Katie bug. You're trying to teach your old man a lesson, aren't you? Well, I promise I'll never—"

"Dad, I'm sick of listening to your empty promises." Years of anger and frustration bubbled up inside me and spilled over. I strode to stand over him, pointing a finger right in his face. "This is it. From this moment on, things are changing."

He opened his mouth.

No way was I going to let him smooth talk me out of this, so I cut him off with the one thing I knew would shut him up. "It's past time you got over Mom."

Sure enough, his mouth clamped shut. He crossed his arms and glared at me.

I mimicked him, not about to be cowed. "I've put up with your drinking and gambling for over twenty years because I felt sorry for you. But you know what? I lost my mom too, and if I can deal with it, so can you."

"A wee exaggeration, don't you think?" He pointedly looked at my ringless finger, then at my pathetic apartment. "Doesn't look like you're dealing with it too well."

Oh—low blow. I recoiled, feeling like I'd been slapped.

"Just calling it like I see it." He sniffed indignantly.

The worst part was that he was right.

Oh, the revelation. The proverbial light bulb went on, bright and unrelenting. I frowned. Damn. I hated that. "You're right."

He blinked. "I am?"

I nodded. "I didn't get over it. Not only have I been trying to fill the gap she left when she died but also the one you left when you abandoned me."

"Now, just wait a second." He scowled, pointing a blunt finger at me. "I never abandoned you."

"You haven't been there for me since the day Mom checked into the hospital the last time."

"I have!" he protested.

No, he hadn't. I didn't even have to try hard to prove it. "When did I have my first date?"

He shifted uncomfortably. "Well—"

"What job did I have in high school to pay for our bills?"

He cleared his throat. "Katie—"

"What did I say in my valedictorian speech at graduation?"

He opened his mouth, but this time he couldn't say anything.

"Because you never came to my graduation, did you, Dad?"

By the look on his face, it seemed like I'd finally gotten through to him. I waited to see if he had anything to say. When he didn't volunteer anything, I went on.

"I've taken care of you all these years to make up for Mom not being here. But Luc's right, I've been letting you take advantage of me. I should have let you take responsibility for yourself." Turns out Luc had been right about a lot of things; I was just starting to realize how much.

The anger and bitterness drained out of me, leaving me just plain sad. I plopped onto the couch next to him and took his big hand in both of mine. I flashed back on how, before my mom got sick, he used to take me on long hikes up Mt. Diablo, just the two of us. He'd hold my hand in his, and I'd feel secure, loved, and protected. He'd listen to my dreams and tell me his in return.

Now, he tried to pull away. I didn't let him. I held tight and waited till he returned my gaze.

Gently, I said, "I've been understanding and giving all these years. Now it's time for you to give."

"You don't know what it's like," he whispered hoarsely.

"Oh, yes, I do. I know better than anyone."

He swallowed loudly, but I could tell he saw the truth in my statement.

I squeezed his hand. "You know what I want more than anything?"

His brow wrinkled suspiciously. "What?"

"I want my daddy back."

He swallowed again. For a moment I thought he was going to pull away and go back to being his normal blustery self. He coughed a couple of times, but then he stilled and nodded. "What do you want me to do?"

I went to my purse and pulled out the information on AA that I'd printed out. I marched back and held it out to him.

He looked at it like it was a poisonous snake.

"I want you to clean up."

"But—"

I shook my head. "It's time, Dad. I'm not giving you any more money."

"But Leon—"

Leon wasn't psychotic like Ivan, so he wouldn't be tying Dad to the train tracks to get his money back. "Leon will wait till you earn enough money to pay him back."

He exhaled in defeat, taking the information with a shaking hand. "Okay, Katie bug."

I should have felt happy, but I only felt tired. It wasn't like my dad had committed to going to the AA meetings. For all I knew, he'd go right back out, find Leon, and increase his debt.

Still, I was hopeful. That damn optimism again.

I sighed. "Dad, I'm late for work."

He nodded, stood up, and headed out. At the door, he turned around, suddenly looking very sober. "I know you don't put much store in my promises, Katie, but I promise I'll try."

Not the amount of conviction I wanted, but it was better than nothing. "That's all I can ask."

He nodded and closed the door behind him.

When I got to work, I was a little surprised they let me in. But I made it to my office and even managed to boot my computer and check my messages before anything happened.

Wha-*bam.*

My door flew open and slammed against the wall. I let out a shriek and jumped up, hitting my knee.

Oh hell—I tore my nylons. Again. I hated ruining a new pair. Frowning, I looked up to unleash my wrath on whoever it was who had caused this catastrophe.

Lydia.

And she looked infuriated.

Gulp.

I sank back down and tried to smile professionally. "Good morning, Lydia. Can I help you with anything?"

"You backstabbing little bitch!"

I blinked. Me?

She stalked closer, her eyes slits of rage. For the first time I noticed that she looked pale except for two burning spots on her cheeks. Her hair flew around her head, wild and messy, and her clothes looked slept in. In other words, she looked human.

Oh shit. The world was coming to an end.

"I can't believe you would do this to me." The closer she got, the more I pushed my chair away to put distance between us. I wasn't entirely sure she wouldn't attack me. "The nerve you had showing up at Harmony by the Sea. He told you, didn't he?"

"Uh—" I backed up until my chair was wedged between the wall and the desk.

"The bastard planned this all along, didn't he? It wasn't enough that he destroyed me all those years ago, he had to come back and rip open all the wounds and pour cyanide in them."

Graphic. "Um, Lydia, which bastard do you mean—"

"Well, I'm not standing for it," she yelled, poking a finger in my direction. "I'm taking him down before he can do it to me again. And you're going with him."

I frowned. "Wait a sec—"

"I can't believe you'd do this to me," she repeated. "I gave you every opportunity to achieve your goals. And what do you do? Stab me in the back." She laughed harshly. "I'll show you what happens when you screw with me. After everything I've done for you. I've made you—"

"Wait a minute." I'm not sure what happened. Maybe it was leftover spunkiness from this morning. Or maybe I was just sick of everything.

I stood up, got in her face, and poked a finger so close that under normal circumstances I would've been scared she'd bite it off. "What have you done for me? You gave me a job and a chance to prove myself, for which I'm forever grateful, but I've slaved for you and what do I have now? Nothing."

I think I might have spit on her with that last word, but I didn't care. I kept going. "I work so much I have no life. I'd do anything for you, which I think I've proven with this stupid assignment you gave me, but here I am on the verge of losing my job. Not only that, but because I rush to do your bidding I've lost my best friend and I'm even further from my dream than I was before."

I frowned. That wasn't true. I lost my best friend because I put work ahead of our relationship. It was my fault completely.

Shit. I shook my head. I needed to fix that. I grabbed my purse and headed for the door.

Lydia grabbed my arm. "Do you think Drake cares for you? Because I can tell you he doesn't. If you think your affair with Drake will guarantee you a position in his company, you're sadly mistaken. He has a history of using people and then tossing them away."

That wasn't like him at all. I frowned. "What do you mean?"

Triumph flashed in her eyes. "Just what I said. Drake's just using you."

Yes, but I was using him too. We had a mutually beneficial relationship.

But Lydia didn't know that.

Still, this didn't make sense. Lydia was ruthless in business, but she was ruthless in a calculated, well-thought-out kind of way. This attack had no calculation to it whatsoever. In fact, I'd never seen her so out of control. I'd never imagined that she could get so out of control.

I cleared my throat and pulled out my chair. "Maybe you should have a seat. Can I get you some tea? My next door neighbor gave me some green tea that's remarkable for—"

"I don't want any goddamn green tea!" she screamed.

Yikes.

I was just about to launch into my horse-whispering voice (not that I'd ever talked any horses down, but I bet I'd be pretty darned good at it) when Drake rushed in.

"What's going on here?" He saw Lydia holding my arm and he scowled. "Let go of Katherine."

She sneered. "Oh please, Drake. You can stop pretending that you care about her. We all know you don't have a caring bone in your body."

He grabbed my other arm and tugged. "You're a fine one to talk."

"At least I know the value of faithfulness." Instead of letting go of me, she held tighter.

"Hey, guys—" I tried to disengage myself from them to no avail.

"That's a laugh. This from the woman who betrayed me."

"Uh, guys—"

Lydia barked a laugh. "Right. As if you didn't betray me first."

"Um, if you guys let go, I—"

They glared at me and pulled at me from both sides.

Okay, maybe it was best if I just shut up.

Drake pointed a finger at Lydia. "I don't know what bullshit you've made yourself believe, but you're the one who sold me out to your boss for that promotion."

I winced. Sounded kind of familiar.

Lydia stepped closer, getting in Drake's face.

"The only bullshit being shoveled around here is your innocent act. I don't buy it for a second."

As I was caught in the middle, it meant I was squashed between their chests. I'm sure a lot of men would have envied my spot against Lydia's breasts, but I just wanted out. Now.

I tried to pry myself out but they yanked me back. So I sighed and decided to hold out for the duration.

"There's nothing to buy," Drake roared. "I don't see how you can label me the guilty party in this farce when I was only ever culpable of loving you."

Oooh. Points to Drake.

And at least the conversation was getting interesting. I looked up at Lydia to see what she was going to come back with.

"Ha!"

I nodded. Not very articulate, but certainly uttered with power.

"You never loved me." Her eyes had gone squinty. "You loved the information I blithely told you about my employer."

"I loved everything you told me!"

"I know," she yelled. "Because it made stealing business from us that much easier."

Drake got a disgusted look on his face. "I never once used the information you told me in confidence. You're confusing me with yourself."

"Liar." She spat the word like it was venom. "I found out what you were doing—my boss told me. Did you really think you were so clever I'd never realize you were just using me? Just like you're using her." She pointed at me.

I batted my eyes and hoped I looked innocent.

"Leave Katherine out of this." His words were halfhearted this time, as if he was working out complex equations. "What did your boss say about me?"

"Save the act, Viggo. You've gotten what you wanted. You know you've won." She tipped her chin up. "You may be a hair from taking over Ashworth Communications, but you haven't broken me."

"I know," he said softly. He let go of me and grabbed Lydia's arm.

Whew. I flexed it to get the circulation going again.

"Lydia, tell me what your boss said."

"Let go of me."

He held her closer. "I never used anything you said to me, Lydia. He must have lied to you." He gave her a wry grin tinged with sadness. "He wanted me out of business."

She snorted (I know—I wouldn't have believed it if I hadn't been there). "He had proof."

"What kind of proof?" Drake asked gently.

Lydia opened her mouth, but she must have had a sudden realization because her eyes became so big I thought they were going to fall out of her head.

Drake nodded. "I thought so."

She dropped my arm.

Yes! Freedom. I stepped away before they could grab me again. But I didn't leave because I wanted to find out what happened. (Shrug. I can't help it—I'm curious by nature.)

Lydia moaned. "I'm such a fool."

(See—I would have missed that sterling admission if I'd left.)

"I can't believe I let him convince me so easily." Her eyes were stripped of their usual coldness, and for the first time I felt like she was an actual woman instead of a deity.

Drake ran a finger down the side of her face and then smoothed her hair back. "I'm still angry at you for believing I'd do that to you, but I understand why you did it. You were hurt." He kissed her forehead. "Though I can't believe how you'd think that of me. I loved you."

She lowered her head.

Oh my God—was that a tear streaking down her cheek?

I clapped a hand over my mouth to keep from gasping out loud. But I was bursting at the seams. I could finally see the appeal of watching soap operas.

Drake lifted her chin. "The thing is, Lydia, I still love you. I came to destroy you as you destroyed me"—he smiled—"but I couldn't do it. It's you I want."

Be still my heart. I sighed. This was so romantic.

Lydia's brow wrinkled. "I thought you and Katherine—"

"It's you I want," he repeated. He pulled her to him and laid a big, wet one on her.

Disgusting. I wrinkled my nose. It was like watching your parents make out. Maybe worse. I snatched my purse and turned to leave.

Drake lifted his head and winked at me.

I closed the door behind me, trying not to think of what they might do on my desk, when I realized one thing. I looked back at the door as if I could see through it. Drake had blue eyes, a goatee, and an excellent job. Hell—he even had a dimple. *He* was the perfect sperm donor for Lydia.

I grinned. I had a feeling that was a project they'd take up as a joint venture.

Chapter Seventeen

Another thing that I realized, having witnessed Lydia and Drake's reconciliation, was how easy it was to waste time. I mean, how many years had they wasted being lonely over a misunderstanding?

Not that I could be critical. Look at me: I'd wasted almost as much time. Stupid. I prided myself on my intellect—how could I be so dense?

And now it might be too late to make things right between Luc and me. What were the chances he'd take me back as a friend (anything more was too much to hope for after the way I'd treated him)? Slim to nonexistent, but I had to try.

I caught a cab and gave the driver an extra twenty to rush me to Luc's loft. I felt a twinge of guilt—I shouldn't have spent the money that way seeing as how I was about to become unemployed, but this was an emergency.

It was the most terrifying ride of my life. I told myself it was the way the cabby was weaving in and out of traffic, but I think it might have been my nerves.

We got there in record time. I ran the entire way from the cab to Luc's home, almost slipping on the slick concrete in the hallway. But I arrived intact, if a little harried, and banged on his door.

Ow. I had to remember to stop doing that.

No answer.

Maybe he didn't hear me.

"Luc!" I pounded with my foot this time, paying no heed to the damage to my shoe. A few scuffs on the leather were the least of my problems.

Still no answer.

I looked at my watch. Luc never scheduled appointments this early, so he wouldn't be in his studio. That meant he wasn't home. Or he was avoiding me.

I pursed my lips. Desperation made me reach into my purse and rifle for my spare key.

Found it. I was sticking it into the lock when the door was yanked open. Losing balance, I stumbled right into Luc's damp, bare torso.

I gasped, putting my hands out to catch myself. Of course, the only place I had to hold on to was Luc's chest.

Wow, it was firm. I couldn't resist a few squeezes before looking up.

I lifted my gaze.

Mistake. Big mistake.

First, his attire—or lack of it—registered on my

mind. The only thing he had on was a towel wrapped precariously low on his hips. He must not have heard me at the door because he was in the shower.

Gulp. If I looked that good in a towel, that's all I'd ever wear.

Then I noticed his eyes and how they gazed at me coolly. Dispassionately. Not an ounce of caring in them.

Panic hit me.

The words *too late* resonated in my mind.

Involuntarily, my grip on him tightened. "I thought you weren't home. I'm so glad you are." I tried to smile.

He lifted a brow and untangled himself from me.

I waited for him to pull me in, to say something— anything. His silence was unnerving—he wasn't quiet by nature.

But I finally realized he wasn't going to venture anything. It was all up to me. Trying not to frown, I asked, "Can I come in?"

He shrugged and moved aside to let me in. I ignored the delicious, clean scent of him—and all that bare skin—and strode for the living room with purpose. I dropped my purse on the floor and began to pace. *How do I start this?*

I guess he'd held his tongue long enough because he said, "I'm surprised to see you here. I would have thought you'd be—busy—this morning."

I wrinkled my nose. "Work's under control."

"I didn't mean work."

"Oh." *Busy.* I blushed at the thought of being busy with Drake. "Oh—um, no. I haven't been *busy* in years."

His glare called me a liar.

Well, he did see me getting out of bed with Drake, after all. But still, if he had any sense at all, he would have seen that for what it was—a diabolical plan for Drake to get Lydia back. And how could he think I'd sleep with Drake and still kiss him the way I did?

I put my hands on my hips. "You're such an idiot."

Oops. That wasn't what I meant to say.

I cleared my throat. "I mean, I'm the idiot, and you were right."

"Was I?" he asked coldly, folding his arms.

For once, I looked—really looked—at him and saw not someone who was being combative or stubborn but someone who was protecting himself.

I'd hurt him.

That insight was like a stab in my heart.

I dropped to the couch, my head in my hands. "I'm such a bitch."

"No argument from me."

I could tell he didn't mean it, so I let it pass. I looked up. "I'm so sorry I didn't see before."

He didn't say a word.

Gulp. There was no other course for me but to continue. "You know how I worked so much because I wanted to buy a house?"

He frowned. "Yeah?"

"Well, you know I did it because I never had a home growing up, right?"

He rolled his eyes. "I may not have taken psychology but I'm hardly brainless."

I nodded and stood up. "I just didn't understand one thing."

He raised one brow.

"Home isn't a place." I stepped closer to him.

His gaze was still shuttered, but his arms relaxed a tiny bit.

I decided to take that as a sign, and I took another step closer so I was standing right in front of him. "Home is you."

Then I socked him on the arm.

"Hey!" He scowled at me and rubbed the spot I'd hit. "What the hell?"

"That's for letting me slave at work all those years and not telling me I was going about realizing my dream the wrong way." I stood up on my toes and pointed a finger in his face. "Why didn't you clue me in about this?"

"Would you have listened?" he asked softly.

"Probably not, but I never knew—" I shook my head. "I never knew how much I loved you."

He just stared at me.

"You know." I swallowed. "Not just in a platonic way, but *love* love."

He didn't say anything.

That's when it struck me. My heart cried out and my eyes filled with tears I stubbornly held back. I hadn't *really* believed it until this moment, but now it was impossible to deny. "It's too late."

Crying was futile. Besides, what did I expect? I'd pimped him out without regard for his feelings or realizing that he was doing it because he loved me. I deserved this.

"Okay." I nodded and tried to smile. "I feel great now that I got that off my chest. Um, maybe—"

I wanted to say maybe he could call me sometime, but that was stupid. Head lowered, I stepped around him to get to the door. I needed out before I started to sob, because once I started I doubted I'd be able to stop anytime this century.

But Luc grabbed my arm.

Startled, I glanced up. His dear face was so close to mine that I blinked in surprise and adjusted my glasses to see him better.

"Do you mean it?" His voice was low and hoarse with emotion.

I wasn't sure which part he was talking about, but since I meant every word of everything I'd said I nodded. "Yes."

"What made you realize?"

I had the feeling he meant that I loved him. "When everything started going down the tubes and all I could think about was that I'd never hear you call me 'squirt' ever again."

A slow grin bloomed on his face. "That's love all right," he said, and then he kissed me.

It was exploratory and hesitant, as if we were both afraid to disrupt the fragile bond reestablished between us. But then something changed and we were all over each other. Luc kissed me voraciously, and I returned it just as hungrily.

Panting, I broke away. "Did you know the tongue is the strongest muscle in the body?"

"Shut up, Kat."

Before I could actually do as he so succinctly

asked, he speared his fingers through my hair and took my mouth.

I'd never had my mouth taken before. It was a revelation—carnal, wet, and all encompassing. It was as if he was trying to imprint himself on me. A tattoo on my butt wouldn't have been more effective.

Even with my attention focused on his lips and the way he was biting mine, I was aware that he'd pulled the pins from my hair and massaged my scalp with both hands. Heaven. I didn't know whether to purr or tell him to get on with it.

Why wait for him to get on with it? I was a modern woman. So I placed my hands, which had been mostly flailing till this point, on his shoulders and groped my way down his arms, his chest, his abdomen, and back up.

His skin was soft underneath his chest hair. I brushed his nipples accidentally the first time, but the way they perked up and he gasped told me I'd discovered something important here.

I did it again, just with the tips of my fingers, to make sure.

Sure enough, Luc's hands tightened in my hair. He broke away, breathing heavy. "Kat."

I grinned and rolled my new discovery between my fingers. "This is neat."

"This is torture. Do you know how long I've been waiting?" Before I could venture a guess, he picked me up and carried me upstairs to his bedroom, nibbling on my neck the whole time. No one had ever nibbled on my neck before, so I was quite distracted by the tingly sensations that shot up and down my spine.

He placed me on his bed and stood at the foot, hands on his hips like a conquering warrior. I did a slow perusal of his body.

Yikes. An excited conquering warrior. The towel around his hips had fallen somewhere along the way and he was completely naked. And tumescent. Very tumescent.

When Kevin and I had had sex, I'd never really gotten a decent look at his goods. We didn't even completely undress. But there was no way Kevin was *that* big.

And the more I stared at Luc's, the bigger it seemed to grow.

Sweat broke out on my forehead. My eyes glued to his equipment, I asked, "Did you know the average depth of a vagina is three to six inches?"

Grinning, he climbed on the bed, grabbed my shoes, and tossed them aside. "Don't worry, Kat. We'll fit."

I frowned at him. "It doesn't look like it."

"I promise." He reached under me and expertly had my skirt unzipped and down to my knees before I could blink.

I grabbed his hands. Suddenly I wasn't so sure this was a good idea. I mean, I didn't know what I was doing. What if he found me lacking? What if sex turned out to be as disappointing now as it had been with Kevin?

I cleared my throat. "Did you know that the modern psychiatric definition of a nymphomaniac is a woman who can't experience sexual pleasure regardless of the number of partners she has?"

He smiled and dropped a kiss onto my lips. "That's not something you're going to have to worry about."

Easy for him to say. He wasn't the one who hadn't had sex in years.

His hands tugged my skirt.

"Luc!" I held tight.

His eyes shined with lust and love and what looked like humor. "Yes, Katherine?"

Wow. I'd never heard anyone say my name quite like that. It made me melt on the inside.

Which gave him the opportunity to divest me of not only the skirt but my nylons and underwear, leaving me buck naked from the waist down.

Using both hands, I quickly covered myself from his hot gaze. "Um, Luc?"

His eyes traveled down my legs and back up to ground zero. I tried not to fidget but it was hard, especially since it felt so weird to still have on my suit coat and everything under it.

He didn't seem to mind the clothes I had on. His gaze bypassed them and went straight to mine. "Kat, I heard somewhere that the tongue was the strongest muscle in the body." And then he bent down, pushed my hands aside, and proved how strong his was.

"Oh. My. *God*." I clutched the comforter on either side of me and hung on for dear life.

His tongue lapped slowly like he was trying to become familiar with the new terrain. Each exploratory lick had me gripping the bed even harder.

In less time than I would have thought, I was close. Close, but not close enough.

I wiggled, trying to get his mouth in the right place. "Did you know the word 'orgasm' is Greek for 'to be excited or lustful'?"

"Are you lustful, Kat?" he asked with a long swipe of his tongue.

"Um. Yeah." I squirmed. Damn it, he missed again. Was he deliberately taunting me? "A little. I could be more."

He did it again. "Are you telling me to get on with it?"

That's one of the reasons I loved him so much—he understood me. I nodded politely—well, desperately, really. "Please."

One thing about Luc—when he decides to do something, he does it wholeheartedly. This was no different.

He nibbled on the exact spot. I gasped. It'd never felt like this—all spinning and hot and desperate. My back came off the bed, it was that intense. Panting, I said, "Did you know the average pig's orgasm lasts for thirty minutes?"

"Let's see if we can give you one that rivals." And he latched on like he was never going to let go.

I screamed, then I screamed again when I felt his finger slide inside me. His other hand wiggled under the clothes I still wore and rolled my nipple.

"Luc!" Just like that, I came. Spots flashed behind my eyelids and for a second I was sure I passed out.

When I came to, Luc kneeled over me, trying to get the rest of my clothes off.

"Damn it, you wear too much," he muttered. He tugged at my jacket sleeve to no avail. He mumbled something else I didn't quite catch—something to the effect that I was wilier than a limp chicken, I think.

I grunted. It was his fault I was in this state. Not that I minded. In fact, I could get used to it.

He cursed again, grabbed the collar of my shirt, and ripped it down the middle.

"That was silk," I protested weakly.

He didn't seem to care that it took five hundred silkworms to make one kilogram of raw silk. He shoved the halves aside, pushed my bra up over my breasts, and stared.

Then he grinned at me as he palmed them. "You don't know what lengths I've gone through over the past fifteen years to catch glimpses of these."

I didn't think I had it in me, but I arched into his hands, instantly ready for more.

"I'd like to dribble oil on you and do this but I can't wait any longer, Kat." With one hand, he reached down and slipped himself in.

Yikes, it was tight. And slightly uncomfortable. But I could tell there was potential here so I squirmed a little to situate things better.

"Wait," Luc said from gritted teeth.

Was he in pain too? I didn't want to hurt him so I stilled. "Maybe we should stop while we're ahead."

"Just try to relax, Kat."

Right. As if I could.

Then he snaked a hand between us and touched me where it counted. Suddenly it was a whole new ballgame, and my team was winning.

The unease disappeared as every cell in my body started to do an excited jig. I clutched his butt (as firm as his chest—I'd have to investigate more later) and swiveled my hips against him.

"Kat?"

I opened my eyes and looked up at him.

Sweat had broken out on his brow and his eyes looked pinched with concern. "Are you okay?"

Okay didn't even begin to describe how I felt. I wiggled a little to show him.

He groaned and flexed his hips into me. "I can't wait anymore. You're killing me."

"Did you know in French orgasms are called 'little deaths'?"

He moaned, laughed, and kissed me—all at the same time. Then he pumped into me, wild and unrestrained and thoroughly delicious. My body took over, undulating in ways I didn't know it could.

Luc cried out and stiffened, still thrusting. It set me off again, a series of earthquakes, the first one catastrophic with each subsequent one weaker until I was a puddle on the mattress with him collapsed on top of me.

He rolled off me eventually and pulled me on top of him. He pressed a kiss onto my forehead. "I think we safely answered the nymphomaniac question."

I grinned. I guess we did. "I didn't quite last thirty minutes, though."

He chuckled, a low rumble in his chest. "That might require a lot of practice. Good thing we have lots of years ahead of us."

I lifted my head and blinked at him. "We do?"

"Yes," he answered positively. Pushing my wild hair back from my face, he gazed at me seriously. "I love you, Katherine Murphy Fiorelli."

I frowned. "I'm not a Fiorelli."

"Not yet." He kissed me, and it was soft and full of promise. "But soon, because don't you think it's about time you came home?"

I smiled, running a finger down his beautiful face. "It's all I ever wanted."

Epilogue

One year later

"Did you know in eighteenth-century England, macaroni was a synonym for perfection and excellence?"

Luc glanced up from buttoning his shirt. "Was it?"

"Yes. That's why the feather in Yankee Doodle's cap was called 'macaroni.'" Frowning, I turned my back to him and looked in the closet. When had it gotten so full? And even with all the new clothes Luc had made me buy before our wedding (my trousseau, he said), I still didn't know what to wear. "Did you know Thomas Jefferson introduced macaroni to the United States?"

His hands slid up my arms and he turned me around to face him. "What are you worried about?"

"Worried? What do I have to worry about? I

mean, other than the fact that my father is down-stairs cooking dinner for us, my boss, her husband, and my baby godson. Not to mention Rainbow." I dropped my head to his chest and moaned. "What was I thinking, inviting all of them over at the same time?"

Luc nuzzled my temple as he stroked my hair. "You were thinking you'd have a nice intimate dinner with the people you care about most."

"I'm insane."

Chuckling, he lifted my head. "Yeah, but you're mine, and that's all that matters."

Then he bent to kiss me, sweet and slow. His lips lingered until he was sure he had my attention—easy to know since I only had on a thin lacy bra and panty set (also from my trousseau). I gave back as good as I got. Soon it became apparent I had his attention too.

I broke away and wiggled my lower parts against his. "Maybe we should just stay up here all night. If we ignore the doorbell, I'm sure they'll go away."

"Two problems with that."

"What's the first one?"

"We have news to tell them." Luc's hands spanned my waist, as if he was measuring my not-yet-expanding belly.

"Did you know that an embryo's heart starts beating by the twenty-fifth day?"

His lips twitched. "I've heard that somewhere."

"Did you know by the second month of pregnancy toes start forming? Right now our baby is growing toes, Luc!"

This time he couldn't hold back his grin. "I know."

"And did you—"

"Kat," he interrupted lovingly, "why don't you save these facts for Lydia and Rainbow?"

"How about if I send them all an e-mail about it?" I brightened. I could break the news *and* list all the facts. I snuggled closer to him and bit the skin right above his collarbone. Sometimes my brilliance amazed even me.

"No."

"No?" I pulled back and frowned. "Why not?"

"Because we need to ask Drake and Rainbow to be our baby's godparents. In person," he added before I could protest. "And didn't you want to tell them we closed escrow on the house?"

Oh yeah—the house. Our house. It was in Noe Valley on a hill overlooking the City. Kind of expensive, but with my increased salary as VP of research at Ashworth-Drake Communications, the mortgage was doable. Luc planned on using the loft as his work studio and expanding his business.

Still, I could include all that in the e-mail too. "What's the second problem?"

"Your dad is already downstairs cooking."

"Oh." Right. "Couldn't we send him on an errand?"

He grasped my hips and did some wiggling of his own. "Not that your idea doesn't have merit."

I pouted and said plaintively, "I have to get dressed."

"Katie bug," Daddy called from the bottom of the stairs. "Where do you keep the bread knife?"

Hell if I knew. I gazed imploringly at Luc.

He smiled. "I'll go help him, you get dressed."

"Thanks." Despite his best efforts, I still wasn't culinarily inclined. We both enjoyed the cooking lessons, though. They were, uh, innovative. I'd never imagined how useful a chopping block could be.

Before Luc could leave, I grabbed him by the shirt and pulled his mouth down to mine to show him how much I appreciated him helping my dad. He'd never been overly fond of Daddy, but in the last year they'd come to a truce. It didn't hurt that Daddy had been in Alcoholics Anonymous for over eleven months now. We'd bought him a computer and he was trading stocks on-line. With his drinking under control, he was actually making money rather than losing it.

I grinned at the dazed look on Luc's face when I let him go. I loved that I could do that to him. I patted his chest and said, "Be right down."

"Uh-huh." He shook his head as if to clear it and lumbered down the stairs to the rest of our loft.

Still grinning, I studied the closet again, looking for the perfect thing to wear. Something nice . . . Something special . . .

"Just the one," I mumbled as I pulled out my red silk dress. It had thin spaghetti straps and was short but not obscenely mini. Tasteful, and when I wore it I felt expensive and luscious.

I slipped into the dress, picked out a pair of strappy shoes to match, and fluffed my hair. I'd been wearing it down a lot lately, especially at home. Luc had a penchant for twining his fingers in my curls, and I found I liked that a lot.

Picking up a tube of lipstick from Rainbow's

new natural cosmetic line, I carefully colored my lips. I'd gotten better at the whole make-up thing under Rainbow's tutelage.

Who knew she and I would have become such close friends over the past year? And now that she'd employed Ashworth-Drake to handle her marketing we worked together too. Kind of. I personally did the research required for her account. (I never knew most lipsticks contained fish scales.)

With a last look in the mirror, I declared myself ready and wobbled down to join the men.

When I walked into the kitchen, they both went silent, gawking at me. Blushing, I looked down. Was my skirt tucked into my panties?

Luc was the first to speak. "Wow."

My dad nodded. "She's as stunning as her mother was."

I smiled at him and squeezed his hand. "Thanks, Daddy."

"Wow," Luc said again.

I would have thought he'd be used to how I looked by now. The new fashionable me wasn't *that* different than the one he'd known for fifteen years. Still, I couldn't help but feel a trill of excitement when my husband looked at me with pure lust in his eyes.

My husband. I loved that. I loved him.

Luc walked over to me and rested his hands on my waistline (he'd been doing that a lot in the past two weeks since we found out we were having a baby). He fingered the silk of my dress. "Kind of fancy for mac and cheese, isn't it?"

I glanced over his shoulder at Daddy. In his

eyes, I could see he remembered all the special mac and cheese dinners with Mom, but instead of pain there was fondness, even if grief still mingled in too.

With a smile, I looked up at Luc and shook my head. "I think it's just right."

About the Author

When Kate was a little girl, all she dreamt about was moving to France and living in a stone castle while painting the Provençal countryside. To prep herself, she studied French, stocked up on berets in every color, and practiced her shrug for hours in front of the mirror.

But then, because indentured servitude seemed more attractive than eating baguettes and drinking wine, she took a detour into the world of high tech. Eventually, that insanity wore off and she decided to try something more stable. Writing seemed the logical choice.

Unfortunately, she doesn't own her castle yet, but she holds out hope that one day soon she can pull her berets out of storage. Keep tabs on her progress by checking out *http://kateperry.com,* or contact her at *kate@kateperry.com.*

By Best-selling Author
Fern Michaels

Weekend Warriors	0-8217-7589-8	$6.99US/$9.99CAN
Listen to Your Heart	0-8217-7463-8	$6.99US/$9.99CAN
The Future Scrolls	0-8217-7586-3	$6.99US/$9.99CAN
About Face	0-8217-7020-9	$7.99US/$10.99CAN
Kentucky Sunrise	0-8217-7462-X	$7.99US/$10.99CAN
Kentucky Rich	0-8217-7234-1	$7.99US/$10.99CAN
Kentucky Heat	0-8217-7368-2	$7.99US/$10.99CAN
Plain Jane	0-8217-6927-8	$7.99US/$10.99CAN
Wish List	0-8217-7363-1	$7.50US/$10.50CAN
Yesterday	0-8217-6785-2	$7.50US/$10.50CAN
The Guest List	0-8217-6657-0	$7.50US/$10.50CAN
Finders Keepers	0-8217-7364-X	$7.50US/$10.50CAN
Annie's Rainbow	0-8217-7366-6	$7.50US/$10.50CAN
Dear Emily	0-8217-7316-X	$7.50US/$10.50CAN
Sara's Song	0-8217-7480-8	$7.50US/$10.50CAN
Celebration	0-8217-7434-4	$7.50US/$10.50CAN
Vegas Heat	0-8217-7207-4	$7.50US/$10.50CAN
Vegas Rich	0-8217-7206-6	$7.50US/$10.50CAN
Vegas Sunrise	0-8217-7208-2	$7.50US/$10.50CAN
What You Wish For	0-8217-6828-X	$7.99US/$10.99CAN
Charming Lily	0-8217-7019-5	$7.99US/$10.99CAN

Available Wherever Books Are Sold!

Discover the Thrill of
Romance with

Lisa Plumley

__Making Over Mike
0-8217-7110-8 $5.99US/$7.99CAN

Amanda Connor is a life coach—not a magician! Granted, as a
publicity stunt for her new business, the savvy entrepreneur has
promised to transform some poor slob into a perfectly balanced
example of modern manhood. But Mike Cavaco gives "raw material"
new meaning.

__Falling for April
0-8217-7111-6 $5.99US/$7.99CAN

Her hometown gourmet catering company may be in a slump, but
April Finnegan isn't about to begin again. Determined to save her
business, she sets out to win some local sponsors, unaware she's not
the only one with that idea. Turns out wealthy department store mogul
Ryan Forrester is one step—and thousands of dollars—ahead of her.

__Reconsidering Riley
0-8217-7340-2 $5.99US/$7.99CAN

Jayne Murphy's best-selling relationship manual *Heartbreak 101* was
inspired by her all-too-personal experience with gorgeous, capable . . .
outdoorsy . . . Riley Davis, who stole her heart—and promptly skipped
town with it. Now, Jayne's organized a workshop for dumpees. But it
becomes hell on her heart when the leader for her group's week-long
nature jaunt turns out to be none other than a certain . . .

Available Wherever Books Are Sold!

Visit our website at **www.kensingtonbooks.com**.